Beyond the Spotlight

A Nanny/Single Dad Romance
Settle Myer

Book Cover by Y'all That Graphic

Edited by: Owl Eyes Proofs & Edits

Contents

To anyone who was ever shamed for being fat: I see you. Love your body. Flaunt your fatness. You don't owe the shamers shit.

Author's Note

This book deals with difficult topics such as grief, death of a loved one (sibling & parental), a brief mention of addiction, the struggles of being a single parent, a mention of adoption due to not being able to have kids (supporting character), minor fatphobia, stalking (not by main character), minor assault (not by main character), attempted kidnapping (not by main character).

This book also has graphic sex, including breath play, spanking, minor bondage, sex toys (nipple clamps & butt plugs), and edging. If you have a specific trigger, please contact the author through her website.

Playlist

Paparazzi – Lady Gaga
  Love Like Ghosts – Lord Huron
  Would That I – Hozier
  Delicate – Damien Rice
  Rivers & Roads – The Head & The Heart
  Falling in Love at a Coffee Shop – Landon Pigg
  Fade Into You – Mazzy Star
  Ends of the Earth – Lord Huron
  Everything – Lifehouse
  The Maze – Manchester Orchestra
  Electric Love – Børns
  Bleeding Love – Leona Lewis
  Mirrors – Justin Timberlake
  (I Just) Died in Your Arms Tonight – Cutting Crew
  (I Just) Died in Your Arms Tonight (Instrumental) – Soft
Notes

ENTERTAINMENT NOW

REY MICHAELSON DROPS OUT
By Angela Borrows

Action star Rey Michaelson announced last week that he was dropping out of the Tyler's Team movie due to a family emergency. Entertainment Now confirms his sister has died.

Michaelson kept his sister out of the spotlight but would often mention in interviews that she became his legal guardian and took care of him after their parents passed away over 10 years ago. We also know that Michaelson's sister gave birth last month, confirmed through a photo he posted on social media showing him holding his newborn niece. Sources tell Entertainment Now that Michaelson may be taking a break from his career to assume custody of her.

Tyler's Team would have been the 25-year-old's first romantic drama. The movie was set to start filming in a month and a half. We've reached out to his team for more information about what this means for his career.

Chapter 1 – Savannah

F uck flying while fat.

I don't do it often, but this trip was unavoidable. This trip takes me to my new life. I pivot my thick body as I walk down the narrow aisle to find my seat, trying not to snarl at all the panicked faces as I approach.

They don't want me sitting next to them.

I get it. Airplanes are the worst. They cram passengers in with little to no leg room, let alone ass room. If you're not a size ten or smaller, you're screwed.

I've been fat my entire life. My parents are big too. They raised me to love myself and my body, despite the world's unrealistic standards for beauty. But despite my unwavering confidence, and not having any more fucks to give, the cruel world does not cater to big bodies.

So, I adapt the best I can: like booking a window seat where I can cuddle up to the plane's wall—even though I'm scared of flying and keep the shade shut and try not to think about the vast nothingness beyond the wings.

Unfortunately, for this flight, I have an aisle seat, which I hate. My elbow always gets hit by people passing by. I learned the hard way to tuck my arm against my side when the snack and drink cart comes through. One killer bruise was one too many.

At least it's not the middle.

I'm lucky there were even seats left on this flight. I bought the ticket last night.

Last night, I was shoving clothes and my most precious belongings into two suitcases and a shoulder bag.

Last night, I left Silo Springs, Arkansas and drove to Joe's Used Car Dealership in Memphis, Tennessee where, ten minutes before closing, I sold my old 2005 Camry for $2,000 cash before taking an Uber to the airport.

Last night, I left my pathetic cheating boyfriend.

I'm not sure why I chose the most expensive city in the U.S. Maybe because New York City is the biggest and the opportunities are endless. Maybe it's because I can be anyone there. Maybe it's because I can hide easier. He'd never find me there, not that the loser would even try. He made it quite clear he's not interested in me anymore.

We dated for seven years. I should have ended things years ago. I'm not even sad about breaking up with him. More like pissed. I'm furious that I wasted so much of my life with him. My rage is in control here and she's making insane decisions.

Like moving to the most expensive city in the U.S. with no job and no place to live except the Airbnb I rented last minute.

My seat comes into view, and I breathe out a sigh of relief upon spotting an adorable little girl sitting in the middle seat. She has orangish red curls and freckles dotting her pale face. She's tiny, too, meaning I won't be crowding her space. My eyes roam to the man next to her and I nearly choke on the minty gum I popped into my mouth after downing a large latte to wake myself up.

Holy hell that man is fine. He takes off his baseball cap and runs his fingers through his light brown hair before securing the cap back in place. He tugs it down low enough as if he's trying to hide his ocean blue eyes and gorgeous face.

My heart beats erratically as a blush snakes up my neck and spills onto my cheeks.

Is it hot in here?

I'm definitely sweating.

What the hell? I've never reacted this way towards a man. Is it because I'm single now? As if my body knows it's relationship free and ready to be dicked?

The man glances up as I stop at their row and lift my shoulder bag to store in the overhead bin. Once done, I sneak a quick glimpse of him and notice he's staring—at my stomach. My black crop top has crept up, showing a sliver of skin. His eyes move down the rest of my body, taking in my sloppy outfit: black sweats rolled at the waist and a pair of gray Crocs.

I pat my dark blonde hair I have piled on the top of my head and smile at him. He clears his throat and shakes himself from his searing gaze.

Did he like what he saw?

I never know with men. They either hate fat bodies, love them proudly, or love them secretly.

I force myself to look away to flag down a nearby flight attendant. "Hi, can I get a seatbelt extender?"

"Of course, sweetie." She places a palm on my shoulder before walking away.

"You sound like my dad's friends' girlfriends," the little girl says the moment I sit down.

"I do? Are your dad's friends' girlfriends from Arkansas like me?"

She nods with her entire head and shoulders.

Her father watches us as if waiting to step in, either because I'm a stranger talking to his daughter or because he doesn't want her bothering me.

"We were there yesterday. There was a lake, and I saw cows and a fairy queen."

"A fairy queen?"

"Yeah. She said I could be a princess."

"Do you want to be a princess?"

"I mean... princesses are cool, but I want to be a knight, like my dad."

My eyes trail to her father again and he opens his mouth to explain, but the flight attendant returns with my extender.

"What's that?" the little girl asks when I take it.

"Addy, what do I say about noses?"

He offers me an apologetic look, which I barely notice because holy crap, he has an accent—British; I believe. It's not that strong, but it just made him ten times hotter. Not to mention this guy is built. Muscle city. His biceps struggle to be held in by the black t-shirt he's wearing. Tight jeans swallow his meaty thighs. My eyes dart down to his bulge.

Damn it. He saw me scoping out his junk. He smirks and blushes and tugs on the baseball cap before turning back to his daughter as she talks.

"Noses are for smelling, not for sticking in places they don't belong," Addy answers in her high-pitched voice while nodding at each word.

So, he has an accent, but she doesn't? Interesting.

"That's right. Now, why don't we leave the lovely lady alone, okay?"

Lovely? Wait. Is he just being British, or does he really think I'm lovely?

"I'm sorry. She's usually quite shy around strangers."

"I don't mind at all." I offer her a reassuring smile and hold up the seat belt extender to show the little girl. "The seat belts on the plane are too short to fit around my tummy. This makes them longer for me."

"Oh, okay. Cool." She looks down at her stomach. "My tummy gets big when I eat too much food. Like ice cream. It's my favorite. Chocolate chip cookie dough with lots of chocolate syrup on top."

She hops in her seat, and I laugh at all this energy at six in the morning.

"I love chocolate chip cookie dough ice cream too. Have you ever had it for breakfast?"

Her eyes widen.

"You can do that?"

I lean in and whisper, "You can..." I glance up at her dad and he's cutting his throat with the tips of his fingers. "... but only with permission from your father."

Her head whips around to the man, who narrows his eyes at me. "Can I, Dad? Please?"

I mouth 'sorry' at him and cover my mouth with my palm to hide my amusement.

"We'll see."

She groans and slams her head back on the seat. "That means no."

"It means, 'we'll see.'"

The remaining passengers board and take their seats. As the plane taxis, the crew makes their final checks. All while my little seat mate chats my ear off.

"What's your name?"

"Savannah, but most people call me Savvy."

"I'm Adeline. My dad calls me Addy, but sometimes he calls me Poppy because my hair is the color of some flower." She tugs on the strands. "Only he can call me Addy and Poppy. I mean, I guess you can, too, but only if you can talk him into letting me have ice cream for breakfast."

"I sure can try, but there's a problem..." Her eyes widen with worry. "I don't even know his name. How can I convince him if I don't know his name?"

She opens her mouth to answer, but her dad cuts her off by jutting his hand out to me. "Reynold."

I accept his greeting, ignoring the way my face heats the moment our skin makes contact. "Nice to meet you, Reynold."

He tilts his head as if perplexed by what I said.

Do people not say 'nice to meet you' in England?

He smirks when I release his hold.

Before my curiosity gets the best of me and I ask him about the weird look, the pilot announces that we're prepared for takeoff. I close my eyes and grip the armrests so tight I'm sure my knuckles are turning white.

"Are you okay?" Reynold asks with a mix of worry and amusement.

I squint open an eye and nod, letting out a long stream of breath. "I'm a little scared of flying. No big deal."

Addy perks up beside me. "I'm scared of flying too. That's why I let Dad sit next to the window. The window scares me. What if it breaks and sucks us all out? What if I see a monster on the wing?"

I suppress a panicked laugh because I've thought the same thing. Well, not the monster part.

"She has... a bit of an imagination," Reynold says apologetically.

Addy holds out her palm to me. "Here, we'll hold hands and be scared together."

This beautiful, pure soul. I want to cry at her kindness. I don't hesitate and take her hand.

"I'm sorry..." Reynold begins, but I wave him off.

"This helps. Honestly."

Once we're safely in the air, Addy releases my hand and pulls out an iPad. "Do you want to play a game with me? It has frogs, and you tap the screen to make them hop or catch flies with their long gross tongues!"

"Adeline," Reynold warns. "Let's leave Savannah alone, okay? Why don't you watch a movie?"

He shoots me a warning with his fierce blue eyes that says don't fight me on this, and I blush way too fucking hard. It's the type of look that promises punishment and makes my little kinky heart dance. Or am I acting like a feral cat in heat because he said Savannah and not Savvy? With his accent, I've never heard my name sound so sexy.

Addy shrugs, then places her oversized headphones on her ears.

"Thank you," Reynold whispers over the top of her head. "I'm not sure what's gotten into her. She never talks this much around strangers. There must be something quite special about you."

He smiles fondly at me, but it's paired with a touch of sadness in his eyes. He looks away quickly before I can ask if he's okay.

At some point during her movie, Addy lies down across her father's lap and falls asleep. Reynold leans his head back while petting her hair, and within minutes he's also dozing.

I wish I could sleep on a plane. Every time I do, my head lolls over and I jolt awake. I pull out my kindle to finish reading a romance about a sexy fat girl getting railed by a wolf shifter and by the time I'm done, there's only about forty-five minutes left in the flight. Both my seat mates are still asleep.

Way too many times I caught myself staring at Reynold's profile: his Adam's apple, his powerful jaw peppered with stubble, his cute nose that has a slight bump in the middle, his long dark lashes, and plump lips, slightly parted. He snores. Not too loud, but enough that the lady in front of us kept turning around with a scowl.

I thought it was adorable.

The plane hits a patch of turbulence and jostles Reynold awake. He wipes drool off his chin with the back of his hand and blushes when he notices me staring.

Damn it. Stop gawking at this man.

Addy also wakes. She blinks open her dark blue eyes—she has Reynold's eyes—and sits up, rubbing them with her tiny fists. He fixes the wayward red curls sticking up all over her hair and my ovaries burst at the sight. Which I find odd since I've never put much thought into having kids. But seeing this man be so caring towards his daughter has my stomach fluttering and my brain filling with thoughts of a family.

Is he married? I didn't see a ring on his finger. Where's Adeline's mother? Questions that are far too personal for me to ask someone I just met, no matter how desperate I am for answers.

Noses are for smelling, not for sticking in places they don't belong.

Addy whines she needs to use the restroom. She seems grumpy, but maybe that's because she just woke up. I get it. I love sleeping and hate getting out of a comfy bed to be productive. I stand so Reynold can herd her out of the row. His arm brushes against my breast when he passes, and I stifle a whimper.

Get it together, Savvy. Are you so touch starved that a simple graze of an arm turns you on?

It doesn't help that the man smells like fucking heaven—woodsy with hints of a spice. I don't know what it is, but I want to bury my nose in his neck and inhale until I pass out.

Reynold and Adeline return a few minutes later. The little girl's grumpiness has vanished, and she has just as much energy as before she fell asleep.

"What's your favorite animal?"

"I'd say a cat. They're jerks, but adorable jerks."

Her face lights up. "Cats are cool, but I really want a puppy. Dad won't let me get one. He says I'm not old enough and they're too much responsibility."

"Well, that's not very nice now, is it?"

I don't miss another glare Reynold shoots my way. I bite my lip to stop myself from smiling because now I'm doing it on purpose. This man turns me on just by existing and the horniness has me wanting to misbehave so I can beg him to discipline me.

The way a fire lights in his eyes as he stares at my mouth makes me wonder if he's thinking the same thing.

"No. Not nice at all." Addy crosses her arms with a humph.

"Flight attendants, please prepare for landing," the pilot announces, and I tense.

"Landing is the worst," Addy says.

"Yeah," I breathe out.

Addy grabs Reynold by the wrist and extends his right arm towards me. "Dad, you hold Savvy's hand this time."

"Addy..."

The plane rocks and rattles and I take Reynolds's hand, threading my fingers with his.

"That's quite the grip you have there, Savannah," he grits out. "Perhaps you could refrain from digging your nails into my knuckles?"

"Shit," I whisper and relent my crushing brace. "Sorry."

"Savvy, you said a bad word. Anytime my dad says a bad word, he pays me a dollar."

I puff out a laugh, her tiny chipmunk voice easing my anxiety.

"Start me a tab."

"What does that mean?"

I shake my head. "Never mind."

The plane makes its descent, and within twenty minutes, we're on the ground. It was a rough landing that had me closing my eyes and holding my breath until we're smoothly coasting down the runway.

"Savannah, we're here," Reynold says softly.

I pop my eyes open, and he's staring at me with a bit of concern. Probably because I'd squeezed his hand hard enough to stop the blood from circulating to his fingers.

I let go and sit up straight in my seat. "Right. Fuck. Sorry."

I cover my mouth with my palms because I keep forgetting there's a child next to me. I'm not used to censoring myself.

"Two dollars, Savvy," Adeline sings. "Hey, your name kinda rhymes with mine. Savvy and Addy. They both end in 'y.'"

She bounces in her seat at the revelation while we taxi to the gate.

"Same with dad's name."

I frown. Reynold doesn't end in a 'y.' Before I think about it or ask what she meant, we roll up to the gate and the seatbelt sign turns off.

"We're here!" Addy squeals. "Savvy, where do you live? We live on the Upside."

"Upper East Side," Reynold corrects.

I laugh. "You probably shouldn't tell strangers where you live."

"But you're not a stranger. You're my new best friend." She gasps. "Would you want to be my nanny? Dad says I need one, but he doesn't like anyone he's interviewed. Pleeeeeease, Savvy! We'd have so much fun!"

"Addy, your nose is wandering again," Reynold says. "I'm sure Savannah already has a job."

I bite my lip to stifle a wince, which doesn't get past him.

"I... don't have one. I'm moving here. I was going to go job hunting tomorrow. Probably find something at a bar or restaurant serving or bartending."

He furrows his brows as if he hates that idea and shifts in his seat to pull his wallet out of his back pants pocket. Shuffling through the contents, he extracts a card and hands it to me.

It has his phone number and name: Reynold Kane.

"We should talk. If you're interested, I mean."

"Okay." My heart races at the thought of seeing this man every day. I don't know how I'd cope. But if he needs a nanny, I'm guessing that means he won't be around a lot.

If it's just me and Addy, then she's right. We'd have so much fun. I realize my cheeks ache with how much I've smiled and laughed this entire trip. I haven't even thought about my asshole ex who couldn't keep his dick in his pants.

I used to babysit in high school. I'm sure nannying isn't much different. Plus, I need a job. The $3,000 in savings I brought and the $2,000 from selling my car will only get me through two months, max. "Yes, I'm interested. When do you want to meet?"

Reynold's eyes widen as if he didn't believe I'd agree. "Tomorrow morning at ten? There's a coffee place near me... wait. Where are you staying? We can meet wherever is easiest for you."

"Oh, um..." I stumble over my words because, technically, I'm homeless. "I booked an Airbnb for a month until I find an apartment. It's in a neighborhood called Hamilton Heights."

He frowns and those perfectly sculpted brows of his pinch again.

"We can meet closer to your Airbnb. There's a coffee place near Columbia University. I used to go there every day while fil—erm—for my job. Here." He finds a pen from the bag he'd pulled from underneath his seat after we landed and takes the card back. After writing on it, he hands it over. "That's the name and the cross streets. Take the 1 train and the subway station lets out right there."

I nod. "Ten a.m. I'll be there."

ENTERTAINMENT NOW

REY MICHAELSON FLIES COACH
By Angela Borrows

Rey Michaelson and his niece Adeline, whom he's had custody of for the past five years, were spotted flying economy to New York City. The two were returning to New York City after attending the private wedding ceremony of Mylan Andrews and Lana Young in Arkansas. Throughout the flight, they were seen chatting with a woman in their row, though it's unclear if she was with them.

This is only the sixth time the movie star has been out in public with Adeline. Half of those public appearances took place over the past year after the two moved to Manhattan. They'd been living somewhere in New Jersey, though the Metal & Mayhem star never revealed where. Entertainment Now has learned that Michaelson is in need of a nanny for Adeline as he prepares for his return to acting.

Chapter 2 – Reynold

Addy and I weave through a crowded sidewalk in SoHo, past people zoned out or staring straight ahead. This is what I love about New York City. It's easy to disappear. New Yorkers get a bad rap for being mean, but they're not. They're just in a hurry. They mind their business and pay me no attention, allowing me to blend in.

We slip inside a posh French bistro where we're meeting my friends, Eloise and Kelly, for brunch. The cool air washes over me when we step inside. It's the end of May, not even summer yet, but it feels like it with a high in the nineties today. The white T-shirt and jeans I'm wearing do nothing more than soak up my sweat.

It's been two weeks since Savannah ghosted me, and I'm still pissed about it. What the fuck happened? She seemed interested in interviewing for the position. Did I push her too hard? Did she accept my card just to be polite? To get me off her back?

Oh, how I want to be hovered over her back, to smooth my palm over her spine and tug on her long blonde hair just to hear her scream my name while fucking her from behind.

I shake my head at the thought. Thoughts I've been having for the past two weeks. I really need to get laid. It's been... too fucking long.

I can't deny how sexy Savvy is. *Was.* Because she ghost-ed me, and I'll never see her again. I'll never see her plush curves. Her plentiful cleavage. Her beautiful ass that has been taunting my dreams ever since we filed out of that plane and she walked ahead of us. She definitely swayed those hips, knowing I was watching.

My attraction to her began when she spotted me on the plane, her doe-like green eyes widening. A beautiful pink blush spread across her cheeks and neck. Then she lifted her bag to the overhead bin, her crop top revealing a sliver of her skin. I nearly lost control when her mouthwatering scent of cherries and crème wrapped around me as I moved past her to take Addy to the loo.

Not to mention how she didn't mind talking to Addy during the flight. She didn't get annoyed by her rambling or her millions of questions. She didn't use the condescending voice adults use when speaking to children. She talked to her like an equal.

Addy has slowly been coming out of her shell since starting preschool this past September and socializing with her peers. She's finding her voice, like when she chastised my friend Jensen at Lana and Mylan's wedding in Arkansas two weeks ago after he called her Addy instead of Adeline. Then she told Jensen's girlfriend she resembled a fairy princess with her dress and flower crown. Her shyness returned when Rebecca told Addy she could be a princess.

Yet, Adeline clung to Savannah as if the two had known each other for a lifetime.

Which is the main reason why I'm pissed. Savannah not only ghosted me, but Adeline too.

I couldn't bring myself to tell her that Savannah didn't show up. I lied and said she rescheduled and we're planning to meet soon. *I lied.* I never lie to Addy. I didn't even lie when talking to her about her mother and biological father.

When Adeline was three, she returned from the park with the nanny and asked why the other kids had two parents and she only had one. How she understood what that meant at just three years old, I'll never know. But I told her the truth.

Then, a year later, she returned home from her first day of preschool, crying because a kid made fun of her for not having a mommy. My heart broke into a million pieces. She was only four. I knew this time when I explained what happened, she'd understand it more.

I told her that her mother got very sick when she was a baby and died. I explained that her mother was my sister, and I took custody of her.

I've loved this child like she's my own. Because she is. She's *my* daughter. I gave up acting five years ago to raise her because her biological father is a piece of shit who left Annalee when he found out she was pregnant. He's been locked up for the past five years of a ten-year sentence on aggravated robbery and assault charges. The idiot robbed a bank with a knife and sliced the security guard on the arm when he got in the way.

My sister met Kyle in Las Vegas while there with her girlfriends for a fun weekend. He was there to waste his money because he had a gambling problem. They fell in love fast and after six months of long-distance texts and phone calls; she moved to New Jersey to live with him. She never told him about her famous and rich younger brother. She stopped telling the men she dated about me because they'd always want something: fame, money, a co-star's phone number. I'm glad because Kyle robbed that bank for gambling money after losing his savings at a casino. He would have used Annalee to force me to give him money.

"Oh, no. What are we pissed about today?" Eloise muses as we walk to the table where she's sitting next to her partner. She sets her camera down and leans back in the chair, tossing her blonde braided hair over her shoulder and crossing her arms.

"I'm not pissed," I say and help Addy into her chair.

"You say that every time we meet, then go on a ten-minute-long rant that proves otherwise," Kelly adds, which makes Eloise giggle.

Kelly and Eloise met at a wedding in Hawaii last year. My friend Mylan Andrews's former bodyguard, Bruno, married Ginger, who is best friends with Mylan's wife, Lana. Kelly was the DJ at the reception and Eloise, who used to be Mylan's assistant, was the photographer. They've been dating for almost a year now. They technically live in L.A., but lately, they've both been booking jobs here in the Big Apple, so I offered one of the guest rooms in my penthouse. In exchange, they watch Addy when needed as I prepare for my first movie role in years.

"I still haven't found a nanny," I begin.

"Here it goes," Eloise chuckles.

"Sexy Savvy never got back to you?" Kelly asks. They chuck off the blazer they're wearing, revealing a black crop top, a curvy body, and tanned skin underneath.

I glance at Adeline, who's not paying us any attention, while she taps away at her iPad. She claims she never listens to our conversations, once telling me that adults talk about boring stuff.

"Please don't call her that," I whine. While venting to them the night after she was a no-show, I let it slip once...*once*... that I thought Savvy was sexy. Then they went on and on about how I had a crush on Sexy Savvy and did kissy faces, smooched on their hands, and sang a song about me and Savvy sitting in a tree with her k-i-s-s-i-n-g. They're fucking tossers.

It's now been two weeks and I'm losing my goddamn mind because I can't stop thinking about her and what I want to do to that body.

"Those are your words, Renny," Kelly points out.

"Yeah, well, she's a pain in my arse because I got my hopes up that she wanted the job and now I'm fucking stressed again."

"Dad, you owe me two dollars." Addy scowls at me for cursing. I grumble and lean over to take out my wallet and extract two bills to give her. She cracks a smile and wiggles in her seat.

That brat. She totally lied about not listening in on our adult conversations.

I glance around the small space, searching for our server. I desperately need water. My mouth is dry as hell, and I'm still sweating after taking the subway all the way from the Upper East Side. I have a driver, but New York City traffic is shite. Not only is the subway faster, but like the crowded sidewalks, people keep their heads down during their commute. To them, I'm just another man with a kid trying to get to their destination.

It's only when I stop moving that people pay attention. Like now. A few restaurant patrons do a double take as their eyes pass over me. I quickly turn back around and pick up the menu to scan the options. I'm craving something sweet, and my stomach rumbles at the description of the Soufflé pancakes with honey crisp apples and toffee sauce.

"Hi y'all, what can I get started for you today?"

I freeze in my seat. It can't be.... My heart drums against my chest at the sound of that familiar Southern twang. Her velvety voice makes my cock twitch as if waking up after keeping it asleep for the past five years.

"Savvy!" Adeline squeals. She jumps out of her seat near the wall and runs around me.

I force my body to move and tear my eyes away from the menu just in time to see Addy crash into Savannah and wrap her arms around her waist. A lump of jealousy lodges in my throat and I push it down. I seriously can't be jealous of my daughter over a simple hug... even if it's with the woman who's been haunting my damn thoughts.

"There's my brave little seat mate!" Savvy beams, scuffing up Addy's already messy red curls.

She's surprised to see Addy and smiles beautifully at her. That bright demeanor falls when she spots me and looks away.

What the hell? What did I do?

Addy steps back and looks up at the woman. She's taller than average. Addy is tall too, already slightly over four feet. Savannah must be around five-nine. My six-foot frame still towers over her.

She's wearing black pants and a white t-shirt with the restaurant's logo on her left breast. Her blonde hair is up in a high ponytail, and I ignore the thought of wrapping the strands around my wrist and tugging.

"Are you here to eat with us?" Addy asks.

Savannah frowns. "Actually, I work here now."

"But I thought you were going to be my nanny." Addy pouts. "Dad said you were meeting soon."

"Oh, did he?" Her head snaps to me and she narrows her piercing green eyes.

"Actually," I begin, swallowing hard, "what I said was something came up, and we had to reschedule."

Savannah sighs and puts on a face of regret when she looks back down at Addy. "I'm so sorry, Adeline. I accepted a job here, so I won't be able to work as your nanny."

I glance at Eloise and Kelly, and they might as well have popped popcorn to snack on as they hungrily watch the unfolding drama.

"My dad can pay you more," Addy says with a whine. "He's got a lot of money."

"Adeline Lee," I warn, but Savannah cuts me off before I can discipline my daughter.

"Oh, I'm well aware of how rich your father is."

She locks eyes with me, and the fire behind them has me squirming in my seat.

"You're a famous actor, right? Something you failed to mention on the plane."

"You didn't ask," I say even though I'm the one in the wrong here.

It's just... she didn't know who I was. She treated me like a normal person.

"Why would I ask if you were famous? You were sitting in coach. Celebrities don't sit in coach. And what about bodyguards? Wouldn't you be traveling with an entourage?"

"Actually, I prefer flying coach. A lot of celebrities do because that's where we're invisible. People scope out first class to see if they recognize anyone famous. Despite living a public lifestyle, I'm a very private man, Savannah. Especially when it comes to Adeline."

And I did have a bodyguard. He sat in the row next to us. Savannah just didn't see him, which is the entire point. My security stays hidden until needed so not to draw attention to me. It's only when I'm recognized while walking through the airport or attending a crowded event that they stay close.

Instead of responding, Savannah clamps her mouth shut. She turns her head to Eloise and Kelly. "What can I get started for y'all today?"

Shit. She's pissed. And the anger looks absolutely stunning on her.

"Um, I'll have Frisée Lardon and a water please," Eloise says.

"House burger au Poivre and a cider," Kelly says next.

Savannah turns to me. "And you, sir?"

I swallow hard, hating the disdain this beautiful woman now has for me, but it also has me wanting to punish her for the tantrum she's throwing. "Soufflé pancakes and French press coffee. Addy will have—"

"Do you want ice cream?" Savannah asks, cutting me off. "Technically, it's brunch, so it's not breaking your *father's* rules."

The way she says 'father' is packed with venom.

Addy stands next to Savannah, holding her hand and staring up at her as if she has all the answers to life. Her face lights up. "Chocolate chip cookie dough?"

"We have chocolate. Is that okay?"

"Yes!" Addy jumps up and down.

Savannah looks at me and smirks, declaring victory. She did this on purpose. She crossed my parental boundary to get a rise out of me because she's mad. But joke's on her. I was going to let Adeline get whatever she wanted today. Only because she's been pestering me for the past two weeks about eating ice cream for breakfast, which I blame entirely on Savannah.

"You're so cool, Savvy," Addy says, giving her one more hug before hopping like a bunny back to her seat. Savannah's face drops, her eyes watering at the sweet, innocent words.

"Um. Okay. I'll be right out with your drinks," Savannah fumbles over her words then turns on her heel, leaving us.

I stand and wave my hand over Addy's head. "Can you two..."

Kelly and Eloise nod, saying nothing about the scene that just played out.

I walk away from the table in search of Savannah. She disappeared behind a wall where I assume the servers go to enter orders for the kitchen. When I round the corner, she's at a touch screen computer, aggressively tapping at it.

"I'm working, Reynold." She huffs, as if expecting I'd follow.

Her saying Reynold and not Rey, despite knowing who I am now, makes my heart flutter. I'm Rey to the world, but sometimes I don't want to be. Sometimes I want to escape and be Reynold Kane again.

"I know but—"

"I can't do this right now."

"Then when?"

"Never. Please, just go. Find someone else."

"I don't want someone else," I growl, my voice loud and desperate.

She sucks in a breath and pauses her work. Some of her coworkers have turned their heads to stare at us. I've got my baseball cap pulled down, hoping they won't recognize me.

Savannah glances around and notices our eavesdroppers. She takes hold of my hand and drags me through the kitchen and out a back door to an outdoor area where the trash is thrown out. She releases her grip on me and starts pacing, her arms crossed.

"You lied by omission. If you had told me you're famous, I wouldn't have accepted your card. I wouldn't have gotten Adeline's hopes up."

"I didn't want to tell you."

"Why?" She stops and drops her arms. "Help me understand."

I take in a deep breath and slowly let it out because I'm so fucking scared to lose this woman. I can't even begin to explain why.

"Because I liked that I was a stranger to you. You saw me and not my fame. People usually put on a worshipping mask when they meet me, but you didn't. Having a normal conversation with you felt like breathing after having the air stolen from my lungs."

A bit dramatic, poetic even, but she's too mad to let the words sink in.

"What was your plan here? Hiding your fame from me? You live an extremely public life that you wanted me to be a part of. You should have told me this when offering me a job that would put me in the spotlight too."

"I know... I... wasn't thinking. I took a chance and hoped I'd be able to explain myself when we met for coffee. I'm sorry, Savannah. Really, I am."

She sighs and turns away from me. I step to her, close enough that I can smell her mouthwatering sweet perfume.

"Is me being a celebrity the only thing stopping you from considering this job?"

"Yes."

"Why?"

She pivots towards me enough that I can see her uncertainty.

"Because there's a reason I moved here, Reynold."

"Tell me," I say, hoping I don't sound demanding. I want her to feel comfortable and safe around me.

She says nothing for the longest time, and I almost think she's not going to.

"You not telling me felt like deceit. I just left a shitty relationship because of a deceitful man. He cheated and lied to me for years. I'm humiliated, and I came here to hide—to start a new life. I didn't tell anyone where I was going. Not even my best friend. I don't need people knowing everything about me, who I'm with, or what I'm doing up here."

I hope the people she's hiding from didn't see the picture another passenger took of us on the plane. Better not mention it. It would likely add fuel to her reasons not to accept this job.

"Why don't you want anyone to know where you are?" I take another step toward her and lower my voice. "Did your ex hurt you?"

The corner of her mouth tilts up. "No. God, no. He's just an asshole with a small dick who couldn't—"

She cuts off her next words and I quirk my brow. So, her ex couldn't get it up? Couldn't make her come? I'll gladly show her how good it could be.

No. Reynold. Stop thinking about this woman like that. You need her to be Adeline's nanny... not your girlfriend.

"Never mind. I just... You and Adeline don't need this. I have baggage. I'm a mess. I never should have agreed to meet with you. Please... find someone else."

"No."

"What?" She scrunches up her nose, and I fight the urge to boop it.

"I told you. I don't want anyone else."

"You know nothing about me!"

"So, tell me." I close the space between us, our bodies mere inches apart. She inhales a sharp breath. "Who are you, Savannah?"

We stare, neither of us looking away as if challenging the other to be the first to break.

"I'm nobody," she whispers after a while. Her green eyes focus on my mouth.

I desperately want to kiss her. Would she let me? Ever since meeting this woman, she's had me in her grips. Her smell, her adorable accent, and her pouty lips fill me with an emotion I haven't felt in years: unadulterated attraction.

I lean in, hoping she'll let me claim this kiss. Instead, I'm met with her eyes widening and her face lighting up with panic.

She punches me.

Chapter 3 - Savannah

I punched Reynold.

Shit.

Did I seriously just punch this man?

"Ow," he growls and grabs his chin. "What the fuck, Savannah?"

"Sorry." I step away from him and cover my mouth with both hands. "Sorry."

He rubs the sore spot and glares at me.

I drop my arms and pace the compact space. "You were going to kiss me, and I panicked, and even though I want to kiss you, I can't. We can't because that'd be inappropriate, right? You want me to be Adeline's nanny. You can't offer me a job and kiss me in the next breath and..."

My words are as fast as my racing heart. I place my palm over my chest as if that will help slow it down. I just assaulted a celebrity. Will he want to press charges? I do *not* need another assault charge on my record.

"I need to leave. I'm probably going to get fired for assaulting you, anyway. I'll just go grab my things now and if you want to press charges, I understand."

He grabs hold of my arm to stop me from walking past him.

"Savannah, calm down. I won't press charges or report you."

I grimace, spotting the red mark forming on his jaw. "But I punched you."

"Yes, you did." He sighs and lets go of my arm, leaving my skin hot from the contact. "You've got a proper right hook too."

"Proper right hook?" I repeat. The words pierce through the anxiety coursing through my body, and I laugh. Full belly snorting laughter.

"Are you seriously laughing right now?" Reynold gapes at me, as I'm unable to control my giggles.

He's not angry, though. He's smiling, failing to hold back his amusement at this... situation.

I breathe in and out slowly, attempting to control myself, and wipe the tears out of my eyes.

"I'm sorry," I say the same time Reynold says, "I'm sorry, Savannah."

"You're apologizing to *me*?"

"Yes. I never should have tried to kiss you."

"Right. You shouldn't have." Even though I've imagined kissing him since the moment we met on that plane. Even though I haven't stopped thinking about him for the past two weeks. "And I shouldn't have punched you."

"Right. You shouldn't have," he says, echoing what I'd just said.

"Clearly an accident."

"Clearly."

We stand in silence, staring at each other for what had to be a minute.

"Okay, well, I need to get back to work," I say, weakly and unsure because I don't want to leave him. "It was... interesting meeting you. Good luck finding a nanny."

Once again, he grabs my arm when I try to walk by him. "Wait..."

My stomach dips at the desperation in his voice.

"I don't care that you punched me–"

"You should."

"But I don't. Call me crazy—"

"You're crazy."

He scowls at me. "Please. Just hear me out."

"What's there to say?" I hold up my hand to list with my fingers. "One: we almost kissed, and that's just begging for disaster. Two: I punched you. And three: you're famous."

Four: he's almost too gorgeous to be real. As if he was sent from the heavens and demanded to be called God. But no. He's not a God. He's Reynold... Rey. A celebrity. He has a freaking Wikipedia page.

> **Rey Michaelson is a 30-year-old TV & Film star. Born in Brentwood, Essex, England as Reynold Michael Kane, he started acting and modeling in London at the age of 14 before moving to the United States at 16. He immediately landed his first role, starring in the hit 80s-themed show, *Metal & Mayhem,* alongside Mylan Andrews and Jensen Boliver. The series was canceled after three seasons and Michaelson went on to star in dozens of high-grossing action movies.**

I stopped reading after that.

I don't know if I could deal with the publicity surrounding his life. I could barely stand having no privacy living in a small town where you couldn't even shit without someone asking what color it was. People saw everything. They heard everything and knew everything. Except, no one knew my ex, Brad, was cheating on me with Cara Calloway, the Gossip

Queen of Silo Springs? Certainly, someone would have said something. Maybe Brad and Cara were just that good about hiding their affair.

Point is... I moved to New York to escape small town gossip. How can I go through that on a global level with a fucking celebrity?

"We'll set boundaries," Reynold says, pulling me from thoughts.

"What?"

"If you agree to be Adeline's nanny, then we'll set boundaries. Strictly professional. No flirting, no near kisses, no right hooks."

I roll my eyes. We shouldn't have to set boundaries. We're adults, for fuck's sake. Besides, what parent would want to hire someone who assaulted them?

"Why me? Why are you so adamant about hiring me? Don't you want someone more qualified who isn't at risk of punching or kissing you?"

He moves towards me, and I step back to keep the distance between us.

"There's no one else," he says.

I scoff, but he keeps talking.

"I met with three other women after you ghosted me. One woman secretly recorded videos and took pictures of me, which I found online an hour later. The next woman had exceptional credentials, having previously worked as a nanny for celebrities. Adeline wanted nothing to do with her. She hid behind my leg and ran off when the woman tried talking to her. And the third person, a college student, was clearly only there because she's a fan. She asked for an autograph and a selfie and ignored Adeline when I tried to introduce them. It's been like this for months."

"What makes you think I wouldn't be like that too? I'm a stranger. You know nothing about me. I could be crazy, or a horrible person. I've already attacked you. I could be a serial killer you know."

He snorts, and I gawk at him. He grins and runs his palm over his injured jaw that has a sexy five o'clock shadow.

"*Are* you a serial killer?"

His jest eases the anxiety coursing through my body. I perch my fists on my hips, packing my next words with sass. "As if I'd tell you."

He laughs, and it's deep. It speaks right to the place between my legs. I should *not* be turned on right now. I can't help it, though. This man makes me act foolish. I want to run into his arms but at the same time, I want to run far away from him. I want to kiss him, but I also want to push him away—and apparently punch him.

"Tell me you'll at least interview for the position."

He tries to close the distance between us once again and I hold up my hand, stopping him.

"Boundaries. Remember?"

He takes the baseball cap he's wearing off and runs his fingers through his hair. Something he did on the plane that I find far too sexy.

"You wanted me to hear you out, so I'm listening. Tell me why you're putting all this trust in me to be your daughter's nanny."

"There's no one—"

"Tell me the real reason, Rey Michaelson."

He flinches the moment his stage name falls out of my mouth and the mask he's wearing drops. The one he uses when going out in public: his celebrity persona where everything is right in the world. The real Rey—Reynold Kane—now stands before me. Vulnerable. Desperate. Scared. I watch his face as he struggles to find the right words.

"I know what it's like to lose everything. To give up a life you've known for years to start a new one. It's terrifying and it can be lonely. I don't want that for you. I want to help because five years ago, I was in your situation."

My brows furrow. "I don't understand."

He pauses and the corner of his mouth twitches. Whatever amused him quickly vanishes and he frowns.

"I got custody of Adeline when my sister died a little over five years ago."

Adeline's not his? After I learned Reynold is famous, I decided not to read more about him and his life. I knew if I did, I'd change my mind and go to that meeting at the coffee place near Columbia University. Now, with him standing in front of me, no longer wearing that protective mask, I *want* to know everything about him.

"I stopped acting to raise her. I uprooted my entire life and left L.A., moving to the East Coast where my sister Annalee lived. I stayed in a small two-bedroom home in Jersey City, New Jersey, I had bought her almost six years ago when she told me she was pregnant, and her ex bailed on her. The house the media never found.

"I had no fucking clue what I was doing. To make matters worse, the coverage surrounding my sister's death, and me taking custody of Adeline, was overwhelming. So, I refused to leave the house with her unless it was needed for a doctor's appointment. I couldn't risk being seen together and having her face plastered all over the tabloids and the internet. The only help I had was the part-time nanny I hired to take her to the park, or to the mall to get candy. She quit a year ago to accept a full-time nannying job with another family."

He pauses and wipes a palm over his face.

"Now Adeline is older, and she's so damn smart. Because of that, I'm honest with her about everything. Before I sold the Jersey City house, I sat Adeline down to explain that I'm famous and how I wanted to return to acting. I asked what she thought about that—about me being gone for most of the day. She was excited. Quite hurt my feelings, really. I never thought I'd get to the annoying dad phase so quickly. Or maybe she's just sick of me being around all the time. She's the one encouraging me to return to acting.

"I bought a penthouse on the Upper East Side. I knew the move to Manhattan would put us back on the paparazzi's radar. They always found me when I was out by myself. Add Adeline into the mix and they go absolutely feral. They caught us three times this past year. The media hasn't tracked down my penthouse yet or Addy's preschool, so I've been able to escort her to school every day."

He looks down at his hands as he picks at his nails.

"That's another reason I'm nervous about returning to acting. Not being there to take her to school, to protect her. Not a day has gone by since she was born where I've been apart from her for more than a few hours at a time. This new movie will have me on set for twelve to sixteen hours a day.

"But Addy has a mind of her own and she's assured me she'll be fine without me. I need someone who connects to her, treats her like an equal, who can talk to her and keep her entertained. You're fantastic at that. So, yes, you're a stranger, but you're the first one Adeline has connected to. It even took her time to be comfortable around Eloise and Kelly."

He turns away from me after his heartbreaking confession and it has me desperate to pull him into a hug. This man needs to catch a break. Plus, I can't stop thinking about Adeline's excited face when she saw me today, her tiny arms wrapping around me. I want to do this. I'm going to do this. For Addy.

"Tell me about the job," I whisper.

He pivots just enough for me to see his profile. It's as gorgeous as I remember from that day on the plane when I couldn't stop staring at him while he slept.

His Adam's apple bobs before he speaks. "We begin filming in two weeks. It'll take about five months, possibly longer. Like I said, I'll be on set for long hours. There will be late nights and early call times. Some weeks, I'll only get one day off, which is why I'll need you to move in."

Move in?

I choke on my response, a strange noise escaping from my mouth.

"You'd have your own room and bathroom. You'd have privacy. I'll pay you whatever price you want."

Any price?

How much does a celebrity nanny even make?

My heart gallops as my head fills with too many questions to sort through.

Reynold's dark blue eyes float down to my mouth. I must be chewing on my bottom lip—a bad habit I've had since high school when schoolwork stressed me out. I wasn't the best student, and I struggled only to barely pass classes and graduate.

"Are you sure about this?" I ask.

"I'm sure. As long as you don't punch me again."

I wince and turn away from him.

Opportunities like this—they don't happen to me. I'm struggling to accept this is real. I grew up poor and worked to survive since I turned sixteen and got a job at the Country Mart grocery store. I didn't go to college because if I hated high school; I knew I'd despise college. I've worked every service job imaginable. And I didn't get handouts. My parents did the best they could to support me and love me and help me whenever needed, but they didn't have much money either.

We'd only moved to Silo Springs, Arkansas, because my dad got a job there. Then the company went under two years later. We couldn't afford to move back to Georgia to Savannah, my namesake and where my parents are from, so we stayed in Arkansas while both my parents worked shitty jobs. It wasn't until after I graduated high school that my dad landed a better job and they finally moved back to Savannah. I didn't go with them because I had a boyfriend and didn't want to leave my friends. I was still trying to figure out my life. My parents begged me to go with them, but I refused. I wanted to live my life, not follow theirs.

Now I'm thirty-five and my life never seemed to get better. Only worse. I'm tired of struggling. Here is this man, offering me the deal of a lifetime. I'd be an idiot to pass it up.

The back door to the restaurant swings open and Reynold freezes in front of me, keeping his back to my co-worker.

"Savannah, there you are," Diana chirps. "We're swamped and need you back on the floor."

"I'll be right there," I say. Diana scowls, then looks at Reynold before her scowl turns into a smirk. I shoo her away and she laughs. She's going to hound me for an explanation when I walk back inside.

"Okay. But before I accept, I want to meet at your place so you can give me a tour and tell me more about what the job entails."

He smiles. Ugh. He's so fucking beautiful. My heart thrashes against my chest as if it already belongs to this man and is fighting to escape to return to its owner.

"Brilliant. Are you available to meet tomorrow? We can go over paperwork, as well."

"Yes. I can meet in the morning."

"Let me get your number." He reaches into his front pocket for his phone.

"I won't ghost you again."

He taps away at his screen, then hands it over to me, eyebrow raised. "Fool me once..."

I roll my eyes and take his phone.

"Why *did* you ghost me? Why didn't you text or call to tell me you changed your mind?"

"Because I was afraid you'd try to convince me to change my mind about not interviewing."

He smiles as if that's exactly what he would have done.

I finish adding my name and number to his contacts and hand the phone back to him. He glances at my information.

"Savannah Monroe. Beautiful name."

I blush and he blushes and we're two awkward people standing in the trash area of a restaurant, staring at each other.

He moves as if he's about to step closer to me, then reconsiders, perhaps thinking about his sore jaw.

The back door swings open again, and my manager, Garcia, pokes his head out. "Savvy," he begins. "We are dying in there."

"Sorry, coming in now."

Reynold clears his throat. "I'll text you."

This time, when I walk past him, he doesn't stop me. And I wonder if he looked at my ass before the door shuts between us.

I told Reynold I wanted to meet at his home, because if I'm going to be working for him, living in his penthouse, spending my every waking moment with his daughter, then I should see where this will all be happening.

He offered to send a car to pick me up, but I refused. We argued over text about that for at least ten minutes before I sent him a ghost emoji and stopped replying.

I take the 1 train down to 85th Street and hop on a crosstown bus to the Upper East Side, getting out on Fifth Avenue and walking a few blocks to Reynold's apartment building. I stare up at the side of the limestone façade. It's got a Renaissance feel to it. I think. I know nothing about architecture, but I'm pretty sure only rich people live along Fifth Avenue across from Central Park.

Reynold must have informed the doorman I was coming because the moment he sees me, he says my name, then leads me to an elevator. He scans a card and pushes a button for the ninth floor, giving me a nod as the doors close on me.

Less than a minute later, they open to a breathtaking foyer with artwork lining the white walls. A woman appears in the hallway before I can focus on each painting.

"You must be Savannah," she says, tipping her head ever so slightly. She's older, I'd guess in her sixties, with her gray hair pulled into a bun at the nape. She's wearing a blue suit with a simple white blouse underneath. Her hands are clasped behind her back. "My name is Brenda. I'm the house manager."

"A house manager?"

She smiles. "I'm in charge of the household staff, keeping supplies around the apartment stocked, calling on any service appointments for maintenance needs, running errands, and whatever else Mister Michaelson needs."

"Oh, so he's rich, rich."

That makes her chuckle. "That he is." She waves me to follow her down the long hallway.

"How many staff does he have?"

"Besides his agent, manager, and PR team, Mister Michaelson has an assistant, stylist, chef, housekeeper, personal trainer, and driver, though he prefers to take the subway. New York City traffic and all." After living here for two weeks, I understand that. The subway is faster. Does he not get recognized? To be fair, I had no clue who he was when we met. I also pay no attention to the other people on the subway. Is that why he likes taking it?

So, if he's okay riding the subway all the time, then why did he not want me to take it here today? Was he being protective? My heart flutters at the thought.

"Right this way. He's in his office."

The hallway has more artwork and a few pictures speckled in. The art is old and looks crazy expensive. I want to stop and look at it all, especially the photos. I see a few with Reynold in them, but Brenda is walking too fast, so I only steal glances.

She stops at a door and knocks.

"Come in," Reynold's deep accented voice calls back.

My heart responds to that voice by galloping in my chest. I'm nervous. *He* makes me nervous. This gorgeous man makes my body respond in ways few others have succeeded in doing.

Brenda opens the door and I walk past her. She closes it right behind me.

"Savannah," he says.

He's standing at his desk, holding a stack of bound papers in his hands. A movie script, I think. He closes it and drops it to the desk, which is covered in even more papers.

I take a moment to appreciate his body. He's wearing a V-neck black shirt that might be a tad too small for him and jeans that ride low on his hips. His light brown hair looks freshly finger-combed, with a strand or two falling over his forehead.

He looks at his watch. "You're late."

I shrug. "Subway delays and I missed the crosstown bus. I had to wait for the next one."

"You should have let me send my driver."

"Aww. Were you scared I wouldn't show up?"

"Not at all."

"Good. Because I said I would."

"And here you are." He gives me a forced smile, his teeth grinding together, causing the muscle in his jaw to dance.

Oh. He's annoyed. Why do I find it sexy?

"Let me give you a tour," he says, and walks out from behind his desk, passing by an acoustic guitar in a stand.

Are you kidding me? Not only is he drop dead gorgeous, but he plays the guitar too? Does he sing?

Lord baby Jesus. I am being tested, and I was never good at tests.

Boundaries, Savannah. Boundaries.

Chapter 4 - Reynold

This is a mistake. I'm far too attracted to this woman to employ her as my daughter's nanny. But I've spent the past five years making responsible, logical decisions when it comes to my daughter's life. This is the first decision where I'm letting my heart take the lead.

Okay, and maybe my dick too.

We really like her.

Did she notice me checking her out? No, she didn't, because she was too busy checking *me* out.

She's wearing a light pink crop top today with a cat riding a unicorn over the right pocket. Her small but ample breasts look fabulous in it. Her nipples poked through the fabric, begging to be taken into my mouth. My hands itched to skim up her thick thighs and underneath the black skirt she has on, to tear at the fishnet stockings so I can sink my fingers into her wet pussy.

Fuck.

I need to stop thinking about her, about her sweet smell filling my nose as I lead her out of my office. My hands are in my pockets to control my achingly hard dick. It leaks with pre-cum and the thought of pulling it out of my jeans and begging Savannah to take it into her mouth crosses my mind.

I shake the thought away.

Boundaries, Reynold. Boundaries.

"Where's Adeline?" Savannah asks as I bring her into the open concept kitchen, dining, and living area.

Dark gray cabinets and sleek stainless-steel appliances line the corner in an L-shape. The huge marble island matches the marble countertops and the bar that looks out over a dining nook. I have a chef who stops by five days a week to prepare dinners for me and Addy, but I'm in charge of breakfast and sometimes lunch if there are no leftovers. This morning, I made waffles and set out a variety of syrups, fresh fruits, and whipped cream, which are still sitting on top of the island.

"Preschool."

She scrunches up her nose. "Aren't five-year-olds supposed to be in kindergarten?"

"She turned five at the end of March this year. She was four when the school year started this past fall, so she didn't qualify for kindergarten."

"Oh." She laughs. "She's pretty freaking smart for a five-year-old."

"That she is. Coffee?"

"Yes, please."

"Are you hungry? I have waffles warming in the oven."

Her growling stomach answers that question, and she wraps her arms around her mid-section. "I woke up too late to eat."

I point at one of the four bar stools at the island. "Sit."

She salutes me, making the corner of my lip turn up at the sass, and I get to work. I pull a black mug from the cabinet above the sink and bring it to the fancy coffee machine I just bought and barely know how to work. I place it underneath the spout and push some buttons.

It does nothing.

After more frustrated button smashing and curse words, Savannah appears by my side.

"Let me."

"No, it's okay. I'll figure it out."

"Reynold." The way my name rolls off her tongue in that adorable Southern accent of hers has me melting where I stand. "I was a barista for five years. I think I can figure out how this machine works."

I nod and step aside and watch as she pushes all the buttons I had pushed. But they work for her. The cup fills up with mouthwatering mocha coffee—my favorite—then she removes it and places it on the countertop.

I can't help watching her as she moves about my kitchen with familiarity, as if this is already her home. She seems comfortable here. Opening the fridge, she takes out the creamer. She even finds sugar in the cabinet next to the oven where my chef, Shirley, keeps spices and seasonings.

Savannah notices me standing there gawking, so I clear my throat and remove the plate of waffles from the oven's warming drawer.

I grab myself a glass of orange juice and sit on a stool while she assembles her waffle. She spreads peanut butter on the top, then adds a cut up banana (my favorite combo). She skips the chocolate, strawberry, and cherry syrups to pick up a bottle of homemade maple (also my favorite) and drowns the waffle in a sea of sweetness.

Before she notices me staring again, I shake my head and clear my throat. "I'll need you to sign an NDA."

"An NDA?"

"You don't know what a non-disclosure agreement is?"

She rolls her eyes. "Yes, but what would yours be for?"

She opens and closes a couple of drawers before finding the one with the forks.

"Basically, the document states you won't share stories about me with the press. That anything you learn about me, or Adeline, and our lives, stays confidential."

"Oh, of course, I would never," she says, cutting into her waffle and taking a bite. She groans her appreciation. My cock jerks, laughably jealous that a waffle is the one giving her such pleasure and not me.

"Great. And I forgot to mention that I'll need to run a background check on you."

She pauses, her fork in mid-air. "Oh?"

"My lawyers are encouraging it. My manager and public relations team, too. Just to ensure you haven't been to jail."

She winces and sets her fork down.

"You've... been to jail?"

"That man at the bar where I worked deserved to be punched."

"So, I'm not the first man you've assaulted?"

She shakes her head. "This guy grabbed my ass."

My chest tightens with regret because I tried to kiss her without her consent. Is that why she panicked? Because of what that man did to her? My regret blooms into anger, not only at myself, but at the lowlife who groped her. *My woman.*

I jolt at the thought. My woman? Except... she's not mine. *She could be.*

Savannah nibbles on her lip, shying away from my re-action. I've been told I wear my emotions, a downside of acting, I suppose. My anger must be seeping through to my face. I just hope she doesn't think I'm furious with her.

"I may or may not have given him a concussion and a broken nose."

Good girl. I know firsthand that Savannah is a fighter. My jaw still aches with the reminder.

"It sounds bad, I know, but this guy was a serial groper. He'd always manhandle women at the bar, and he touched me inappropriately far too many times that I let pass. One time, I caught him jerking off at the side of the bar while looking at a picture he took of my ass on his phone."

"Jesus, Savannah."

She takes a sip of her coffee and I lick my lips, wondering how sweet her mouth would taste right about now.

"I know," she says and stands, planting her hands on the counter. "I shouldn't have agreed to meet with you. I'm not qualified. I don't know what I was thinking. I should have known you'd need to do a background check..."

"One arrest in defense—"

"It wasn't just one. But I swear all my arrests were worth it and totally justified."

"How many times have you been arrested?"

She lifts her eyes, locking them with mine.

"Four."

I flinch. I didn't mean to, but she saw it.

"Yeah, that's what I thought." She walks around the island. "I'm just going to leave now."

I catch her arm before she passes me, and back her up against the counter, planting my hands on the marble top to cage her in. She sucks in a breath and her pupils dilate, letting me know the move didn't scare her but turned her on. Good. I don't want her to fear me.

"Tell me everything."

She lets out that breath she'd been holding and my mouth waters at the sweet maple, peanut butter, and banana scent.

"My first arrest was in high school for running naked through the hallways on senior prank day. The school resource officer caught me. Since I'd just turned eighteen, I was arrested and charged with public indecency. That shit went on my record. Second time was for vandalism, but to be fair, Callan Ray cheated on my best friend Justine with her cousin who he knocked up. So, we slashed his tires like Carrie Underwood said we should, and spray painted 'cheater' on the side of his house. Third time was at a protest in Little Rock for reproductive rights. Fourth time was the serial groper I told you about."

I'm leaning in close enough I could kiss her. She looks down, and I take her chin between my fingers, lifting her head. I want nothing more than to take all her worries away. To worship her like she deserves so she can forget about her old life and the wanker who cheated on her.

"Never be ashamed—"

"I'm not ashamed," she says, lifting her chin higher. "I'd do it all again in a heartbeat. But after telling you all this... and after punching you..." She shakes her head. "I shouldn't have come. I'm wasting your time."

She tries to move out of my cage, but I don't budge. She places a palm on my chest over my heart. Can she feel how fast it beats for her?

"I don't care about the things you did."

"You should."

"Everything you did was for someone else. You protected your friend who was cheated on. You fought for reproductive rights. You sent a sex offender to the hospital and stopped him from groping other women at the bar."

She raises a brow. "What about streaking through the halls of my high school?"

I smirk, the image of a naked Savannah crosses my thoughts.

"You're totally picturing me naked right now, aren't you?"

I shake my head. "Not at all. That would be quite inappropriate."

She rolls her eyes and I remind myself that I can't repri-
mand her for the action. Would she let me spank her? Tie
her up so I can fuck her at a punishing pace?

"So... should I go?"

She flutters her eyes, nibbling on her lip. The urge to stare
at her mouth overcomes me.

Is she doing that on purpose?

"No, Savannah. You haven't said anything to change my
mind."

I finally release her, and point to where her food sits on the
island.

"Finish eating."

She nods and returns to her stool like an obedient good
girl.

She hasn't technically accepted the job, and I keep approaching the boundary line. It's a test, and I keep waiting
for one of us to fail and cross it.

*You are a responsible adult, Reynold. You are perfectly ca-
pable of not thinking about fucking the nanny.*

Once Savannah is done eating, she stands with her plate
and coffee mug. I attempt to grab the dishes from her, but
she twists out of my reach.

"I've got it."

I'm not sure what to say as she goes to the sink to rinse
them off. I'm usually the one taking care of others. Even

when I have Eloise and Kelly over, I never allow them to help me clean up after breakfast, lunch, or dinner.

I would have done the same for Savannah, but she literally dodged me like a damn NFL player.

Why do I find it equally infuriating and sexy?

"Let me show you the rest of the penthouse," I say the moment she closes the dishwasher.

"Wow, it's... bright in here." Savannah's eyes scan the pink walls of Adeline's room.

"Yeah. She's been nagging me about repainting. She's out of her princess phase and wants the pink walls and bedding gone. Her new favorite color is orange, and instead of dolls, she wants puzzles and art stuff because she loves drawing during art time at school."

"What time is she done? I was hoping to see her today."

"Four. You're more than welcome to stay here for the next five hours."

"No," she says way too fast. "I have work at two."

I open my mouth to tell her to quit, but snap it shut because that's not my place.

"Four seems late for preschool."

"The school offers extended education hours. Adeline was so eager to learn, I registered for a four p.m. release instead of the typical three."

Savannah fingers through the books on Addy's small bookcase, some falling off the shelves because between me reading them to her at night, or her reading them herself, she's always asking for more books. I'd never deny her more books, but one of these days, we need to go through them all to see if she wants to donate any of the ones she's already read.

We leave Addy's room and walk through the ensuite bathroom we share to enter my bedroom.

Savannah turns circles around the large space, blushing and biting her lip—something I've noticed she does often when she's nervous... or turned on. I'd kill to know what she's thinking about. Is it my scent infused throughout the room that's causing her cheeks to redden and her nipples to harden in that sexy crop top she's wearing today?

She scans her eyes over the décor. I tried to keep it simple. Movie posters hang on the white walls from a few of my favorite roles. A couple of award statues sit on my bookcase—no Oscars or Golden Globes but I won 'best fight' at the MTV Movie Awards one year. Before I officiated Mylan's wedding, that was probably the last time I'd hung out with my friend. He fell asleep during the show and his drooling face was turned into a meme. I text it to him sometimes, a lot more now that we're rekindling our friendship.

Mylan, Jensen, and I were best friends when we were teens. We worked on a show together called *Metal & Mayhem*. We played three outcasts forming a band. I always found it funny that Mylan was cast in a role that required singing even though he can't carry a tune for shite. The producers either used my voice or hired a professional singer to dub over Mylan's voice for the songs we sang on the show.

After the show got canceled three seasons later, our careers took off, and we slowly grew apart. Jensen and Mylan stayed close a lot longer than I did with either of them. I still kick myself in the arse for not being there for Mylan while he struggled with his addiction.

"I never asked you what part of Arkansas you're from," I say, distracting myself from my thoughts.

"Silo Springs."

"Wait, really?"

"You've heard of it?"

"I was just there for Lana and Mylan's wedding. I officiated it."

"Wait, is that what Adeline was talking about on the plane? With the faerie queen?"

I nod.

"Wow. What a small world. I worked at Lilies Bar & Grill. Lana was my boss before she moved away. I heard the wedding was gorgeous. They had the ceremony on a cliff at the lake, right?"

Before I can answer, she sighs dreamily and keeps talking.

"I wish I could have gone, but as you know, they only invited family and close friends."

Mylan met Lana Young when he was cast in the movie *Tyler's Team*. He got the role when I dropped out to care for Adeline. The movie was based on a true story of a college football star who died of cancer, and Lana was his fiancée. Mylan met Lana in Silo a few weeks before filming and asked her to help him with the character. They fell in love, and she helped him with his addiction.

To think I could have been in the same town as Savannah and met her sooner.

"Would Lana be willing to be your reference? I could call her."

"We worked together for at least three years, so I don't see why not." She beams at me. "I was there for all the madness when they filmed the movie. I worked a few shifts when Mylan came in to hang out with Lana. We had Rockstar Karaoke on Saturdays with a band playing instead of a track. Man, Mylan is a horrible singer, isn't he?"

"The worst."

"Can't dance either. Anyway, I remember all the fans and media showing up. You couldn't go anywhere around town without someone sticking a microphone in your face to ask about Mylan or Lana or the movie. Maybe that's why I reacted to you being famous the way I did."

She picks up a photo of me holding Adeline on the day she was born. I'm smiling as I look down at the tiny human life, wrapped like a glowworm in a pink blanket. I expect her to ask about that day or about my sister and how she died. Instead, she sets the frame down and looks away, clearing her throat.

"Does that mean you're friends with the guy who directed *Tyler's Team*? I can't believe he's dating Rebecca Taylor now. Everyone in Silo Springs thought they hated each other with how much they fought over the screenplay for the movie. Rebecca's book was fantastic, so I can't even imagine how hard it was cutting and changing stuff. They did a good job though. I never officially met Rebecca. We didn't go to school together since I'm five years younger. Have you met her?"

"I have. She's lovely. And, yes, her boyfriend Jensen is my friend. I worked with him and Mylan on a TV series when we were teens. I'm working with Mylan again on this new movie. It'll be the first time we've worked together on a project since *Metal & Mayhem* was canceled."

Her face lights up, eyes sparkling. "Is Lana going to be in New York with him during filming? I'd love to reunite with her."

"I believe so. We can invite them over for dinner."

"We?"

Bloody hell.

Did I just say that like we're a couple planning double dates with our friends?

"*I* can invite them over..."

She frowns and turns away from me to inspect some of my awards. Aside from the popcorn statue, I also have a People's Choice and Critics' Choice Award. She runs her fingertips over the nameplate of each one—over my name—as if not believing it's real. That I'm real.

She leaves the bookcase to walk back to me, stopping a foot away... leaving distance between us.

I almost reach out to pull her closer. Almost.

"I accept the job."

Oh, right. The job. I've been giving her the tour as if she already agreed.

"But these moments between us..." I hold my breath, waiting for her next words. "They need to stop. We need to reinforce the boundaries. Keep this... professional."

"Right, yes, of course."

My heart drops because even though I agree it's what's best, I'm selfish and would risk it all to have her.

"I really want to…"

"But?"

"I wouldn't be able to stop, and I need this job and I think Adeline needs me, so I can't risk that by… you know."

"Right. Boundaries."

"Boundaries," she echoes.

"Good."

"Great."

We stare at each other, silently, as if waiting for the other to change their mind. When neither of us says another word, Savannah purses her lips.

I desperately want to fight her on this, but I won't. I'd never push a woman to do something she doesn't want to do. Or something she wants to do but can't for whatever reason.

"Let me show you which room will be yours."

She drops her shoulders. Disappointment flashes across her face, but she's quick to plaster on a smile as I lead her out of the room.

I have a feeling this agreement of ours won't last long.

I hope it doesn't.

Chapter 5 – Savannah

I 'm on a break during my final lunch shift at the French bistro in SoHo when my phone dings with a text message.

Hot British Guy

> **Do you have a toilet paper preference?**

I made the mistake of telling Reynold I moved to NYC with nothing but two suitcases and a shoulder bag full of clothes, shoes, a few books, and personal items. The next day, the texts started.

He bombarded me with a million questions about supplies I want stocked in my bathroom. Everything from shampoo, conditioner, skin and hair care products, make-up, and even tampons and pads. Then he asked about my favorite foods and snacks to fill the cabinets and fridge in the kitchen and meals I wanted prepped by his chef. He even asked me my favorite color, which I assume he will implement in my room.

I tried telling him a million times not to buy me anything, but he ignored those texts. When he offered me his credit card to go shopping for new clothes, I called him.

"I don't need new clothes, Reynold."

"You told me all your clothes fit into one bag. I want you to have more."

"Then I'll buy them with the salary you *pay me for being* Addy's *nanny."*

"Part of the contract you signed, which you clearly failed to read, states that your employer covers wardrobe allowances. Just as your employer is covering all your food and transportation costs."

"My employer can go—"

"Stop fighting me on this, Savannah. I have more than enough money. Buy the damn clothes."

He's so freaking demanding sometimes, and even though he hung up on me before I could continue arguing, my curiosity got the best of me, and I googled his net worth. Despite taking a break from acting for five years, he'd filmed enough movies, making more and more with each one, to keep his bank account well fed.

Yeah. He's stinking rich. Like, multi-millionaire rich.

Me

Are you seriously asking me about toilet paper?

Hot British Guy

Yes

Me

I don't give a shit. Lol. Get it?

Hot British Guy

...

Me

Fine. Surprise me

I follow it up with poop and toilet paper emojis.

He sends an eye roll emoji because 'surprise me' has been my answer to a lot of his texts.

Hot British Guy

I just want to make sure you have everything you need before you arrive

Me

You've done more than enough

Hot British Guy

I can always do more

When I don't answer, he sends another text.

Hot British Guy

Don't forget. The car will be there at 3. The driver will help bring down your belongings

Me

I won't forget. And I don't need help. I got the bags up the stairs and inside the Airbnb all by myself. I'm perfectly capable of bringing them back down. Stop. Worrying.

Another eye roll emoji.

Hot British Guy

Just trying to help

It's been like this all week. I'd respond to his text messages, adding silly emojis, and he'd send back the eye roll one. I tried sending a GIF once, and he reacted to it with a 'thumbs down.'

Filming for Reynold's new movie begins in a week, but he has a final table read scheduled for tomorrow morning. He also has fight training sessions and other movie-related errands to take care of. He has a busy week ahead, and he didn't want to ask his house manager, Brenda, or Eloise and Kelly to watch Adeline. They've been helping him out enough.

He officially hired me after running the background check, which found all the arrests I informed him about. He'd called to tell me that his lawyers and public relations team did *not* like that I had a record. They urged him to find someone else, but he refused.

Since I start tomorrow, that means I'm moving in today. He wanted me to move in last week, but that was not happening. I needed to distance myself from the man after our tension packed 'moments.' I'm hoping with him being on set for hours upon end, we'll rarely cross paths. It's for the best because I just know I'm not strong enough to control myself around him.

Reynold also suggested I quit the French bistro job, and he'd cover whatever I would have made this past week. As tempting as that offer was, my pride wouldn't allow it. I'm about to enter his rich world where he's literally paying for everything, including my six-figure salary (I almost fainted when I read $150,000/year on the contract), my food, and my transportation. And apparently my freaking wardrobe. I needed this week to mentally prepare for all that.

Reynold is giving me this opportunity of a better life after years of struggle and it's going to take some time to get used to. I'm also struggling to get used to the way he cares. I feel pampered. Spoiled. Never in my life has anyone treated me like he does. While I enjoy messing with him over the text messages, he's doing everything in his power to make sure I'm comfortable in his home. A part of me feels it should be the other way around. But then I remember this man is rich as fuck, and he can afford to buy all these things.

After my thirty-minute break, I serve my last two tables. By two p.m., I'm walking out the door and hopping on the 1 train back to my Hamilton Heights rental. I packed everything up last night, so five minutes before the car arrives, I lug my suitcases down the three flights of stairs.

An SUV pulls up to the curb as I'm exiting the building, struggling to keep both roller bags upright. Next thing I know, a tall, skinny man with deep brown skin is grabbing my luggage and carrying it for me.

"I'm George," the man says, loading my two suitcases into the back and taking my shoulder bag to add to the stack. "I've been driving for Mister Michaelson for the past five years. It's very nice to meet you, Savannah."

"Please, call me Savvy."

"Of course," he says and offers me a kind smile, causing wrinkles around his brown eyes.

He opens the back door for me, and I duck my head to get in. Holy crap. This is nice. It has seat warmers, small TV screens in the headrests, and a mini fridge stored in between the driver and passenger seats.

"This is so weird," I mumble.

George chuckles as he merges into traffic. "Give it a week, Sunshine, and you'll think nothin' of it."

His deep voice and adorable New York accent calm my nerves. Not only am I anxious about entering this world of fame and money, but I'm also scared to see Reynold again. It's been a week and I couldn't stop thinking about him... and how badly I want to kiss him (even though I punched him when he tried). His intoxicating woody and spicy scent mixed with whatever body wash and shampoo he uses when he caged me between his arms. His warm breath that smelled like coffee and maple syrup from the waffles he ate that morning.

I spend the entire commute daydreaming about doing naughty things with my new boss, and suddenly we're pulling up to the front of Reynold's building. The beautiful limestone façade almost seems magical. Is this real? Certainly, I'll wake up from whatever fever dream I'm having.

George opens my door, pulling me from my thoughts. I attempt to retrieve my luggage from the back, but he shoos me away.

The building's doorman walks out with a cart and stops in front of me. He's a short white man, big like me, wearing a suit, hat, and white gloves. Sweat lines his head below the brim of the hat.

"This must be Savannah Monroe. I'm Peter." He also has a New York accent, but it's not deep like George's. It's a bit nasally and reminds me of the characters from *The Sopranos,* which Brad used to make me watch. I suppose, to me, everyone from New York sounds like the characters from that show.

Peter hands me a card.

"This is the key to the elevator that gives you access to the Penthouse." He chuckles. "Don't look so scared. Mister Michaelson is the nicest tenant we have in this building."

Peter walks on, rolling the luggage cart to the SUV. George, who I didn't realize was still standing next to me, pats my shoulder. "Go on in and we'll bring your bags up. Don't you worry, Sunshine."

That's the second time he's called me Sunshine, which is also my dad's nickname for me because of my blonde hair. I miss my parents. It's almost been a year since I've seen them. I really need to plan a trip to visit. George's nickname is like having a little piece of home here with me. Despite my anxiety about this... strange new life of mine, I smile, letting a wave of calm wash over me.

"You can do this, Savannah," I tell myself. "Reynold is your boss. A man. He's just a man." *A stupidly gorgeous man who you can't stop thinking about.*

I leave George and Peter behind to haul up my luggage, which I still find strange letting them do for me. Inside the elevator, I tap the key card and the doors close, jerking slightly as it ascends to the top floor.

Laughter hits my ears when I enter the apartment and I follow the sound down the hallway to the open concept kitchen, dining, living area. Reynold stands at the island with two people I recognize from the French bistro.

"Sexy Savvy!" the one with tanned skin says. Their hair is shaved on the sides and longer on top. They are short and curvy. More mid-size than plus-size like me.

I blush at their words and dart my eyes to Reynold.

"Kelly," he warns. Kelly bursts into a fit of giggles with the stunning blonde woman at their side joining in on the joke.

Kelly holds up their hands. "Your words, Renny."

"You said that about me?" I choke out.

"He sure did," Kelly blurts before he can answer. He flips them off, which has the two cackling even harder.

The blonde woman stands and walks to me with her hand out, which I take. "Hi, I'm Eloise and this is my partner, Kelly." She points her thumb at them.

"Nice to meet you two."

Kelly joins us. "Oh, no. The pleasure is all ours."

"Would you two knock it off?" Reynold growls.

"What's wrong, Renny? Are we embarrassing you?" Kelly teases.

"As a matter of fact, yes, you are," he says and crosses his arms.

Kelly and Eloise look at each other, then erupt into another fit of giggles. Reynold tosses up his hands and rolls his eyes. He walks off, stopping at a table just inside the kitchen.

Once Eloise composes herself, she places a palm on my shoulder. "It's really fun to mess with him."

Reynold's back is to us as he shuffles through a pile of mail, ignoring us all. "Oh, I know exactly what you mean."

He throws the stack down on the table with a smack. "Could you not egg them on, Savannah?"

I salute him. "Sir, yes, sir."

Eloise and Kelly lose it, and I cover my mouth to hide my laughter. The corner of Reynold's mouth twitches as he struggles not to smile too.

"Where's Adeline?" I ask, scoping out the living room. It's Sunday so she wouldn't be at school.

"In her room, taking a nap," Reynold answers. "We went on a bike ride through Central Park earlier today and it wiped her out."

The elevator dings announcing my luggage arriving and I leave the kitchen, walking past Reynold so I can retrieve it.

I don't make it far before his large hand wraps around my elbow. "Let me do it."

"No, it's fine."

I attempt to keep walking, but he moves in front of me, and I nearly crash into his chest.

What the hell?

"Move out of the way, *Rey*."

His eyes widen, clearly not a fan of me calling him Rey.

"Let me help, *Savvy*."

I narrow my eyes at him, and we face off in a game of chicken. Who will back down first?

Both of us have lived lives where we've been independent, taking care of others before ourselves. He wants to help me, but he's *been* helping. Too much. I can't even breathe without him asking if I need more oxygen pumped into my body.

I poke my finger into his muscle-bound chest, attempting to push him back. "I can get my luggage myself."

He smirks, amused at this little spat we're having, and gently wraps his long fingers around my wrist to stop me from poking him. "Stop being stubborn and just let someone take care of you for once."

I scoff and rip my arm out of his grip. "Or you could stop being an overbearing asshole."

He sucks in a breath and clamps his mouth shut. I immediately regret calling him an asshole. He's not an asshole. The opposite. And he's right. I'm being stubborn. I don't mean to be, but I've never needed to rely on anyone, so I'm struggling to hand all this control over to him.

"Mister Michaelson, if you'd just point the way..." Peter says, standing like a deer caught in headlights.

"Right," Reynold says and finally breaks eye contact with me.

"Reynold," I whisper, but he's already stalking away, with Peter following.

By the time I force myself to walk to the room where I'll be staying, Peter has unloaded my luggage and is rolling the cart past me to head back down to the lobby. He nods and I offer him a weak smile.

I lean my shoulder on the door frame and watch Reynold try to balance my bags next to the dresser, then give up and lay them down. When he turns to leave, he spots me and freezes.

"If there's anything else you need..."

"Reynold... I'm sorry—"

"It's fine, Savannah."

"No. It's not fine. You're not an asshole. I'm the asshole."

"What about overbearing?"

"Oh, no, you're definitely overbearing," I say with a smile, and he barks out a laugh, which has my cheeks warming with a blush. "It's just... you've done too much for me already, and I'm literally here to help *you*."

He doesn't respond right away, but he swallows hard, and I watch his Adam's apple bob in his throat.

"I know," he says quietly.

I walk into the room, closing the distance between us. The need to touch him, to place my palm over his heart again and feel it thundering underneath my hand like it did a week ago, is nearly debilitating. Still, I stop myself before reaching out.

"Can you promise me something?"

He holds his breath and nods.

"Promise you'll stop worrying about me."

His shoulders sag, and I can see the argument on the tip of his tongue, ready to burst free. He keeps the fighting words to himself.

"I'll let you know the minute I need help. Okay?"

He searches my eyes for the longest time, going through some sort of inner battle.

"Okay. I promise."

A fter Reynold leaves, I unpack. It doesn't take long since I don't have many belongings. I place my three pairs of shoes in the built-in cubbyholes in the walk-in closet that's big enough to fit a full-size bed inside, then hang my skirts, dresses, and shirts. I'd have to hang up a hundred more outfits just to fill this thing up. My underwear, tights, and pants all went into the white wooden dresser that I'm guessing is an antique.

As expected, Reynold painted the room a beautiful teal: my favorite color. The green sheets and comforter on the queen-sized bed explain why he asked if I had any other favorite colors.

I check out the bathroom next, which he stocked with all the products he asked me about. He bought my favorite coconut shampoo and conditioner, brown sugar body wash, face cleaner, shaving gel, razors, and a teal loofa. I pull the green towel off the rack and hold it up against my body.

Extra-large.

I didn't even ask for towels and if I had, I would have requested the biggest ones he could find. He really thought of everything, which makes me feel like such an asshole for calling him an asshole.

A perfume bottle sits next to a brand-new pack of toothpaste and a toothbrush, and I pick it up. Amber Romance from Victoria's Secret. How did he know? I spray myself with my favorite scent and leave the bathroom.

I walk over to the floor to ceiling windows and gasp when spotting a balcony, which I didn't see when I first toured the apartment. Reynold also failed to tell me about it. I unlock the deadbolt and step out to the sounds of honking since this room faces Fifth Avenue. It also has a breathtaking view of Central Park. Two chairs and a small table fit on the small deck, and I'm already imagining sitting out here to watch the sunset.

"Savvy?!" a tiny voice calls out to me.

I leave the banister of the balcony and return to the room, closing the door and locking it. Seconds later, Adeline runs into my room and slams into me with one of her ferocious hugs.

"I'm sorry," Reynold says, trailing behind. "I tried to tell her not to bother you."

Adeline plants her chin into my stomach to look up at me. "Am I bothering you?"

I wink at her. "Never."

She releases me and turns to Reynold, crossing her arms. "See, told you Dad."

He raises his brow and gives me a pointed look. I shrug and he shakes his head with a smile that does things to my body:

his blue eyes light up and a cute half-moon forms around his mouth on one side.

"Dad made dinner, and he said you have to join us. He said you have to sit next to him too." Adeline's energetic words rush out. She takes hold of my hand to lead me out of the room.

Guess I'm going to dinner.

"Adeline Lee, you know that's not what I said. I said we'd ask if she wants to join because it's not required," Reynold sighs.

Addy giggles and pulls my arm so I can lean down. Next to my ear, she whispers, "Eloise and Kelly told me to say all that."

"I heard that," Reynold growls. He grabs Adeline by the waist and starts tickling her. Addy laughs and squeals and she releases my hand to run away from her dad.

He chases her while snarling like a monster and she screams all the way to the dining area where Eloise and Kelly are sitting and dinner is being served.

I feel like I'm intruding on a family dinner.

Reynold helps Adeline in her chair, then sits next to her. I stand off to the side.

"What's wrong?" he asks.

"I think I'm just going to..." I point my thumb over my shoulder.

"Sit down, Savannah."

Fuck. Why'd he have to say it all sexy and demanding like that? He pulls out the seat next to him and I sit like a good girl.

I blow out a breath and silently question why I'm here. Was this a mistake? Because after everything he's done for me—the room, the towels, the perfume—there's no way I'm not crossing the boundaries we've set.

Chapter 6 - Reynold

S avannah is quiet during dinner. She appears uncomfortable at first. I'm assuming it's because of whatever prompted her to try to back out of joining us. She only relaxes when we start eating and share stories about our lives.

"How'd you two meet?" Savannah asks Eloise and Kelly and takes a bite of creamy spinach stuffed salmon.

"I was the photographer at Ginger and Bruno's wedding in Hawaii and Kelly was DJ'ing," Eloise says with a smile and a blush. "I'd just finished my duties, and I really wanted to shake my ass on the dance floor, so I go up to their booth and request a Bad Bunny song."

"Someone always wants to hear a Bad Bunny song," Kelly adds and shakes their head.

Eloise giggles. "Kelly scowled just like they're doing now, and I took out my phone—since I'd already put away my camera—and started taking pictures."

"I hate getting my picture taken." Kelly's scowl deepens.

"They said, 'you better delete that photo.' And I said, 'make me.'" Eloise waves the fork in her hand around as she speaks. "After some arguing back and forth, I said, 'I'll tell you what; you play Bad Bunny and I'll delete the photo.'"

"I played Bad Bunny," Kelly finishes the story with a face splitting grin.

"And I didn't delete the photo," Eloise says, smirking. "We flirted all night and have been together ever since."

"That's so sweet," Savannah says, her hand over her chest as if the story was too much for her heart to take. "I was supposed to go to Ginger's wedding. We worked together at Lilies Bar and Grill in Silo Springs. I couldn't make it, though."

"Didn't Lana pay for everyone's tickets and rooms?" Eloise asks.

"Yeah," Savannah answers. "It's a long story."

I want to ask if it's because of her ex, but she would tell us if she wanted us to know. So, I keep my mouth shut, not wanting to make her uncomfortable.

Savannah's leg brushes against mine and it's not the first time it's happened tonight. I desperately want to grab it and run my palm up and down her thigh. I can't stop thinking about touching her, which I want to do all the time.

I tune out Eloise talking about upcoming photo shoots for fashion magazines and watch Savannah as she listens intently. She smiles and nods and asks questions when appropriate. She truly cares about my friends' lives.

Kelly speaks next, talking about auditioning for a DJ'ing residency at One Note SoHo, a high-profile club where the rich and famous frequent. A club I've been to with Mylan and Jensen. I remember that night. Mylan had just lost a role in a movie because of his addiction, and he'd gone out to drown his sorrows in booze and drugs. I met him and Jensen there, but I didn't stay long because I had an early flight the next morning. I left before Mylan lost control.

He's been sober for five years now. This movie I'm about to film with him is his first role since he left acting to recover. It's my first role since leaving to take care of Adeline. We can help each other during filming—support each other and bond. We're still working to rebuild the friendship that was fractured because of our busy lives and tragic life happenings.

I'm pulled from my thoughts by Adeline's excited voice. She's made her way into Savannah's lap and is rambling on about preschool and the friends she's making. She talks about recess and art and learning French. It's a posh preschool that teaches five-year-olds different languages. She also wants to enroll in violin lessons. She talks about more things that all merge as her excitement to share her life with this woman grows.

My chest tightens and my throat aches as I watch them together. Adeline didn't grow up with a motherly figure in her life. She had no one to connect with, aside from me and the part-time nanny who was only around for a few hours a week.

I sheltered her life mostly from the media, but also because I didn't want to confuse her. I didn't date anyone these past five years because my previous relationships never lasted. I couldn't bring a woman home to meet her then chance Addy becoming attached.

I've been so alone.

Savannah grabs my knee and squeezes, making me jolt. "You okay?" she mouths as Addy continues to babble in her ear.

I smile and nod, and she squeezes my knee one more time before letting go.

This is why Savannah is different. She's the first person in a long time to see past my fame, which is her least favorite thing about me. She sees the real me, not the one I manufactured for the world.

I check my phone. It's nearing nine. "Okay, Poppy. It's time for bed."

Eloise and Kelly stand, calling it a night and retreating to a guest room.

"I'm not even tired, Dad. Can I please stay up and hang out with Savvy?" Adeline whines, which is immediately followed up with a yawn. She blinks her dark blue eyes, struggling to keep them open.

"I'm tired too, Adeline," Savannah says. "We'll hang out tomorrow after you're done with school. It's going to be so much fun. We should probably sleep, though, so we'll have enough energy."

She fakes a yawn and stretches her arms over her head, which pushes her breasts up high and reveals part of her stomach.

I ignore my cock jumping at the sight.

"Okay," Addy grumbles and hops off Savannah's lap.

I lead the grumpy child to her room. She picks out a book about a flying dog for me to read. I only get a couple of pages in before she passes out. I kiss her on the forehead, tuck the blankets under her chin, and return to the kitchen to clean up.

Savannah has already cleared the table, wiped it down, and is now rinsing off the dishes and putting them in the dishwasher.

I open my mouth to protest her help but clamp it shut after remembering her words from earlier. She's right. Having her here helping with the things I spent five years doing on my own has already lessened my stress. Can she help with my sleepless nights?

"Thank you for cleaning up," I say, my voice making her jump.

She drops a plate, and it shatters on the floor.

"Dammit to hell," she says in that sweet honey accent. She squats down to pick up the pieces and I rush over to help. "For such a big man, you sure are quiet on your feet."

I take the broken plate from her and stand to toss it in the rubbish. When I'm done, she's already back to putting the dishes in the dishwater.

"Your accent gets thicker when you're scared," I muse.

"It does not."

"*It does not,*" I mimic in a Southern twang, which I'm brilliant at if I do say so myself.

She playfully pushes at my arm and I still at her touch. My cock twitches at her nearness, her sweet smell, and sexy, sultry voice. If I move at this moment, I'll take her in my arms and show her exactly what her touch does to me.

"Yeah, well, for a British person, your accent isn't very Britishy."

"That's not a word."

"You know what I mean," she says and tries to hide her smile.

I join her at the sink and hold out my hand for the dish she's rinsing off.

"I moved from England when I was sixteen. Now I'm thirty. Most of the characters I play are American. My accent isn't what it used to be."

"Do you hate that?"

I shrug. "It's just who I am now."

"Is that why Adeline doesn't have an accent? Because she's always lived here?"

I nod. "She had one at first because of me. Then she started watching American cartoons and kids' programming and she wanted to talk like her favorite characters. She's also been in preschool since September, so any trace of an accent she once had is now gone."

"You sound sad about that."

"I'm..." my voice catches in my throat. "I was at first, but then I realized Adeline probably would have had an American accent even if my sister had lived. Annalee had no intention of moving back to England. So, Adeline would have grown up without a British accent."

She hands me a wine glass. "At least she doesn't have a country bumpkin accent like mine."

"I like your country bumpkin accent. It's cute."

"Cute?" she says an octave higher, almost sounding offended. "Not sexy?"

Her tongue swipes over her plump bottom lip, which draws my attention to her mouth. It parts slightly, a perfect 'o' as she notices my response. Can she hear my heart beating this close? Does she realize how badly I want her at this moment?

I clear my throat. We set boundaries for a reason.

"My final table read is at nine tomorrow morning at Kaufman studios in Queens. Adeline usually wakes up around seven. Preschool starts at nine. I'll make her breakfast before I leave at eight, but you might have to get her dressed. So I'll need you awake before I leave."

"Of course."

"And I hired two bodyguards who will escort you and Addy—"

"Like suit and tie, secret service type bodyguards?"

I shake my head but can't help smiling. "No, like dressed-in-regular-clothes-and-staying-back-so-not-to-seem-too-obvious bodyguards."

She giggles, and it's such a pure sound that I almost want to start rattling off jokes just to hear it again. I think I'm hilarious, but I'm British. My humor is rather dry. Not everyone gets it.

"If you and Addy go anywhere after school, Sarah and Henry will protect you. I've done my best keeping her out of the spotlight, but over the past year, they've caught us in public together. Enough that the paparazzi might recognize her now. Though, without me beside her, she might have more anonymity. It's possible no one will spot you two together at all."

"What if they do find us?"

"Sarah and Henry will keep them back and my driver, George—you met him—will be nearby waiting in case you need a fast getaway. You are not obligated to answer the paparazzi's questions. That's up to you. My publicist team can send you some things to say if you'd like."

She nods, nervously chewing on her bottom lip.

"Don't worry," I say, tapping her chin and she releases it. "I don't expect you to have any issues with them. They don't know where we live or where Addy goes to school, at least not yet. The few times they've spotted me with Addy, we were running errands around Manhattan. Someone once saw us at the Bronx Zoo and sold the photos to the tabloids. It's possible something like that could happen if a fan recognizes her, but it's highly unlikely."

She relaxes her tense shoulders slightly.

"I'll be home around six because I have fight training, then meetings with my PR team after. My chef Shirley will be here by four to make dinner. There will be leftovers for lunch if you need, but I'll leave money in case you want to order takeout."

"Reynold," she begins. "I don't think you can prepare me any more than you already have. I've got this."

My near-constant anxiety melts away at her words. "Right. Yes. Sorry."

"Tell me what your movie is about."

I suck in a breath of surprise. "You really didn't Google a thing about me, did you?"

"No. After I found out you're famous, I decided not to. Is that why you give me a weird look when I ask about you? Answers I should know because they're on the internet?"

"Yeah, even after people find out who I am, they go online to research me. Why didn't you?"

"I don't know..." she shrugs. "I guess I want to get to know Reynold, the single father from the plane and not Rey, the A-list celebrity who the media exploits because something tragic happened to him."

"Thank you for that." She hands me the last plate. I place it on the rack, put a detergent pod in its holder, then start the dishwasher.

"For what?"

"For treating me like I'm a normal man."

She smirks. "Oh, Renny. You are nowhere near normal."

I grimace at her using Eloise and Kelly's nickname for me, which causes her to giggle again. Why is she so damn adorable?

She dries off her hands before sitting on a stool at the island. "So... the movie?"

"Oh, right. It's an action flick. I play a heartbroken widower attempting to seek revenge on the men who killed his wife. Mylan is playing the detective assigned to stop my character."

"How did the wife die?" she asks, eyes wide. She rests her head in her palm, elbow perched on the marble surface.

"She was a secretary at a company that was laundering money and became the scapegoat to hide her bosses' crimes."

I lean my hip against the counter, arms crossed.

"That sounds intense."

"Yeah. I have a lot of stunts in the movie, mostly fight scenes. Since I perform my own stunts, I'll be working with a choreographer over the next week to block the shots. We've had a few sessions already and I'll have more throughout filming."

"I must confess... I'm not a fan of action movies. I'm more of a rom-com gal. Or documentaries. I love a good crime doc. Is that why I didn't recognize you on the plane? Because you only star in action movies? Have you acted in any romances?"

I flinch at the question, and her brows crease because she saw it.

"*Tyler's Team* was going to be my first romantic drama."

Before she can offer her sympathy or ask questions about that part of my life, I clear my throat. "I should head off to bed."

I turn to leave, but not before seeing her frown at my abrupt need to end this conversation.

"Reynold," she says. I pause and glance over my shoulder. "I know I talk a lot, but I also love listening."

I nod once and smile. I plan to take her up on that offer.

When I'm ready.

"Good night, Savannah," I finally say and leave her standing in the kitchen.

I'm the last to arrive for the table read this morning. I woke up to Savannah and Addy in the kitchen making pancakes. They had music blasting, giggling like schoolgirls, and were covered in batter: their hands, arms, clothes. Savannah even had a drop of batter on her nose. I couldn't help myself when I wiped it off with the pad of my thumb and stuck it in my mouth. The move made her blush beautifully.

I didn't want to leave, so I stayed until the last possible second, which made me late.

I take the last seat at the table next to Mylan. He's looking great. I remember seeing photos of him splashed all over the tabloids during the worst of his addiction and he appeared slimmer, paler. Now he's bulked up with muscles that could almost rival my own. He's shaved his curly hair to the buzz cut required for his character. His wife, Lana, was not happy about that.

He smiles, his blue eyes lighting up as we greet with our not-so-secret handshake that we made up as teens with Jensen. Three palm slaps, two fist bumps, a fist to the chest over the heart.

"How was the honeymoon?" I ask.

"Man, two weeks was not long enough." He slinks down in his seat and ruffles the pages of the script with his finger-tips. "Lana and I could have stayed in Greece for a month if I hadn't booked this role, but..." He shrugs. "It was time I returned to acting. I've missed it, and I'm pretty sure Lana is tired of me being around all the time."

"Isn't she coming up here next week?"

"Yeah, but she's not staying long. Maybe a month and a half."

I frown. From what Jensen has told me, Lana keeps him grounded and distracted from his disease.

"Don't give me that look, Ren. I'll be fine. I'm happy and madly in love with a woman who fulfills me in ways booze and drugs never could."

I grimace. "Sorry, I didn't mean..."

"I know. You're just worried, and I don't fault you for that. Honestly, it happens all the time. People tend to remember mistakes and hardships."

He's right. I'm worried for my friend who I lost a lot of years with because of our busy lives. When *Metal & Mayhem* ended, I was nineteen and already had a full year of projects booked. I stayed too busy to hang out with Mylan and Jensen, enough that I don't think Mylan even considered me a friend anymore. Being there for him, caring for and protecting him, like we did as teenagers, is all I want now that he's back in my life.

My phone vibrates with a text message, and I take it out of my pocket to read it.

Sexy Savvy

See what you missed after you left?

She sends a photo and I belt out a laugh.

Sexy Savvy

I let Adeline do my makeup before taking her to school. What do you think?

She looks like a clown. Literally. Bright blue eyeshadow and red lipstick that has more around her lips than on it.

Me

Did you go out in public like that?

She sends the side-eye emoji followed by another picture of her walking down the sidewalk with Sarah and Henry trailing behind.

Yep. She went out in public like that.

Me

Weren't you worried about paparazzi? Perhaps it's not a good idea to draw attention to yourself

Sexy Savvy

Addy dared me to. I had to

Me

Wait. How does she know about dares?

Sexy Savvy

That's what I asked, and she said the kids at school learned from their siblings and taught Addy. They dare each other all the time at recess

Another picture comes through. Central Park is behind her and a few people standing nearby stare with amused looks on their faces.

My fans

They're clearly jealous

Savannah sends me two emojis: one of a crown and the other of a hand getting its nails painted.

"There's only one reason someone smiles at their phone like that."

I lock my phone's screen and put it back in my pocket.

"I don't know what you're talking about."

"Who's the girl?"

I sigh, attempting and failing to hide my smile. "There's no girl. I was smiling at something my daughter did."

"Liar. Show me."

The movie's director enters the room at that moment, followed by a team of producers and other key crew members.

Mylan leans into me and whispers, "Is it the nanny? The one you called Lana about?"

My eyes widen because of course Lana told Mylan that I asked about Savannah. Lana did sound a little too excited talking about how she's an excellent and reliable worker. It wasn't until she mentioned Savvy being funny and beautiful and newly single that I got a little suspicious of this glowing recommendation.

"It is! I knew it," Mylan hisses. The director—a man in his forties who's going to be the next Michael Bay with all the action movies he directs—is talking about... well, I'm not sure because I'm not paying attention.

Did I really have 'a look' on my face reading that text? Clearly, since Mylan called me out on it. I don't think I've ever had that look when talking to a woman; that goofy, can't stop smiling, can't stop thinking about them look.

The table read went on without a hitch. It took three hours for the cast of ten men and five women to read through the lines while the director, producers, and script coordinator made notes for scene changes.

Everyone lingers after to chat. Mylan and I are the youngest cast members, aside from the woman playing my wife. Victoria Bedford has a few romance movies on her credits, but this is her first action film, though she won't have a lot of screen time. The majority of her scenes are flashbacks, which we're filming towards the end of production. She's five-five and petite with long, dark blonde hair and green eyes.

I wouldn't say I have a type. I consider attraction and beauty to be unconditional. I've been attracted to a wide variety of women because each one had something wonderful and exciting about them. All different and individual in their own rights.

And then there's Savannah. A phenomenal and gorgeous plus-size woman who makes me feel alive like no one else. She makes me laugh when the past five years have been full of heartache.

The chemistry between Victoria and me is perfect for the role. It'll help audiences sympathize with my character when Victoria's character is killed, but it's all professional on my side. Not so much for her.

She's definitely flirting with me.

"I haven't been to the city in years. You should show me around when we're both off. Or this weekend before filming starts?" she says, her voice a pitch higher in that sexy, trying-to-woo-me voice.

"Oh... um... I'm pretty busy so..."

She shrugs and lays a hand on my forearm. "We'll play it by ear."

She winks, then walks away. I don't even watch her go.

If it were Savannah, though...

"Wow," Mylan says next to me. Did he just witness that? "She wants your dick."

I scoff at his crudeness.

"Unless... it belongs to someone else?" he adds, smirking. He was totally being crude on purpose to get a reaction out of me.

"I am not talking to you about this," I say and roll my eyes, which makes Mylan grin, the wanker. "When is Lana arriving again? Savannah wants to reunite, and I thought you two could come over for dinner."

"Like a double date?"

"No, like four friends eating dinner together."

Mylan chuckles and shakes his head. "She flies in late on Wednesday next week. We're down for dinner. It'll have to be a night we both get done filming early though."

That could make organizing a dinner difficult. Sometimes the filming schedule changes the night before. It's possible Lana and Savannah will have to hang out without us. The two of them can play tourist around New York City. Addy would love that too. Though, Lana is as famous as me and Mylan, so Savannah might be hesitant to be seen in public with her. I'm sure Lana is bringing the disguises she and Mylan like to wear in public to hide in plain sight.

I shouldn't worry. Lana will have bodyguards on top of the two I hired for Savannah and Addy.

"Sounds good, brother," I say and bring Mylan in for a hug.

He waves as he leaves and I'm not far behind, hopping into the car with the new driver I hired so George can stay with Savannah and Adeline. Xavier gives me a nod and drives off, heading to Midtown from Queens where I'm meeting the movie's stunt coordinator and fight choreographer. Mylan and I have a big fight scene at the end of the movie, but our practice session isn't for a couple of days.

It's barely noon and I'm already exhausted. This fight practice is going to kick my ass, especially since it's been well over five years since I've done workouts this intense.

I just wish I were back home with Adeline and Savannah.

We'll be filming for at least five months. It's going to be a long five months if I already miss my daughter this much.

And the woman I just met three weeks ago.

ENTERTAINMENT NOW

MYLAN & REY'S RETURN TO ACTING
By Angela Borrows

Mylan Andrews arrived at JFK on his private jet, sporting a buzz cut for his new movie, A Man's Revenge. He plays the role of a NYPD detective who investigates the death of a woman believed to be linked to the mob. Andrews stars alongside his Metal & Mayhem co-star, Rey Michaelson. Michaelson is playing the husband of the murdered woman who is determined to find his wife's killers.

This is the first film for Michaelson since he took a break from acting five years ago to take care of his niece after the death of his sister. Entertainment Now reached out to his PR team who says he's hired a live-in nanny to assist with care while he's on set.

This is also the first movie for Andrews after he went into a year-long recovery program for his alcoholism and drug addiction. He's been focusing on his nonprofit, Beyond the Bright Lights over the past few years, helping others in their recovery. When asked about concerns of a relapse, Andrews's manager Tony Wadeson said, "Absolutely not. That time in Mylan's life has passed."

Chapter 7 - Savannah

I never considered how bored I'd be while Addy was at school for seven hours.

The days drag on.

The first day, I walked through Central Park. Sarah and Henry tagged along, despite me insisting they didn't need to. I bought us hotdogs and sodas from a nice man with a cart and we sat at the Bethesda Fountain, eating in silence, because neither of them is very chatty. Then we walked to a field, and I sat underneath a maple tree, reading a spicy romance book on my Kindle before it was time to pick Addy up.

The second day, I walked across the Upper East Side to a cute little park along the East River. I sat on a bench, watching the rushing water and ferries zooming past. I never imagined New York City to be so peaceful. No honking cars or boisterous crowds, aside from the dozen or so people on a run, jog, or walking their dog along the waterfront.

Now it's day three of this new job.

I finally gave in and used Reynold's credit card to go shopping for clothes. I searched for some local plus-size stores and found a place called Wray on the Lower East Side. It was heaven. They had sizes from XXS up to 6X. I'm 2X. I've got an apple body shape—small breasts and a big belly. I tried on so many clothes: angel maxi slip dresses, sundresses, dresses that had cutouts in the front and back, crop tops, skirts, jeans.

I bought every single thing.

The store is pricy, but I found a few items on sale. Still, I spent upwards of $2,000.

Back in my room at the penthouse, I send Reynold two pictures, one of me holding up the bag, showing the store's name and another of the receipt.

Me

Thanks sugar daddy

I follow up with a kissy face emoji.

We've been getting bolder, amping up our flirting with each text exchange. He even sent a winking face emoji the other day. The 'sugar daddy' text is definitely in violation of the boundaries we agreed on. I'm hoping he'll call me out on it. Deep down, I ache to be punished for my bad behavior.

I'm about to set my phone down, since he never texts back until hours later because he's busy training, but this time he responds immediately. My face heats and my stomach clenches with anticipation.

Hot British Guy

> **You went to a store called Wray? Do you miss me that much?**

Me

> **Don't think you're special. Besides, the spelling is different**

Hot British Guy

> **Show me what you bought**

Me

> **Aren't you busy fighting someone or something?**

Hot British Guy

> **I'm on a break. Show me**

Me

> **Fine Mr. Bossy Pants**

I take out all the clothes and lay them out on my bed. I snap a picture and send it to him. The three dots that let me know he's typing pop up. They disappear, then pop up again.

Hot British Guy

That's not what I meant

Me

Huh? What else could you mean?

Hot British Guy

I want to see them on you

Me

You... you want me to try them on?

Hot British Guy

Yes

Me

Try them on and send you pictures? Of me? In the clothes?

Hot British Guy

That's exactly what I want

Me

I bought lingerie too

I didn't, but I want to see his response.

Me

Shall I model that for you, too, sir?

Hot British Guy

Before he can make more demands that I'd surely give in to, I send another text.

Me

I'm afraid you have a very important job to do, and I can't distract you by sending Sexy Savvy Selfies, which is in clear violation of the boundaries of our working relationship, therefore, I decline your order to model my clothes. #boundaries

I know I'm teasing him, but he started it. I'm the innocent one here, I swear.

Okay, maybe not since, technically, I called him sugar daddy.

He replies with an eye roll emoji.

Hot British Guy

See you tonight at dinner, Savannah

I fall back onto the bed on top of my clothes, clutching the phone to my chest like I'm some high school girl with a crush. Thirty-five years old and I've never had a man make me act so giddy. I told him I want to remain professional, but every day, every flirty text, I'm considering amending the boundaries or dropping them altogether.

When Reynold walks into the Penthouse hours later, just after seven, he's sweaty, and there's a bruise forming under his eye. He also has minor cuts on his lip, eyebrow, and cheek.

I stand from the stool at the bar in the kitchen. "What the hell happened?"

"Savvy, you owe me a dollar," Addy says, not looking up from the picture book she's reading. She's propped up on her knees, arms folded on the counter, hovered over the book.

"Hell isn't a bad word," I say.

"My teacher said it was when I said it."

"Why did you say... nevermind." I turn back to Reynold.

"Mylan happened." He opens the fridge and grabs a bottled water. He unscrews the lid and pours the cool liquid down his throat. "You know how he's a terrible dancer?"

I nod.

"He's bad at fight choreography too. I'm sure you know that the fights in movies aren't real. We're not supposed to make actual contact, but Mylan slipped up twice and punched me."

I cover my mouth with my palm.

"It's not funny."

I clear my throat. "Right. Of course."

He scowls because I can't stop smiling, even as I walk over to him and grab his hand. "Let me clean you up."

"It's fine. Don't worry about it."

Ignoring his protest, I drag him into the bathroom.

I sit him on the closed toilet seat while I search his medicine cabinet for the supplies I'll need. Then I step between his legs and get to work. I start with the cut on his eyebrow, soaking a cotton ball with witch hazel and dabbing it on. He jerks slightly, either at the cold liquid or the sting from the disinfectant. Once satisfied it's clean, I cover it with one of Adeline's Hello Kitty bandages.

I repeat the process for his lip.

The restraint I have while tending to these minor wounds is impressive. He smells so fucking good. His sweat mixed with that spicy wooden scent of his is making my panties wet enough I might need to change them. My nipples harden and poke at the fabric of my bra. Can he see them through my white T-shirt?

I'm carefully dabbing his lip with the witch hazel while avoiding eye contact when he suddenly seizes hold of my wrist.

"You should go."

He swallows hard, his Adam's apple dancing with the movement.

My nearness must be affecting him too, or maybe he sees my reaction to him.

"Please, Savannah, before I cross the boundary we set."

What if I want him to cross the boundary? We've been approaching the line and one of us is bound to cross it sooner than later.

I stifle a groan when he stands and walks around me. I suppose he's right. We set those boundaries because of me. Because it's what I wanted.

I leave the bathroom and relieve my pent-up sexual tension in my bedroom.

Reynold avoids me after the bathroom non-incident. Not going to lie, that hurt. I take it as a sign and stop flirting with him through text messages. He didn't text-flirt with me either.

Reynold and Adeline spent last night painting her room orange. She invited me to help, but I declined, telling her I didn't feel well.

Now it's Sunday night. While Reynold and Addy ate the dinner he cooked, I walked to a nearby pizza place to grab a slice and ate it while strolling casually through the neighborhood. When I return to the penthouse, Reynold is in Addy's room, putting her to sleep.

I head to the library, the one room I've been spending most of my time in. I don't watch a lot of TV shows or movies. Brad always took the remote and would watch shows only he liked. I gave up on asking him to watch a rom com with me. Now, I'm perfectly happy cuddling up with a book and disappearing into worlds where magic, shifters, and mafia bosses live.

When Reynold showed me the library during his tour, I squealed with joy. Tall bookcases, packed to the brim, hide the walls. Each side has a rolling ladder to reach books placed higher up. I walk to one case, examining the titles—all classics and, if I had to guess, first editions as well. My finger traces along the spines. Not a speck of dust to be seen. I haven't found one I want to read yet. I've mostly been coming in here with my kindle and curling up in the oversized chair in the corner to read.

"Do you have a favorite?"

I jump and yelp at the sound of Reynold's voice behind me and twist around, clutching my chest.

"You scared me, you big ole jerk."

He's standing in the doorway, his shoulder perched on the frame. He's wearing gray sweats, and it takes everything in me not to look down at his dick outlined by the fabric.

Get it together, you horny wench.

A smile stretches across his stupidly handsome face. "Big ole jerk? That's a new one."

I face the bookcase again, trying to hide my reaction to him. Walking along the wall, I let my fingertips skate over the spines again. I love the feeling of a book underneath my touch. I imagine all the hands it's been in, the joy it brought to others, and the long life ahead for it.

"I'm not a classics girly," I say, answering his initial question. "I had to read them in high school, and it turned me off because it felt like work instead of an escape."

"What *do* you read then?"

I'm far enough away from him now, so I turn back around and raise an eyebrow, planting my hands on my hips, ready for his judgement. The types of books I read used to embarrass me, but not anymore. I take pride in being a sexual person—though it's been a while since I stopped sleeping with Brad months ago. It still pisses me off he was fucking Cara while fucking me, which is why I went to a free health clinic the day after arriving in NYC to get tested. Thankfully, I'm disease free.

"Romance books... Ones full of sex." Ones that helped me discover what I like—what turns me on.

"Is that so?"

"Yeah, the smuttier the better."

I shouldn't be confessing this to my boss, who I can't stop thinking about. Who I can't stop flirting with over text messages despite the boundaries we've set. But the way his eyes light with fire, a desire, a need... it urges me to keep going.

"Books with kinks: spanking, breath play, edging, praise... punishment."

He grinds his teeth, making the muscles in his jaw dance.

"Interesting."

It's all he says before moving towards me. Slowly. Almost like he's stalking me where I stand with my back to the bookcase.

"Is that all you read?"

"Mostly."

"What's your favorite romance trope?"

"Um... enemies to lovers."

He's right in front of me now, looking down at my frame. He's not much taller than me, but he makes me feel so small. I try to back up, but the shelves stop me. My palms flatten on a row of books. The musk of old pages hits my nose at the same time Reynold's scent takes hold. Fuck, he smells good. It's woodsy, cedar, I think, with something else. A spice that I can't name.

"Enemies to lovers, huh?" He plants a hand on the shelf above my head. "Is that why you like to push my buttons?"

"I don't know what you mean," I barely breathe out. He's mere inches away from my mouth. I lick my lips and the movement catches his eye.

"You don't?" He taps his thumb on the wooden shelf above my head. "What was it you said to Adeline about ice cream for breakfast? And getting a puppy?"

I swallow hard, my mouth suddenly dry. He smirks because he knows exactly what he's doing to me right now.

"Refusing to let me send a car to pick you up for your interview? The ghost emoji you sent me and not responding to my texts after?"

"Yeah. No idea what you're talking about," I whisper. He smiles this time, a predatory smile, and my legs almost give out.

"The sugar daddy text?"

"Nope. Wasn't me. Must have been autocorrect."

He leans down, his mouth next to my ear. "You're such a horrible liar, Savannah."

I stifle a moan at the way he says my name: musical and dreamy.

If he kissed me right now, I'd let him.

But he doesn't. Instead, he straightens up and extracts a book from the shelf above my head. He steps back and turns it over in his hands before giving it to me.

"Pride and Prejudice. Your classic enemies to lovers. Were you required to read that in high school?"

"No," I say and hold the book against my chest. "But I saw the movie."

"Read the book. It's better." There's a hint of demand in his voice, an order that I will no doubt submit to. He stuffs both hands back in the pockets of his sweats and I try not to look at his biceps straining against the fabric of his shirt. "It's not... *smutty*, but a good read for sure."

"Yes, sir, er, sure. Okay. I'll read it." He has me flustered and he damn well knows it based on the cocky smirk on his face.

He walks backwards, heading to the door without breaking eye contact with me.

"Good night, Savannah."

The moment he's gone, I exhale and cover my face with my palms.

What the fuck was that?

Chapter 8 - Savannah

I wake up around seven thirty the next day, make Addy breakfast, and take her to preschool. Reynold starts filming today. It's now ten a.m., but his call time isn't for another two hours. He slept in, which he never does. His fight training must be exhausting.

"Ham, cheese, pepper, and onion omelet with a side of bacon," I say and hand Reynold a plate when he finally shuffles into the kitchen. He pauses, frowns, then sits at the island where we like to eat. "Mocha coffee with a splash of creamer. Just how you like it," I add, setting down a mug next to him.

"Thank you. But you know you don't have to cook for me, right?" he says, his voice scratchy and sexy from sleep. He cuts into his omelet and takes a bite, closing his eyes while he chews.

"I know I don't *have* to, but sometimes people *want* to do nice things."

I dry my hands on the towel and set my hands on my hips.

"Besides, I cooked everything before I took Adeline—my actual boss—to preschool this morning. I put yours in the oven to keep warm."

"Addy is your boss, huh?"

"Yep!"

He shakes his head and devours the omelet in five more large bites. He washes it down with his coffee then stands to clean off the dishes.

"Tonight will be a late night. I probably won't be home until two in the morning."

After placing the rinsed off dishes in the dishwasher, he closes it and leans against the counter, arms crossed. My eyes drop to his muscle-packed forearms before floating back up to his face.

He lifts his finger, homing in for an entire monologue as he does, but I hold up my hand to stop him.

"I see you're about to go barking off instructions..."

He snaps his mouth shut and frowns.

"It's been a week and I think I got a handle on things. Addy gets out of school at four. I'll be there at three-thirty, just in case. I'll have your super scary and intimidating body-guards, Henry and Sarah, with me—"

"They're not even scary—"

"They've been escorting us for the past week to and from preschool while you were off doing your little fight thing. They'll continue to escort us any time we're out in public.

"Shirley will be here by four to cook dinner. After dinner, we'll watch a movie or go over her schoolwork if she has any. Or maybe we'll practice her French. She gets a bath before bedtime, which is at nine. She'll pick out a book for me to read and then I'll tuck her in, safe and sound." I lean against the island, arms crossed, matching his pose. "Does that cover everything?"

He pushes away from the counter and stalks toward me. Trapping me in his arms, he leans in until his mouth is just inches from mine.

"Smartass."

"Is it ass or arse, British Guy?"

"British Guy? Really? How clever."

"You hate it, so I'm using it from here on out."

He lifts his right hand off the marble countertop and pushes a piece of hair off my face.

"Always pushing my buttons, Savvy." I cringe and he smiles, knowing how much I hate him calling me Savvy. Just like how he hates me calling him Rey. He's Reynold, and I'm Savannah. It's our thing. The jerk.

"What about our boundaries?"

"Fuck the boundaries. I've been wanting to cross that line for a while." His lips tickle mine. "And after last night... you talking about the sexual books you read, listing the kinks that had me imagining every way I could implement them on you... Last night, I decided I hate the boundaries. Now... it's up to you. Do I cross it, or do we go back to being professional?"

I shiver with anticipation and squeeze my thighs together because holy shit, this is hot.

"Tell me what you want, Savannah. You're in control here."

I'm in control? My breath hitches because I've never had a man give me control. Brad took, took, took. All I ever wanted was to feel appreciated. Wanted.

"Do it. Cross it."

His mouth crashes against mine and I fist my hands in his shirt as he strokes my tongue with his. His arms wrap around me tightly and I melt against his chest. When his hand snakes down my back to grab my ass, I moan into his mouth.

Fuck. This is a great kiss.

Is this really happening? Am I making out with my hot boss? No, a hot *celebrity*?

God, he's a good kisser. It's as if his tongue is familiar with my mouth and knows what I like. As if he's somehow memorized the feel and taste of me.

This is it. We're not going back. This kiss is a gateway drug, and I'm already craving more.

I place my palm on his chest and push him away. He steps back and the air in the room rushes between us. I cover my mouth with my palm because if I keep kissing him, I won't stop.

"I thought..." His words trail off. He stares at me, confused, waiting for me to explain. "You said cross the line. You kissed me back."

"Worst kiss of my life."

The concern drops from his face and something feral takes over. He cages me in again, a cocky smirk plastered on his face—the same one he gave me last night. He gently grabs me by the throat as he leans down until his mouth brushes mine.

"Why are you lying to me?"

"Who says I'm lying?"

"What's going on inside that head of yours? Do you not want this?"

I lick my lips, hungry for more. More of his kiss, his taste, *him.*

"I want this. God, do I want this."

He grabs my waist and pulls me flush against him. I skim my hands up his arms and along his neck, and he closes his eyes at my touch.

How long has it been since he's been touched by someone?

"Then why did you stop?"

I secure my grip at the nape and pull him down, ready for him to kiss me again.

"Because I won't be able to stop. What if someone walks—"

"Well, isn't this interesting?" Eloise muses, entering the kitchen like a silent mouse.

Reynold groans and takes a step back. Neither of us heard the elevator ding. If I hadn't freaked out and stopped us, how far would we have gone?

"Did we interrupt something?" Kelly says, following Eloise to the island.

"I should head out." Reynold sighs, agitation from our interruption masking his face.

"Do you two want omelets?" I ask Eloise and Kelly, attempting to avoid their pressing questions.

"No, thank you. We've got a flight to catch," Eloise says. "I have a few shoots in L.A. and Kelly has a DJ'ing gig in San Diego. We'll be back at the end of the week, though. Lana will be here too. We should all do dinner one night."

"It's already in the works," Reynold says and grabs a small duffle bag. He looks at me. "Call or text if there's an emergency. Or if you need anything. Anything at all. My assistant will monitor my phone while I'm in the middle of scenes."

I salute him. "Sir, yes, sir."

He narrows his eyes at me because he *hates* when I do that. His reaction only eggs me on because it's packed with a promise of punishment. He takes his phone out of his pocket, then taps away at the screen. He's already down the hallway and walking into the elevator when my phone vibrates next to me on the island's countertop.

Hot British Guy

Brat

I smile at the screen, blushing because that word packs too much power behind it.

"Wow," Eloise muses and I jerk my head up, already forgetting these two were here. Reynold makes me forget a lot of things when he's around. "Cheesing at your phone like it's the finest wine."

What does that even mean?

"Are you two hooking up?" Kelly adds, which garners a slap on the shoulder from Eloise. "What? You want to know too. I'm just more forward than you are."

I roll my eyes at them. I'm glad Adeline is at preschool right now, though she claims to ignore our adult conversations. We're also careful not to flirt when she's here.

"Aren't y'all gonna be late for your flight?"

Eloise giggles. "That accent of yours gets thicker when you're embarrassed."

"My accent is thick, period."

"Mhm," Kelly hums.

"Okay, byeeeeeee you two."

After that encounter with Reynold, I head to my room to take a cold shower.

I pick Adeline up from school at four, with Sarah and Henry trailing close behind. Reynold was right about them wearing street clothes. Both still have fancy earpieces, which makes me feel like I'm the president being protected by secret service members. Henry, who I swear is Jason Momoa's doppelgänger, even has the sunglasses. Sarah looks like she could battle the Terminator and win.

Addy wants ice cream, so we stop at a place that has a buffet of sweet toppings. She piles sprinkles, marshmallows, gummy bears, and chocolate syrup on top of her chocolate chip cookie dough ice cream. I keep mine simple and add strawberries and cheesecake chunks to my vanilla ice cream. Even Sarah and Henry indulge.

The four of us sit at a table, digging in. I snap a photo and send it to Reynold.

He responds immediately with a gif of Shaq, shimmying his shoulders and smiling with the text 'yummy' at the bottom.

Did he just send a gif? No way. His first ever gif? Why does that fill my body with tingles and make me want to giggle and kick my feet?

Naturally, I make a big deal about this.

Me

Congrats on sending your first gif!

I add a gif of Leonardo DiCaprio from *The Great Gatsby*, holding up a glass

He sends one back of Elle Woods in *Legally Blonde* saying, 'What, like it's hard?'

Two gifs in a row? He's out of control!

Me

How's work?

Hot British Guy

Exhausting. It's an hour straight of action shots, then waiting while they reset the scene, then more action shots and... well, you get it

Me

Hang in there, BG

The three dots pop up, then disappear. I smirk, proud of myself for confusing him.

Hot British Guy

BG?

Me

Yeah. British Guy=BG. Remember? It's how you're saved in my phone

I follow up the text with a goofy face emoji and a winking face.

I leave out that I have him saved as 'Hot' British Guy. He knows he's hot. Besides, Eloise and Kelly told me I'm saved as Sexy Savvy.

He sends back his favorite eye roll emoji. There's my proper Brit.

Hot British Guy

About to start filming again

Me

Okay. Break a leg

Savannah. That phrase is meant for stage actors. Not action stars who might literally break a leg

Me

Tomato, to-mah-toe

"Are you texting my dad?" Adeline asks, scooping a big bite of ice cream into her mouth.

"I am. How did you know?"

"You were smiling at your phone like he does when he's texting you."

My face heats. He smiles when texting me?

Why do I suddenly feel like I'm in high school and found out my crush likes me back?

Adeline moves on from that conversation, as if she didn't just drop a bomb on my head. She talks about her day at school, saying her dad agreed to let her learn the violin (her best friend is also taking lessons.) She talks about her art class, which is her favorite thing about preschool. She brought home a painting, and it's surprisingly good. It's not the usual family standing outside a home, surrounded by green grass, flowers, and sunshine. Instead, it's of Reynold, Adeline, and me holding hands in front of tall New York City buildings. She even painted a yellow taxi on the street instead of a dog.

It's going on the fridge as soon as we get home.

Shirley is making dinner by the time we return to the penthouse. Tonight's menu: chicken carbonara with garlic bread and steamed veggies.

My stomach growls at the savory aroma.

Reynold texts throughout the night asking how things are going. I respond with pictures: Addy and me eating, Addy and me watching a movie, Addy taking a bath with a crown of soapsuds on her head, and me holding up the book she chose for me to read.

She falls asleep by nine thirty, and I head back to the kitchen to clean up. Then I crash on the couch, grabbing *Pride and Prejudice* off the coffee table. I started it last night after he plucked it from the shelf. I was hooked from page one. While Addy was at school today, I settled into the comfy chairs on the balcony in my room to continue reading it. I have about eighty pages left.

I finish after an hour and text Reynold to let him know he was right about the book being better than the movie. The phone chirps seconds later. My heart thrashes against my chest in anticipation.

Only... it's not from Reynold, as I expected. It's from an unknown number... from Arkansas. Dread fills my lungs. There's only one person who it could be because I've stored the numbers of everyone who's important in my life.

I left Silo as quietly as possible. I quit my job as a server at Lilies Bar & Grill by texting my manager, Emily. The only person I called—and it wasn't until a few days later—was my best friend, Justine. I told her about Brad cheating and how I couldn't stay in Silo Springs anymore. She understood. She's been there for me through the good and the bad, but she's married with two kids. Our friendship relied on her getting a babysitter so she could hang out or me coming over to chill with her, the kids, and her husband, who always seemed annoyed that I was there.

She was ecstatic to see me escape the small-town life. She always said I was meant for something greater. She also hated Brad.

I planned to never think about that fucker again, so how the hell did he get my number?

Unknown Number

> **Savs. It's me. Brad. I miss you. Can we talk?**

It's been a month since I caught him and Cara drunk as skunks, making out in her car in the parking lot of Lilies. I was off work that night and bored, so I went up there to hang out with Justine. Brad was supposed to be working a shift at the gas station up the road, but confessed they fired him a month before.

Lying. Cheating. Limp dick loser.

Me

> Who? Sorry, I think you have the wrong number

Unknown Number

> **I know this is Savvy. I got your number from Justine's phone when she wasn't looking**

Damn my best friend for not having a lock on her phone and always leaving it on the counter at the bar while she's working. She's going to get that thing stolen someday.

Me

> I don't want to talk to you. Don't text me again

He tries calling, and I send it to voicemail.

Unknown Number

> **Please. Let me explain**

Me

> There's nothing you can say to get me to understand or accept what you did. Our relationship has been over for years. Leave me alone

Unknown Number

> **I know you're in New York from the phone number. What are you doing**

there? Are you with someone? Who?
I'll treat you better if you take me
back. Please, Savs

I hate that nickname. I don't respond and block the number, then toss my phone on the couch. He's acting crazy. Why can't he leave me alone? He has someone else now. Why can't they go run off and live happily ever after together?

Dammit. I need to tell Reynold about this. He won't be happy. I told him Brad wouldn't come looking for me. I'm still sure he won't because he can't afford to fly up here to chase me. Still, Reynold needs to know. I'm his daughter's nanny, and I'm responsible for her safety.

I turn on the TV, needing a distraction, but I can't focus anymore, so I head to my bedroom to go to sleep. While I'm getting ready, I hear a quiet knock.

"Savvy?" Adeline's small voice sounds as she opens the door.

"What's wrong?" I ask, walking out of the bathroom.

"I can't sleep."

"Aww. I'm sorry Adeline."

"Will you call me Addy? Like my dad does?"

She hugs me, burying her face in my stomach. I pet her messy red curls. "Of course, Addy."

"I want to sleep in Daddy's bed. Will you sleep with me too?"

I gulp. Her dad's bed?

"Oh, um, sure. Do you want water first?"

"No, thank you."

She takes my hand and leads me to Reynold's room. Why didn't he warn me about this? He should have said something if she has a habit of sleeping in his bed. Especially since she wants *me* to join her.

She tells me to sleep on the left side because that's 'dad's side' and I do. I tuck us in and inhale Reynold's scent on the blanket and pillow. Addy cuddles up to my side and within seconds, she's fast asleep.

Her warmth, the soft sheets, and the heavenly mattress have me struggling to keep my eyes open.

I startle awake to a huge presence in the room.

"It's just me," Reynold whispers.

I lift my head, disoriented. Oh, right. I'm in Reynold's bed. Now he's home, standing on Adeline's side.

"Sorry. She woke up upset and wanted to sleep in here. She asked if I'd come with her. I meant to text you to warn you, but I fell asleep."

"It's okay, Savannah," he says quietly so as not to wake up Adeline.

"Why didn't you tell me she does this?"

"Because she doesn't." He squats down and pets Adeline's hair, smiling at her with all the love the world has to offer. "She's never wanted to sleep in my bed."

He clears his throat. Unshed tears fill his eyes, shining in the light of the lamp that Addy made me keep on because she's scared of the dark.

"I didn't mean to wake you. You can stay here. I'll go sleep in a guest room."

I sit up some more.

"No. This is your room. I'll leave."

"Daddy?" Adeline grumbles.

"Hey, Poppy."

I rarely hear him call her that. He tends to do it when she's tired or whiny. It's cute and makes my heart burst because it reminds me how sweet this man is. How he gave up everything to care for her. Does he realize how amazing he is at being a father?

"Will you sleep with me and Savvy?"

"Oh, Darling. I don't think—"

"Please," she whines.

Reynold finds my eyes and silently, apologetically, asks for permission. I nod and offer him a sleepy smile.

I don't even remember him getting into bed because the moment I lie back down; I fall asleep.

Chapter 9 – Reynold

I wake up to a warm, soft body cuddling my side.

Savannah.

Her arm is thrown over my stomach, her legs intertwined with mine, and she's using my chest as a pillow.

God... this is amazing.

My hand moves up and down her back and she sighs, tightening her arm around me. I lean down and bury my nose in her hair. Coconut from the shampoo and conditioner I stocked in her bathroom.

I want to stay like this forever.

What time is it, anyway? I don't have to be on set until eleven. It's going to be another late night. Though, if it means coming home to Savannah in my bed, I don't mind one bit.

I carefully reach for my phone on the bedside table.

A few minutes before seven.

The muffled sound of a TV pierces through my sleep fog. Adeline must have woken up to use the toilet and went back to her room to watch cartoons. I should wake Savannah, but she looks too peaceful right now. And I'm selfish. I'd keep her here all morning if I could.

Her palm slides to my stomach, flattening where my shirt has crept up during sleep. I nearly groan, feeling her silken and warm skin on mine.

I continue caressing her back and she matches my movements by slowly smoothing her hand up and down my abs.

"Savannah," I whisper.

"Hmm?"

"Are you awake?"

"No," she mumbles. She doesn't stop running her palms over my stomach, getting dangerously close to my cock, which grows hard with every stroke she makes.

I place my palm over her knuckles.

"I highly suggest you stop doing that..."

"Or what?" she challenges, not stopping.

I roll us over, putting Savannah on her back, allowing me to tower over her. She gasps, her green eyes lighting up with lust, making her pupils expand like the dark of night. She focuses on my mouth, and I lean in, ready to claim those pouty lips, but she places her hand on my chest to stop me.

"Addy?"

I hop out of bed and lock the doors, then rush back, all within seconds.

Savannah covers her face with her hands, laughing. "Someone's eager, aren't they?"

"Five years, Savannah."

I lean in once more to claim my kiss, but she stops me *again*, her palm covering my mouth this time.

"No kissing."

I tilt my head in question.

"Morning breath."

I peel her hand away and press my lips along her jawline, then down her neck to her collarbone. She sighs and fists her fingers in my hair. I move the fabric of her tank top down to expose one of her breasts.

"Is this okay?"

"Yes. Don't stop."

Her rose-pink nipple puckers and I pinch it, then pull it. She moans and arches her back.

"I'm going to need you to be quiet, Savannah. Do you think you can do that for me?"

She whimpers and nods.

"That's my girl."

While working one nipple with my fingers, I cover the other with my mouth, flicking my tongue and sucking hard. Savannah grabs a pillow and smashes it against her face just in time to muffle a moan when my teeth graze over the sensitive nub.

"You're doing such a good job, Savannah."

I move my hand down her stomach until the fingertips slide underneath the band of her sleep shorts.

"No underwear?" I ask, discovering her bare underneath.

She shakes her head, the pillow still over her face, as I find her wet pussy. She shuts her legs on my arm.

"Open these back up."

She whines but does as I say, allowing me to tease her.

"Please, Reynold," she says into the pillow, stifling her voice.

"Fuck you're soaked. I'm so proud of you."

She groans at my praise, and I reward her by plunging a finger in. I pump slowly before adding another.

"Do you hear that?" I ask, her pleasure filling the silent air. "This is what I do to you."

I pinch one of her nipples hard while flicking my thumb over her swollen clit, causing her to buck off the bed. I press down and massage while fucking her with my fingers. When I add a third finger, her pussy clamps down.

She's close.

I slow my thrusts and remove my fingers so I can press the pad of my middle finger to her puckered hole. "Do you want me here?"

"Yes," she moans.

"Have you ever had anyone here?"

She shakes her head.

"Let's fix that then."

I use her pleasure for lubricant, then slowly push my finger in. Her heels dig into the mattress, and she attempts to move away at the invasion. The headboard stops her from getting far.

She's tight and I don't want to hurt her. We'll work on this. I'll make sure she's well stretched out before taking her arse with my cock.

I'm kneeled between her legs, one finger carefully entering her arse until it's an inch deep. I draw it out and spit to give it more lubricant, then press it back in. Anchoring my finger there, I use my other hand to continue fucking her cunt. I pump harder, faster, relishing the soft moans from beneath that pillow. When I thrust one last time, curling my middle finger to hit her g-spot, she explodes with an orgasm. Her pussy latches on, sucking hard, and her arsehole clenches around my middle finger. I let her ride out her release before removing my fingers from all her holes.

She drops the pillow from her face just in time to watch me lick her pleasure off the fingers that were just inside her pussy. I groan at the taste. Better than I could have ever imagined.

My dick aches to be inside her. Not yet though. Would she let me fuck her mouth? I could have her watch as I jack off. Would she let me come on her face? As if reading my thoughts, Savannah sits up and reaches for the band of my sweats. Her fingers curl around the elastic and my heart kicks in my chest.

"Dad? Savvy? I'm hungry," Addy's faint voice calls from her bedroom.

Savannah's eyes widen, and she lets go of the band. She scrambles to adjust her clothes and cover herself.

"She didn't hear us, did she?" she asks in a voice a pitch higher.

"Doubtful. You were quiet, like the good girl you are."

She groans. Her hair is a mess, standing every which way around her head. I lean in to kiss her, but she slaps her palm over my mouth again. This time, I lick it, and she squeals before peeling it away.

"Asshole," she grumbles. Her eyes fall to my chest, and she grimaces. "I drooled on you?"

I glance down at the wet spot on my white shirt and smirk. "It appears so."

"I didn't mean to... cuddle with you."

"I'm glad you did."

Her phone's alarm blares, and she twists her body to snatch it off the bedside table.

"Fuck. I need to make breakfast and get dressed to take Addy to school."

She attempts to get out of bed but gets caught in the sheets. I lay back, an arm behind my head, and watch the frantic woman. She's too adorable. When she finally rights herself, she adjusts her pajamas and blows a piece of hair out of her face.

"It's only seven. You have time," I offer.

"Right. Okay."

We stare at each other for the longest time.

"You're freaking out about this, aren't you?"

She fidgets on her feet and opens her mouth, then clamps it shut. "Maybe we shouldn't have done that."

"Tell me why. Voice your concerns, Savannah."

"Last night we were kissing. Today your finger was in my ass."

I cover my mouth to hide my smile. She's being serious, but all I can think about is how wonderful she looked coming on my fingers.

"Are we going too fast? Are we going too far over the boundary line?"

"Right. The boundary line. We could readjust it." I quirk my eyebrow, giving her the chance to tell me what she wants.

I will do anything she wants.

"I... I don't know. Maybe. Let me think about it."

We stare at each other some more. As if both of us are waiting for the other to make another move.

"Daaaaad, Savvy, I'm hungry!" Adeline calls from her room once again.

Savannah sighs and breaks eye contact with me. Before she walks past me out the door, I stand and grab her wrist.

"And Savannah?" I pull her to me and brush my lips against hers. "I don't give a fuck about morning breath."

I slant my mouth over hers, and she melts into me. The kiss is quick, not wanting to break her 'no kissing because of morning breath' rule. I don't even slide my tongue in like I want to.

Savannah disappears to her room to shower and change, so I get Addy dressed, then we head to the kitchen so I can cook breakfast.

I pause at the fridge.

Adeline painted us? Me, her, and Savannah, and we're all holding hands.

"Poppy, I love this."

"Thanks Dad! Savvy hung it up on the fridge last night," she says. She's sitting on a stool at the island's counter, swinging her legs while playing an educational game on her tablet.

My heart beats as thoughts of a family dance through my head. I grew up with loving parents who were taken from me too soon. Then my sister became my legal guardian. She was young, only eighteen, and barely an adult herself. She supported me in my modeling and acting career and moved us to the U.S. when I was sixteen so I could follow my dreams. Now she's gone too, and I've assumed this parental role by myself. It's been so fucking hard.

To see the three of us together through my daughter's eyes, as if we're a proper family, squeezes my heart. Which is ridiculous because I've only known Savannah for a month. She's my daughter's nanny. She wouldn't want...

I'm absentmindedly whipping up scrambled eggs, bacon, and toast while drowning in my thoughts when Savannah walks in. Fuck, she looks fantastic. She's brushed her straight blonde hair, and it falls over her shoulders. She's wearing a light pink sun dress that has a corset built in, covered in white daisies. Her cheeks are still pink, and I hope it's the afterglow from the orgasm I gave her.

"You cooked? I was going to do that."

I set out three spread options for the toast: grape jelly, strawberry jelly, or butter.

"I know, but I got here first."

I plate Addy's food, then Savannah's, setting both on the island's counter in front of them. After preparing my plate, I sit diagonal to Savvy, so I can see her.

"It's not a competition, BG," she muses while spreading grape jelly on her toast.

My favorite.

"Really? I'm just British Guy? Even after you and me..." I pause and glance at Addy, who's not paying us any attention.

"My apologies, sir." Savannah giggles and digs into her food.

I desperately want to respond to that brat, but I suppose I must be appropriate while my daughter is around.

After about five minutes of us enjoying breakfast, Savannah sighs. Concern plagues her face.

"I have to tell you something."

She sets her napkin on the plate and slumps her shoulders. I straighten, not at all liking how nervous she is by the way she chews on her lip and flips her phone over and over on the counter.

"My ex texted me last night. He knows I'm in New York. I told him to leave me alone then blocked him, but... I'm worried he might try to contact me again."

I relax slightly. "How did he get your number? Didn't you change it?"

"I did. I changed it to a New York number after I moved here. Brad said he got it from my friend's phone when she wasn't looking."

"Do you think he'll come up here to find you? I know you said he didn't hurt you, but could he?"

She shakes her head. "He's an idiot and as intimidating as an ant. Plus, he's too broke to come up here." Her eyes flicker to Addy. "But..."

Now I'm following her train of thought.

"Sarah and Henry won't let anything happen to you or Adeline. *I* won't let anything happen to either of you. Okay?"

She nods, not totally convinced. "Okay."

"Good." I finish my food and take the plate to the sink to wash off and place in the dishwasher. "I have three more late nights this week. Lana flies in on Wednesday. You two should hang out. Friday night we'll have dinner. You, me, Addy, Lana, Mylan, Eloise, and Kelly."

"Okay."

"Do you have Lana's number?"

"No."

"I'll send it to you. I'm sure she'd love to play tourist with you and Addy. You haven't done that yet since arriving, correct?"

"Not really."

I sigh at her short answers and defeated demeanor. She's still concerned about her ex. I walk to her side and cup her cheek, my body blocking hers, so Adeline can't see what I'm doing. "Don't worry. I'll take care of this."

Her eyes widen. "What do you mean? What are you going to do?"

I swipe my thumb along her jaw, then over her lips. She parts them ever so slightly and I fight the urge to slide the tip in.

"Savvy, can we leave now?" Adeline asks, interrupting the moment.

Revoking my privacy as a parent hasn't been an issue until now. I haven't wanted to be intimate with anyone for the past five years. Now that Adeline is getting older and finding her independence... now that I'm returning to acting... my *needs* are hitting me full force.

I suppose I'll just have to get creative with my plan to flirt with, and steal kisses from Savannah. Especially since she's allowed me to taste her.

Before Xavier drives me to Queens for my eleven a.m. call time, I take out my phone and call Lana. I ask her if she trusts anyone on the police force in Silo Springs to keep an eye on Brad. I explain that he texted Savannah, and she curses in my ear. She tells me she always found him to be a creep. Lana reassures me, saying she'll call the police chief to have Brad watched. If that tool even tries to leave town, I'll know.

Savannah insists I shouldn't worry about her ex. Still, I'm not taking chances. After what happened this morning in my bed, I have an overwhelming need to protect her.

Chapter 10 - Savannah

Two whole days. That's how long it's been since Rey and I...

I'd catch myself staring at his hands... his fingers... those magical fucking fingers that made me come. My body count isn't what I'd consider high. I've only been with ten men my entire life. Brad was vanilla and boring. He tried to pleasure me with his mouth and fingers, but he could never hit the right spot, so I'd fake it. Then, when he passed out, I'd take my vibrator into the bathroom to finish what he started.

The other men weren't as bad as Brad, but no one... *no one* has ever made me orgasm during foreplay alone.

I told Reynold we should slow down. I've spent the past few days convincing myself it's for the best. Adeline sure is testing me, though. Every night, she'd wake up an hour after I put her to bed and beg me to go sleep with her in Reynold's room. Once she dozed off, I'd leave her there and go back to my room.

I have a feeling she's doing this on purpose. Reynold said she never wants to sleep in his bed. She's a clever little girl. I know she understands more than she leads on. She pretends not to listen to adult conversations, but she's always recounting every detail, every word said from preschool. I know she listens to, and sees, everything.

Reynold told me Addy was the one encouraging him to return to acting. He said she's independent, and no longer needs him around all the time. Is she putting on a show of missing him for my benefit? Is she trying to play matchmaker?

Reynold is also testing me.

I'd find him brooding in the kitchen while making breakfast, then he'd whisper in my ear.

If only you'd been in my bed this morning. My mouth is far more talented than my fingers.

Damn him.

Still, I stayed strong. I want this. I do, but it's all happening too fast. I worry about losing this job. What if we hook up and it's horrible, or we hook up for weeks and he finds someone else to fuck, or we hook up until he gets bored, then decides he doesn't want to see me working around his home and fires me? Or if he doesn't fire me, it would be awkward and then I'd have to quit.

Okay, my thoughts are creating worst-case scenarios. Especially the one about the sex being horrible. I don't think Reynold is horrible at anything. And I've known him long enough to know that he wouldn't 'wham, bam, thank you ma'am' me. He wouldn't treat me like a booty call. That doesn't mean it wouldn't get awkward if something were to happen. How could I see him every day knowing his dick has been inside me?

It's Thursday morning now. Lana is meeting me at Addy's preschool and we're going to do some tourist stuff. First up: The Statue of Liberty.

I almost don't recognize her as she walks up to me with her bodyguards trailing. She's wearing a blonde wig, high-waisted jean shorts, and a tucked in pink t-shirt that says New York City on it. A fanny pack sits diagonally across her chest. She looks like a mom who got stuck in the eighties. I almost tell her she sticks out like a sore thumb, but it's New York, and I saw similar outfits while working in SoHo for a few weeks.

We could be sisters. We're about the same size. I'm wearing overall shorts and a crop top underneath. I have my long blonde hair up in a ponytail since it's the beginning of June. Even though temperatures are in the upper eighties, we're going to be walking around in the sun all day. I'm already sweating thinking about it.

"Savannah! It's so good to see you!" Lana brings me into a crushing hug before pulling away. "You look fantastic."

"Me? You're absolutely glowing!"

Lana waves me off. "That's just an org—"

She stops and cringes.

"Sorry, I was about to TMI you."

I laugh. "No, please! TMI me! I want all the details."

We walk arm in arm while Lana tells me about her morning activities with Mylan that left her with a post-orgasm glow. Sarah and Henry stay close behind. Lana's two bodyguards walk ahead. It's so very clear that we're being protected, and I try not to think about it potentially drawing attention to us.

To avoid morning rush hour traffic, we take the subway down to Battery Park. With the train cars crowded as hell, Lana and I are more like sardines encircled by bodyguards.

We pass the time catching up on life. We talk about her work with the Tyler's Team foundation. The charity she co-founded helps families going through cancer treatments. Since the release of Rebecca's book and movie, the foundation has been flooded with donations. She's been busy helping manage that and doing press appearances.

We also talked about Brad cheating on me. How it was a blessing in disguise because now I'm living a life I could never dream of in New York City.

Tickets for the crown sold out months ago, which is fine by me since I'm scared of heights. Lana had her assistant make a call and name dropped to get us pedestal access, which was also sold out. Thankfully, we don't have to wait in the long lines, being herded to a ferry like cattle, because Lana rented a private boat to take us to the island.

We follow a sidewalk until reaching the front of Lady Liberty. Lana snaps a few photos of me posing like the iconic statue. Then she has one of her bodyguards take a few of us together.

Next, we walk down yet another sidewalk to the entrance for the pedestal. Tourists are everywhere. My anxiety spikes, but no one pays us attention as they document their core memories. Just as I'm doing.

It's surreal. I never once believed I'd see the Statue of Liberty in person, looking up at her green stained copper body as if I'm an ant and she's a giant about to step on me. She represents those who sought freedom and a new life.

My throat aches with tears because this is my life now. I've never felt more free.

After taking a few pictures and sending them to Reynold, we head to the statue's café for lunch. Since there's not much seating inside, we sit outside. A few times, seagulls tried to steal our French fries. I'm terrified of birds and kept screaming, which put Lana in a giggling fit.

After lunch, we head back to the Upper East Side to pick up Addy.

My phone vibrates with a text.

Hot British Guy

You're such a tourist

He sends two emojis: the Statue of Liberty and an arm holding up a phone as if it's taking a selfie.

I bark out a laugh because he's come so far from his eye roll emoji. Why does that make the butterflies in my stomach stir? Maybe it's because he's led a life of responsibility for the past five years. He's a serious man, but now he's letting his walls down and showing his true, goofy self.

Me

I love this city! We're going to the Brooklyn Bridge after picking up Addy

Hot British Guy

She's never been. She'll love it

I heart the text but before I put my phone away, he sends another.

Hot British Guy

New York City looks good on you

Heat spreads through my body and spills into my face. I glance at Lana, who surely sees me turn beet red. She's smirking.

"Okay, out with it," I say with a sigh, knowing she's been waiting to ask me this question all day.

"What's up with you and Rey?"

"Nothing is up with me and Rey."

"I don't believe you."

"He's my boss."

"And?"

"And nothing. That's it." I shrug.

"Did I ever tell you you're a horrible liar?"

I gasp, clutching my invisible pearls. "Why, Lana Young, I would never."

"Actually, I took Mylan's last name, so it's Lana Young-Andrews now."

My face lights up, eager to ask about the wedding and the honeymoon since we didn't talk about it on the train ride down. She holds up her palm.

"We're not talking about me, though. We're talking about you lying about how you feel about Rey."

I humph and cross my arms, slumping down in my seat on the subway.

"Did you know he called me about Brad?" Lana contin-ues.

"What?"

She nods. "Rey called and asked if I knew anyone in Silo to keep an eye on Brad and make sure he doesn't leave town to come up here and find you."

"He did not."

"He did, and I told him Chief Hallows would take care of it."

My mouth gapes open.

"A man wouldn't do that for just anyone. You're special to him."

"He wants to make sure Adeline is safe..."

She shakes her head. "Mylan says every time they're doing a scene together, and the director calls cut, Rey rushes over to his assistant to check his phone. His face lights up when there's a text from you. He talks about you all the time."

"We've known each other barely a month."

Lana waits for me to confess.

"Okay, fine. We've had... our moments."

"I knew it. Spill."

I tell her everything, from the almost kiss to me punching him, the flirty texts, the kitchen kiss, and the morning we woke up cuddling (and the TMI that came after).

"But it's all happening too fast and I'm wondering if we're making a mistake getting involved."

"Why?"

"Like I said, he's my boss. I need this job. What if we get together and it doesn't work out? I'd have to quit."

"Then Rey would make sure you're taken care of. He wouldn't leave you high and dry."

She's totally right. I've told myself the same damn thing.

"Is there another reason?"

I bite my lip, giving myself time to form an answer. "He's a celebrity."

Lana blinks at me.

"Right. You've been through this. It's just... the paparazzi... I hated all the small-town gossip in Silo. The idea of it happening on a greater scale because of who Rey is... I don't think I could handle it. I don't think I could stand seeing my image on the internet and having assholes comment about my weight. I love who I am, but that doesn't mean I want others to bring me down."

Lana nods while listening. She places her hand on top of my knuckles.

"I get it. But you could see it as an opportunity to show the world that big bodies deserve to be romanced, even by celebrities. Fatphobes hate it when we're happy, so flaunt your fatness. They're hiding behind some computer, spewing off hateful comments while you're living your best life. Ignore the haters, don't read the comments, and enjoy the man who can't stop smiling at his phone while texting you."

"You make it sound easy."

"It's not. It never will be. But you'd have me to talk to about it. And I can introduce you to Jensen. He grew up dealing with body shamers. But most of all, you'd have Rey and Adeline, and I'm pretty sure they're the only ones who matter."

"You and Mylan matter. And Eloise and Kelly, too. All his friends."

Lana smiles as bright as the sun today. "Can't forget Rebecca, Ginger, and Bruno."

"Oh my God, how is Ginger? Isn't she about to pop?"

"She's got at least one more month, possibly less. She's having a little girl. They're naming her Gracey after her mother. That's why I can't stay long. I'm going back just before she gives birth."

We fawn over that for a few minutes and as we exit the subway and walk towards Addy's school to pick her up, Lana says, "Look. I know you two just met. You say you want to take it slow, so tell him that. Get to know each other first and see where it goes."

"Going slow is the problem. I'm struggling to keep my hands off the man as it is."

Lana giggles. "I get that. It only took me four days after meeting Mylan to give in." We stop at the school's gate, waiting for the kids to get out. "Talk to Rey. Lay out some ground rules. Tell him your concerns. Most importantly, have fun."

She wags her eyebrows at me, and I blush, thinking about all the fun things I want to do with Reynold.

I scan the waiting area and wave at a few parents or nannies that I've chatted with over the past few weeks. A man I don't recognize stands off to the side. He's wearing a baseball cap that's pulled down over his face.

He must be someone famous because that's exactly what Reynold did when I first met him. He was trying to hide in plain sight.

"Savvy!" a tiny voice calls out my name.

Addy leads the pack of tiny humans as they exit the building. She runs towards me, carrying a piece of paper in her hand. Her orangish red curls bounce with every step.

"Here!" she holds out the painting. "It's you and Dad."

I choke on my words as I scan the art. I knew it. She's such a little matchmaker! The painting is of me and Rey in stick figure form, holding hands. We're standing next to the kitchen island, which has stacks of pancakes on top. We're both smiling and have hearts for eyes.

"This is so good, Addy. I'm putting this up right next to the other one."

Adeline spots Lana next to me. She gives her a shy wave, then grabs my hand and clings to my arm.

"Addy, you met Lana. You went to her wedding in Arkansas."

She peers around me, giving Lana a cautious scan.

"The wedding lady had red hair."

Lana leans over and cups her hand over her mouth to whisper. "I'm the same person." She lifts the blonde wig to show her. "See, red hair underneath. I'm just playing a game of hide and seek with the paparazzi."

Addy's small shoulders loosen.

"I hate the papa-rat-sees." That shyness just seconds before starts to fade. "My dad tries to hide from them too."

"Do you want to play hide and seek from them now? We can go explore the city," Lana says, still whispering. "And don't worry, we have four bodyguards to keep those rats away."

Addy nods enthusiastically and jumps up and down. Lana winks, then stands.

We hop back on the subway to the Lower East Side and enter the Brooklyn Bridge from Manhattan. It takes forty-five minutes to walk across between the crowds, stopping to take photos, and casually strolling, in no hurry to get to the other side.

My feet ache by the time we reach Brooklyn Bridge Park. I've never walked so much in my life. It's worth it, though. The New York City skyline from this vantage point is breathtaking. The day is clear, except for a streak or two of white clouds across the bright blue sky.

It's peaceful. No honking cars. Only the waves crashing against the stone barrier. A warm breeze washes over me and I close my eyes, inhaling deeply.

"Wow," Lana says beside me. I pop open my eyes. She's holding up her phone with a picture of me on it.

Wow is right. The sun highlights my profile. I have a double chin, but it's never bothered me. The first time someone tried to bully me about it, I was ten years old.

I said, 'Two is greater than one, so I'm better than you.'

Reynold had no problem with my double chin either. My face heats remembering his lips peppering kisses along my jaw and down my neck. Across all the places on my body the world told me was bad.

I send Reynold the picture along with the ones Lana took of me and Addy with the NYC skyline behind us. Then we grab some ice cream from a cart along the Bridge View Lawn and sit on a bench to scarf it down.

"Huh," I say, noticing a man lingering a few feet away.

"What is it?"

"That man." I discreetly nod my head in his direction. "He was at Addy's preschool."

Lana narrows her eyes.

"Does he seem familiar? A parent maybe?"

I shake my head. "I've never seen him before. And he doesn't have a kid with him right now."

Lana sighs. "Probably just a fan. It happens sometimes. I don't know how they find me, even with the wig on."

"That's annoying. Kinda scary too."

Lana calls over one of her bodyguards, Frank. She whispers in his ear, and he nods. He takes Sarah with him to confront the man. But as they head towards him, he walks off.

"Want us to chase after him?" Frank asks.

"No. Just keep an eye out in case he returns." She turns to me. "Did you get a good look at him?"

"I think he had dark hair. Not too tall. Built but not bulky."

Frank nods at my description and huddles with the rest of the bodyguards.

"Hey," Lana says, quietly. She places her palm on my hand, which I realize was shaking. "Fans are mostly respectful. Sometimes they get excited and linger too close. That man probably has a crush, either on me or Mylan. He was likely too shy to come up and talk, so he followed us around, staring. I'm sure he's harmless."

I let out a long breath. "Right."

"Savvy, I'm hungry," Addy whines. Her face is covered in chocolate ice cream. I take a picture of the adorable mess and send it to Reynold. He hasn't answered the other texts. He must be busy on set.

"Why don't we get pizza?" Lana suggests.

Adeline's face lights up and she jumps up off the bench and bounces on her feet.

As we walk to the famous Grimaldi's Pizzeria, I keep glancing over my shoulder. My nerves are wrecked now. I know Lana said not to worry, but that guy gave me the creeps. What if he wasn't here for Lana? What if he's a paparazzo and recognized Addy as Rey's daughter? Could he have been following us and snapping pictures of her this entire time?

ENTERTAINMENT NOW

LANA TAKES ON THE BIG APPLE
By Angela Borrows

Lana Young-Andrews flew into New York City Wednesday to spend time with her husband, Mylan Andrews, who began filming his new movie this week. Young-Andrews spent Thursday playing tourist, wearing one of her many infamous disguises. She visited The Statue of Liberty with a blonde woman who appears to be the same person in the photo of Rey and Adeline on the plane from Memphis to New York City last month.

Young-Andrews and the mystery woman were later spotted at the Brooklyn Bridge with a little girl that Entertainment Now has confirmed is Michaelson's niece, Adeline. The three were spotted snapping photos and eating ice cream before visiting the famous Grimaldi's Pizzeria. We've reached out to Michaelson for comment about the woman's identity but have yet to hear back.

Chapter 11 - Reynold

"I'm hiring more bodyguards."

Savannah's head jerks up as she's setting the table for our dinner with Mylan, Lana, Eloise, and Kelly.

"That's unnecessary, Rey."

I hold back the growl at her calling me Rey. She knows how much I hate it. Rey belongs to the world. Reynold belongs to Savannah.

"Sarah and Henry should have noticed that man."

"He blended in with the other parents at school. He wasn't doing anything suspicious."

"Then they should have seen him following you at the Brooklyn Bridge."

Savannah was furious when I said I would fire them for this reason. It was really cute the way her face turned red, and she clenched her fists at her side. How her nostrils flared with every heated word she flung my way.

She sighs, puts the last plate on the table, and walks back to the kitchen where I stand. I plant my hands on the kitchen island, furious. The fact that Lana's bodyguards didn't notice him either... what if he had attacked?

"Do you really think it's a good idea to have three or four people following me and Addy around?" I inhale her sweet scent. I want nothing more than to wrap my arms around her. Stand here and hold her until our legs give out, but she's been distant ever since the morning she woke up in my arms. "Don't you think that will just point a target on our backs? Sarah and Henry are good at keeping a low profile because it's just them. But four people? It'll be too obvious."

That's why the extra bodyguards I hire will stay discreet. She'll never know they're there, only stepping in when needed. I'd already considered hiring the hidden security but decided against it. I didn't want to potentially scare Savannah or have her think she was in danger. Now I have a reason.

I feel helpless. I fear this happening all the time while I'm away on set.

I shouldn't have gone back so soon.

"Hey," she whispers and skims her palm up my arm and shoulder to rest against my neck. I stand up straight, allowing her to move in front of me. My hands fall to her hips, and I tug her against my body. "This isn't your fault, Reynold."

She latches her hands at my nape.

"We'll lie low for a while, okay? I'll take Addy to school, pick her up, and come back home. That's it. Just to be safe."

Before I can respond, she kisses me. My entire body relaxes.

She's kissing me?

I don't even care why she changed her mind. I take advantage of this gift she's given me and stroke my tongue over hers. She sighs into my mouth as I massage her lips with mine. My palms explore her backside, up and down and over her round arse. I squeeze the plump cheeks and grind my quickly hardening dick into her stomach.

She threads her fingers in my hair and when I squeeze her ass again, she responds with a gentle tug. The quiet sounds she's making, her soft moans and breathy whimpers, have me wanting to fuck her right here on the counter.

I pause the kiss and lean back. "Why?"

"Either I answer, or we keep kissing because at any moment someone could walk—"

I crash my mouth against hers, understanding the urgency in this private moment. Adeline is in her room watching the telly, and our dinner guests will arrive soon.

I lift her off the floor, and she yelps as I set her on the island's countertop, making her taller than me. Her legs wrap around me, and her fingers return to my hair.

I move my hands underneath her shirt to the small of her back, sliding a palm up her spine until I find her bra. She shakes her head, telling me not to unclasp it. I smile against her mouth, nipping the bottom lip at the same time I snap the band against her skin.

She groans at the pleasure infused pain, squeezing her legs around my body, letting me know how much she liked that. Before I can shove everything off the island's countertop and devour her, the elevator dings, announcing our guests.

Savannah slowly ends her kisses and pulls back just enough to rest her forehead against mine.

"Not worried about being caught?" I ask.

She smiles and palms my cheek. I close my eyes at her touch, remembering how wonderful it is to connect with someone so intimately.

"Not anymore, Reynold."

The loud voices and laughter of Mylan, Lana, Eloise, and Kelly enter the apartment the moment the elevator doors slide open. Savannah anchors her hands on my shoulders to inch off the counter, her body sliding down mine in the most delectable way.

I take her chin between my finger and thumb.

"Tomorrow is going to be a long day at work, but Sunday I'm off." I give her a soft kiss. "Sunday you're mine."

I step away from her just as our friends enter the kitchen. Mylan leads the pack, holding a leash. His golden retriever, Banana, trots beside him. He pauses at our disheveled looks. Savannah is flushed, her clothing wrinkled and in need of adjusting. My reflection in the appliances shows my hair sticking up on all ends.

Lana, Eloise, and Kelly pool around Mylan and Banana, mouths gaping as they watch us recover from that heated moment.

Mylan points his thumb over his shoulder. "We can come back, or…"

"I'll go get Addy," Savannah says with a blush and heads down the hallway. She pauses to hug Lana.

Their body types are similar, but Savannah might be thicker. Lana also has dark red hair that's currently braided and slung over her shoulder. Savannah's blonde hair is up in a messy bun, which I absolutely love, especially how baby hairs fall around her oval face.

"If you stare at her any harder, you'll start drooling," Mylan says, slapping my back as I watch Savannah walk away with Banana. Lana promised she'd bring the pup over for Adeline to play with.

I ignore my friend and finish bringing dishes to the table. Shirley prepared a few options for us. Lemon chicken, honey garlic salmon, Italian salad, mashed potatoes, corn, and a pasta salad dish.

Dinner is loud, everyone talking over each other with exciting stories about their lives. I showed everyone the photo I took of Mylan asleep on set the second day of filming. That man can fall asleep anywhere, I swear. He was curled up on a cushioned mat used for falls during action scenes.

Mylan one-ups me by passing around his phone, showing everyone the video of me smacking face first into a layer of plastic that he hung on my trailer door. He loves pulling pranks on set. I wasn't even mad that I fell on my ass and bruised my tail bone. It reminded me of our time together filming *Mayhem*.

I wish Jensen was here. He's on tour with Rebecca for her new book. They have a couple months left, but he promised me they'll come visit at some point. Maybe in October when the Renaissance Faire is being held in Fort Tryon Park. I've been a few times, including last year, and I always dress as a knight. The costume is still in my closet.

Would Savannah want to go?

She must sense me staring at her profile because she reaches her hand over and squeezes my knee. I want to snatch her hand and move it up my leg to my cock, but that wouldn't be appropriate. This woman makes me want to do a lot of inappropriate things.

I glance at Adeline sitting next to Savannah. My daughter doesn't even want to sit next to me anymore. I thought I'd be sad about that, but the way she lights up when Savannah is in the room, how she giggles and smiles at all the things this woman says... I wonder if this is what it would have been like if my sister had lived. Is this what it looks like when a little girl has a mum?

I take Savvy's hand and weave my fingers with hers and bring them up to my lips to kiss her knuckles. No one notices, and even if they did, I wouldn't care. Savannah blushes wonderfully and chews on her bottom lip. I wink and rest our hands in my lap as we continue chatting with our friends.

"Do you have any plans on Sunday?" Lana asks Savvy. "I was thinking we all do brunch and go shopping. Or we could go on the Staten Island Ferry or out to Coney Island."

Savannah glances at me before answering.

"I do have plans... um..."

Lana saw the suggestive glance. She sees Savannah's cheeks reddening.

"Adeline, have you ever been to a candy store?" Lana diverts.

Addy's eyes widen, and she nods enthusiastically. "My old nanny took me all the time. We went for my birthday last year. I got so much candy, my tummy hurt when I ate it all."

"Well, would you want to come with me and Mylan to Times Square on Sunday? There's not one, but two candy stores there. M&M's and Hershey's! You can buy all the candy you want... I mean, if that's okay with your dad."

Adeline turns to me. "Can I Dad?"

"Sure, Poppy."

Addy jumps in her seat. "Savvy, will you go with us?"

"Actually," Lana begins, "Savvy is going to be busy... um ... with your dad."

"Wait, what?" Mylan asks, confused. "What are you two doing that you can't come with?"

Lana punches his leg underneath the table, and he winces.

"They're busy," she grits through her teeth, trying to get Mylan to follow along. "Working on a very important project. But maybe Eloise and Kelly want to come."

Adeline giggles. "Will you, Elly and Kelly?"

Adeline was thrilled when she came up with Eloise's nickname, realizing it rhymed with Kelly's name.

"We'd love to." Kelly grins, catching on to what Lana is setting up.

Thankfully, my daughter doesn't ask about the important project because then we'd have to fib some more.

"We can also take Banana to Central Park where you can run around with him," Lana adds.

"Yay!" Addy sings and Banana barks. He's been sitting at her feet all night, waiting for her to drop food. Addy totally snuck him bites of her chicken.

Mylan, still confused, darts his head back and forth between everyone. It's only when Lana whispers in his ear that his face transforms from surprised to understanding to that annoying smirk he does when he likes to tease. The same one he gave me at the table read when he prodded me about smiling at Savannah's texts.

Everyone sticks around to chat well after dinner. Eloise and Kelly are flying to Europe this fall for a slew of gigs. Lana and Savannah make a list of touristy things to do while she's here. I am absolutely not jealous that I can't join them either.

Okay, just a little jealous.

By nine, it's time for everyone to leave since Mylan and I have a five a.m. call time.

Eloise and Kelly retreat to their guest room, assuring me they'll have their own place soon. I tell them no rush, but I'm sure they're more than ready for privacy. They've been apartment hunting and have narrowed it down to two places: one in Brooklyn and one in Chelsea. Mylan and Lana head back to their hotel in Midtown.

After I put Adeline to bed, I return to the kitchen to find Savannah cleaning up.

Her back is to me, rinsing off dishes to load into the dishwasher. She's humming a song I don't recognize, nodding to the beat in her head, and swaying those delectable hips of hers.

I creep up behind her and slide my hands around her midsection, prepared to kiss her neck when her head rears back and slams into my chin.

I grunt and grab my face, pain knifing through my jaw. Then I start coughing. Damn. Did she knock the air out of me too?

"Reynold! Oh my God! I am so sorry."

"That's the second time you've clocked me in the jaw."

She rushes to my side and inspects my injury, scowling. "Yeah, well, you shouldn't walk up on unsuspecting women like that."

She finds a frozen steak in the freezer, wraps it in a paper towel, and gently places it on my injury.

"I thought it'd be sexy, not scary," I whine.

Her face softens and a tiny smile breaks through, easing the adrenaline likely pumping through her body.

I wrap my hand around her wrist and lower the steak from my jaw.

"Tell me why you kissed me earlier. You've been avoiding me for days. What changed your mind?"

"Because I like you, Reynold Michael Kane," she says.

I suck in a breath at her saying my full name. It sounds like a song coming from her mouth.

"I haven't felt this way about anyone. Not even my ex. I think that's what spooked me. To have this overwhelming need for someone who you barely know. Then when we went from kissing to..." She bites her lip instead of finishing the sentence and I wonder if she's remembering what it felt like to have my finger up her arse. "I talked to Lana about it, and she convinced me to give it a try."

I lean in, my mouth close enough that I can smell the wine from dinner on her lips.

"And what exactly is *it* you want to try?"

Pink paints her cheeks in the most beautiful shade. "Whatever you want."

I lean my head on hers, refraining from kissing her because if I start, I won't want to stop and I have to be on set in seven hours.

I'll need more time for the things I want to do to this woman.

"Are you sure?"

"Yes."

There's a hint of hesitation in her voice.

"But?"

I lift my head to see she's chewing on her lip as she does when she's nervous... or turned on.

"I really need this job."

"Okay?"

"And what if... I don't know. What if it doesn't work out, and it gets weird, then I'll be forced to quit?"

I stand up straight and take her hands in mine.

"Tell me what will make you feel better about this decision, and I'll do it. I'll do whatever you want Savannah Beth Monroe."

She licks her lips and blushes. Did my saying her full name turn her to mush like when she says mine? She doesn't call me out on using her middle name, which she never told me. I got it off the background check.

"I, um... do you think we could have..." She sighs. "Sorry, this is weird..."

Oh. Now I understand what she wants.

"Would you like me to ask my lawyers to draw up a contract?"

She nods.

"Done. When we start dating—"

"You want to take me out on a date?"

"I want to take you out on a million dates. I want to fuck you. I want whatever you give me. And if we were to end things and you feel you no longer want to be a part of mine and Addy's life, then I will pay you a year's salary."

"A year? Reynold, no, that's too much."

"It's not and you will accept it."

"So overbearing."

I smirk and run a finger over her jaw. She flutters her eyes.

"Oh Savannah, you have no idea how domineering I can be. Is that what you want? Would you like me to tell you what to do?"

She peers at me with hooded eyes.

"Remember the types of books I told you I like to read?"

"Of course."

"I want you to do all the things I listed."

Chapter 12 – Savannah

Reynold came home from set today looking like death, coughing, and running a fever. He couldn't make it through his scenes without hacking up a lung, so the director sent him home.

He has a cold.

I should have known something was wrong with him last night when he kept clearing his throat and sniffling. I figured it was just allergies.

He insisted he was fine and tried to clean up the living room after Addy and I built a fort, but I dragged his ass to the bathroom. I shoved cold medicine down his throat, then tucked him into bed.

He fell asleep right away.

It's now almost ten at night and he's still passed out. I'd long fed Addy leftover salad and chicken from dinner last night. We watched a Disney movie, and she fell asleep in my lap. I carried her to her bed, and she woke up long enough for me to read her a book about a family of bears moving from the woods to the big city.

I'm exhausted, but before heading to bed, I stop by the library to pick out a new book to read. I flip the light switch and take in the room's beauty. It doesn't matter how many times I've been in here; I always find it magical. It reminds me of a study in a Victorian home. Floor to ceiling cases of old books fill two long walls. I scan the spines from afar, pausing at the spot where Reynold backed me against the shelves.

Heavy red velvet curtains cover the windows lining another wall. A small antique desk sits in a corner with a short bookcase behind it. Pictures of Reynold and Adeline and a few of his parents and sister clutter the top shelf.

There's another acoustic guitar in here, different from the one in his office. It's part of a tiny band corner with a bass guitar and a Fender Stratocaster electric guitar (which I know is an expensive brand). Can he play all these? I am dying to hear him.

I scope out the top of his desk, which is littered with movie scripts (just like the desk in his office), then walk over to the floor to ceiling bookcases. After reading *Pride and Prejudice*, I figured I could give the other classics a try. Except, this time, I see Reynold's added some new books.

Spicy romance books.

Books by authors with the filthiest smut. I've already read a handful of these, but the rest are new to me or on my 'to be read' list. How did he know?

"Did he seriously buy these for me?"

"I did."

I jump at Reynold's scratchy voice filling the silent air of the room.

"Goddamn it, Rey! Stop scaring me!"

He's standing, arms crossed, leaning on the doorframe with a mischievous look on his tired face. I know he's tired because he didn't react to me calling him Rey.

"How did you know what books I wanted?"

He starts coughing and that sexy book boyfriend pose disappears. He latches a hand on the frame to hold himself up.

"Reynold," I scold, and he frowns at me. I close the distance between us and palm his forehead once he's done coughing. Yep. Still burning up. "Why are you awake? You should have called or texted me, and I would have helped you with anything you needed."

"Anything?"

"Yes, you stubborn fool."

That damn smirk returns. "I had to use the loo. Would you have held my cock while I took a piss?"

I push at his chest, and he stumbles back slightly. I grab his arms to anchor him.

"Come on. Let's get you back to bed."

He doesn't argue and allows me to lead him to his room. I leave him sitting on the bed to grab more medicine and a glass of water.

He's curled up in the fetal position when I return.

"Am I going to die?"

I huff out a laugh and sit next to him.

"It's just a cold, Reynold. Haven't you had a cold before?"

"Not one this bad," he mumbles into his pillow.

"Maybe it's the flu. You're around people more now that you're back at work. Your body was mostly isolated for five years, right?"

He nods.

"And with Addy at preschool, kids are a cesspool of germs. I'm surprised you didn't get sick sooner than this."

He slowly flips onto his back and rubs his palm over my thigh.

"Thank you for taking care of me."

I move a lock of hair off his forehead. "Of course."

"The last time someone took care of me was sixteen years ago. It was a month after my parents died. My sister was so stressed. She was barely eighteen and halfway through Upper Sixth—that's the equivalent to senior year of high school here in the U.S.—when she was given custody of a fourteen-year-old boy. Then I got a stomach bug. I had it for three days and she never left my side."

I palm his cheek, then slide my hand up into his hair so I can rake my nails over his scalp. He closes his eyes and sighs at my touch.

"How did she die?"

He doesn't answer for the longest time.

"A few months before filming for *Tyler's Team* started, I flew to New Jersey to help Annalee during her last month of pregnancy. She didn't have anyone to take care of her. Kyle abandoned her the minute he found out she was pregnant, and she said all her friends were busy and she didn't want to bother them.

"She hated the idea of me helping her. The kid brother wasn't supposed to take care of the big sis. Still, I came. The doctors kept her in the hospital for the last month of her pregnancy because she had peripartum cardiomyopathy: a weakened heart. After she gave birth, her symptoms got worse. I'd been sleeping on the couch in her hospital room, Adeline next to me in a bassinet. I woke up to the sound of Annalee's heart machine crashing and Adeline wailing."

My hand is still in his hair, absentmindedly petting him the entire time.

"I'm so sorry, Reynold."

He finally opens his eyes and I expect them to be pained, full of grief. Instead, he smiles as if relieved I'm here with him, listening and supporting him.

"Call me Reynold again."

"Reynold," I whisper.

"Mmm. Never stop, okay?"

I salute him. "Sir, yes, sir."

He chuckles, which makes him cough violently, reminding me he's super sick.

I point at his chest. "Take your shirt off for me."

He quirks a brow. "I like how this is sounding."

He struggles to strip so I help. Despite his skin being hot to the touch, he starts shivering the moment the shirt is off.

I grab the jar of Vicks VapoRub I had delivered while Reynold was asleep.

"This will help you breathe better." I take a dollop of the ointment on two fingers and spread it over his chest. He hisses at the sudden coolness of it.

Once I'm done, I wash my hands in the kitchen, then grab an ice pack from the freezer and wrap it in a towel.

Reynold's eyes are closed again when I return, and I'm certain he's asleep, but when I sit back down on the bed, he lifts his hand and rubs my bare leg... up my inner thigh.

I try to ignore the somersaults in my stomach caused by his touch and place the ice pack on his forehead.

"Watch those hands, buddy. You're burning up and totally not sexy right now."

Lie. Still sexy. Maybe even more with how needy he's being. The tough action star, taken down by the common cold.

Men are such babies.

"I had plans for you," Reynold murmurs. "I was going to sex you up so good."

I snort. "You're delirious."

"Will you sleep with me tonight?"

I bite my lip because I want nothing more. But he's sick and I'm pretty sure he's contagious.

Ugh. Fuck it. I'm probably already sick, especially after that kiss last night.

My throat *is* a little sore now that I think about it. Does the cold virus act that fast? Or did Addy get us sick?

"Okay. Let me give you more medicine and then we'll go to sleep."

I wake up the next morning coughing.

I knew it.

My skin is slick with sweat, and my lungs are burning. I sit up on the edge of the bed, glancing over my shoulder to make sure I didn't wake Reynold but find he's not there. Before I stand to search for him, he appears in the doorway.

He's holding the same medicine I gave him yesterday.

"You were coughing all night, tossing and turning. I got you sick," he says, not at all sounding sorry. "Now *I* get to take care of *you*."

He can barely get the words out before he's hacking. His typically tanned skin is still pale and there are bags underneath his beautiful blue eyes.

"How will you take care of me while you're still sick? Don't worry about me. I'll be fine."

"I'm sure you will be fine, Miss Independent, but I'm still taking care of you."

He sits next to me on the bed and removes the lid to the bottle of cold and flu medicine. He pours the recommended amount into the plastic cup and hands it to me. Then he pours his own into a small paper cup that Addy uses to rinse out her toothpaste. He holds his up like it's a shot glass.

"Cheers."

We clank and down the medicine, both of us blanching at the chalky taste.

I sigh and fall back onto the bed. Reynold does the same. "Who gets sick in the summer? So lame."

We lay there for a few minutes in silence. Well, not really because we're both wheezing from congestion and coughing up mucus.

"How can I watch Adeline like this? What about your work?"

He finds my hand at my side and weaves his fingers with mine.

"Brenda's here with her now."

I always forget about Brenda. Reynold says she works remotely most of the week, only coming over to accept deliveries or to stock supplies. I also never see his housekeeper. She stops by to clean once a week, typically when no one's home.

Reynold brings our hands up to his mouth and kisses my knuckles. "I can't go back to work until a doctor clears me. One, they don't want me getting the other cast and crew sick, and two... my role is active, so I need to be at one hundred percent health before I return. I need to be able to run, jump, and perform all the stunts. They've rearranged the production schedule to film scenes I'm not in. I should be able to go back in a week, maybe two."

"Addy's not sick, is she? Or any of our dinner guests?"

I checked on her last night before snuggling up with Reynold. She seemed fine. I felt her forehead and listened to her breathing. There was no sign of a fever or congestion.

"Addy is as loud and talkative as ever, and no one else got sick. But no one else was making out with me either, so..."

I hear Adeline's muffled laughter from the other side of the door.

"Lana is taking her tonight. She wants to convince Addy to go spend the week with her at her hotel while we recover. Lana said she needs practice."

"Practice?"

He nods. "Mylan and Lana are considering adoption, and Lana is going to be a godmother to Ginger's baby."

I'm so happy that Lana and Mylan decided to adopt. Last year she did an exclusive interview with Entertainment Now. She talked about getting pregnant in high school, losing the baby, and having an emergency hysterectomy. She'd always wanted kids but had no one to share the parenting experience with until she met Mylan.

"Come on." Reynold stands, pulling me from my thoughts. He holds out his hand. "I'm going to make you some soup."

I scowl.

"Us. I'm going to make *us* some soup."

I roll my eyes but take his hand and follow him out to the kitchen.

"Savvy!" Addy squeals and runs towards me.

"Adeline Lee," Reynold warns in that punishing voice that gets me all hot and bothered.

Addy stops in her tracks.

"You need to stay back. We're sick, remember?"

"I want to be sick too," she whines.

"Oh, Addy," I begin. "Being sick is no fun. That means staying in bed and not going out for ice cream or hanging out with Lana and Banana."

I giggle at the names rhyming. Lana said Mylan named the dog Banana after her childhood nickname.

"I get to hang out with Banana today?" she says with hope.

I nod and Addy jumps up and down.

"Do you want to have a sleepover with Banana and Lana too?" Reynold adds.

"Will you and Savvy be there?" she asks with a frown.

"Savannah and I have to stay here to get better," he explains. I can see how he struggles to not walk to her, take her in his arms, and reassure her. "We only need a few days, at most four, then you can come back."

Adeline's eyes widen. "That's a long time."

Reynold laughs to shake off his hesitancy. I'm assuming it's the first time he'll be away from her since she was born.

"I know, Poppy, but it'll pass in no time. Lana wants to take you on adventures."

Addy's face brightens at that, and she hops around again. "I love adventures. Can I wear my knight's costume?"

"You sure can," he says, then turns to me. "I bought her one after our trip to Arkansas, and she's been wanting to wear it ever since."

"Because I want to be a knight like Dad," Addy giggles. She runs off into the living room and jumps feet first onto the couch. This is the second time she's mentioned Reynold being a knight. The first time was on the plane.

"I do the Renaissance Faire up at Tryon Park in the fall. Addy joined me for the first time last year. She was a tiny princess, and I was her knight. The costume lets me blend in and feel normal, if only for a day."

Normal. He seems to want normalcy, but he's a famous actor. Didn't he realize fame came with the job?

He must have seen the question on my face.

"I used to revel in the fame... the publicity. I didn't mind the paparazzi because I wanted to be seen. It all changed five years ago when..."

When Adeline was born, and his sister died.

"Sometimes I wonder if I still want to act."

"You do."

He raises a brow at me. "Oh yeah? You know what I want?"

I blush at the double meaning of that question.

"I know you get so excited anytime you talk about this new movie. You talk my ear off at breakfast, reliving the scenes you filmed the day before. You missed acting."

He opens his mouth and holds up a finger like he does when he's about to argue with me, but it's interrupted by a cough. I fill up a glass of water and hand it to him.

"Okay, soup time."

He takes a huge sip, then a deep breath. "Soup time."

Chapter 13 – Reynold

Despite feeling like death, spending time with Savannah is absolute bliss. We sleep a lot, only waking to eat or shower (though not together because I know I wouldn't be able to control myself).

We snuggle up with tissues, soup, and tea and binge TV shows and movies. I convince her to watch some of my action films. I've never been alone in a room with someone while they watched me act. Except when I first started acting, and each role was new and exciting. My parents would make a big deal out of me being on the telly, and we'd gather around in the living room to watch whatever show I was on. One time they invited our neighbors over and my dad yelled, "That's my boy," when I came up on the screen.

I knew I didn't need to impress them because they'd tell me I was great, even if I wasn't.

It's different with Savannah. She's the first woman I'm excited to share this part of my life with. Probably because she isn't remotely interested in the fame side of me.

Yet, she smiles every time I come on the screen, engrossed in every word I say. She becomes emotional when I die because sometimes, I play the bad guy who gets killed by the good guy.

Then there are the sex scenes. I've never been shy about my body. I'll bare ass at the drop of a coin. I even went full frontal for a movie once.

Two films we watch show my backside while I'm fucking a woman. Savannah bites her lip and blushes. Her breathing picks up and I want to grab her to make our own sex scene, but she made it quite clear how miserable and not sexy she feels.

Between sleeping, eating, and watching TV or movies, we don't do a lot of talking. I never thought I could enjoy someone's company, despite barely uttering a word to each other. Still... having her near me, her body flush with mine, and her head resting on my shoulder is intoxicating.

By day three, our coughs are nearly gone. We're in the kitchen, eating actual food instead of soup. I asked Shirley to come early today for lunch. She prepared chicken quesadillas with chips and salsa.

"What did you do while raising Addy since you weren't acting?"

I pause, the question seeming to come out of nowhere. I take a bite of food and chew while forming my answer because I never talk about this part of my life with anyone.

"Well, the first year, I mostly slept. Addy woke up a lot throughout the night, so I was always tired. Any chance I got to sleep, I would.

"When she turned one, I hired a part-time nanny. She'd take her to the park and while they were gone, I'd do some voice over work for commercials or books. I bought all the equipment and turned a closet into a recording studio."

I shrug.

"Other than that, I didn't do much else. I worked out a lot. Mostly to relieve stress and... other things."

She blushes, knowing exactly what I meant by 'other things.'

"Why didn't you go to Ginger and Bruno's wedding? You said you were invited, but you couldn't go?"

She takes a sip of her lemonade to wash down a bite.

"Brad didn't want to go because he said Lana hated him. She did, but I wasn't going to admit that. Then he got pissed when I told him I was going without him. We got into a big fight, which ruined my excitement. I flew to Georgia instead to stay with my parents for a few days. I needed a break from him. Now that I think about it, that's when I first suspected he was cheating. I remember him being weird when I got back. As if he was guilty about something. I never noticed anything off with him until that day."

I want to murder him. How could anyone cheat on this woman?

"That was the last time I visited my parents too. I haven't been back because I felt ashamed. They told me to break up with Brad—they weren't fans of his either. So, I didn't want to see their disappointed faces when I showed up and told them we were still together."

I take her hand in mine. "If you want to fly down and visit them, you can take all the time off you need."

She shakes her head. "It's fine. I talk to them on the phone and text them both a lot. They're supportive in everything I do—even when I think I'm a disappointment. I should have known better. They're never disappointed in me or in anything I've done. Not even when I told them about moving here on a whim. They were honestly excited for me."

We finish eating while sharing more of our lives, including some of our favorite things. Our tastes are similar. We both like banana and peanut butter waffles with maple syrup and playing old school video games. She was way too excited when I told her I have Mario Kart. We both love anything artsy. For me, it's music, acting, and reading non-fiction books. For her, it's fashion, styling outfits, and reading anything but non-fiction books.

We share things we hate like people who are rude to service industry workers and books with cliffhangers (more so her since I don't read a lot of fiction books anymore, but I am quite curious about her spicy romances.)

I ask her when her birthday is (so I can spoil her when that day comes). February twentieth, which makes her a Pisces. I'm a Scorpio; my birthday is November fourteenth.

She snorts. "Scorpios are sex maniacs."

"Yes... we are." I relish the way her face turns bright red.

I'm counting down the days until I can show her just how much of a Scorpio I am.

Adeline returned from hanging out with Lana two days ago, and Savannah resumed her nanny duties. The set doctor cleared me for work then I met with the fight choreographer to make sure I'm okay to do action scenes. After lying around in bed for nearly a week, returning to physical activities left my recovering body exhausted.

Returning to set also meant time away from Savannah. I want our first time together to be special. I'll have to negotiate with my friends to take Adeline for the night. I know they would. It's clear they want whatever is happening between Savannah and me to work out just as much as I do.

I've missed her in my bed. Last night, she slept in her room saying she didn't want me tired and distracted today since it's officially my first day back. I didn't fight her on it because she's right: all I want to do is finish what we started before getting sick.

"What are you pissed about?" Mylan asks when he sits down in a director's chair beside me. He just finished a scene, and the crew is resetting for the next, which includes an intense police questioning between mine and Mylan's characters.

I shrug. "Just wish I was home."

"With Savvy?" Mylan wags his brows.

Yes, with Savvy. But I don't respond to that.

"Thank you for taking care of Adeline while we were sick."

"It was no problem. It helped solidify Lana and my decision to adopt."

I smile. "Really? That's amazing news, Mylan."

His happiness dulls slightly. "Remember when we were teens, and we'd go out, get drunk, fuck around, get into trouble?"

"Of course. Best time of my life."

"What the hell do I know about raising a kid? I was a mess growing up because of my parents. What if I'm like them? What if my kid ends up being like me?"

"You mean caring, strong, and selfless?"

"You know what I mean, Ren."

"Mylan," I begin, "you're not the same man from five years ago. You realize that, right?"

He nods, still not entirely convinced he's good enough to be a parent.

"Look... you're going to have doubts every single day. When I got custody of Adeline, I thought for sure I'd fail. Then the first time I held her after my sister died, she grabbed my finger. She wrapped those tiny digits around, gripped hard, and smiled at me."

"It was probably gas," Mylan offers.

I punch him in the arm, and he hisses.

Wanker.

"What I'm trying to say, you fucking twat, is in that moment, I fell in love, and I knew I could do it. I could be a parent to this child who wasn't mine. She wasn't mine, but now she is, and five years later, she's alive and happy because of me.

"So, yeah, I *do* think you'll be a good father. You're nothing like your parents because you've learned from your mistakes, and you've righted your wrongs. Plus, you'll have Lana, and I know she doesn't put up with your bullshit."

Mylan chuckles. "Truth."

We don't talk for a minute while Mylan checks his texts and I respond to a few from Savannah. She took Addy to Central Park after school, and they had a picnic in Sheep Meadows. A pang of missing this moment rips through my stomach. I should be there with them.

I've missed out on a lot of important things in my lifetime because of my career. Because I was chasing fame.

"Mylan," I begin, and my friend lifts his head. "I'm really sorry I wasn't there for you."

"Ren, you don't need to..."

"When *Metal & Mayhem* wrapped, I had a lot of projects lined up. I barely had time to breathe, let alone hang out with you and Jensen. I missed you guys so much and it hurt to see you two get closer without me. It's my fault though. You'd both text me and invite me to things, but I just couldn't find the time."

"You were doing what was best for you and your career."

I drop my eyes down to my lap where I'm picking at my hangnails.

"I suppose... but it was fucking lonely."

I made friends, but they weren't like Mylan and Jensen. Not authentic. What's worse is how I had to read the tabloids about the people who came into Mylan's life when me or Jensen weren't around. They'd get close to him, pretend to be his friend, then take advantage of him. They'd betray his trust and leak secrets about him in exchange for money.

Mylan slaps his palm on my shoulder. "What matters now is that you're here. I'm here. We're doing this movie together and after, we'll keep in touch, right?"

"You bet your arse, mate."

"Maybe you can move back to L.A.," Mylan says.

It's something I've considered, but I buried Annalee in New Jersey. I take Adeline to visit her grave once a month. I raised Addy on the East Coast, and I'm not sure if I'm ready to move her away just yet.

For the next week, I stay busy filming. The days were long, making up for the ones I missed. Today was my last long shoot before I have two days off.

Two days.

I plan to spend every single minute of them with Savannah.

I return home at one in the morning to find Savannah in my bed. It's like a reward after a trying day at work. I slip in quietly, making sure not to wake her, and pass out the moment my head hits the pillow.

When I wake, I'm rewarded with a body curled up against my side.

Something I've noticed about Savannah is how she tosses and turns in her sleep. She did it a lot when we were sick. She woke me up once by kicking me in the shin. I couldn't fall back asleep after that, so I watched as she jerked around, attempting to get comfortable.

She doesn't seem to do it when Adeline is in the bed with her, though. It's as if her body knows to keep still. Except Addy isn't here now, and Savannah has wormed her way over to me and slung her arm over my stomach.

I smooth my palm over her bare arm and kiss the top of her head. She smells like coconut and peaches.

She smells as good as she tastes.

I only got a small taste, and I've been craving more.

"Good morning, BG," she mumbles into my stomach. I laugh and it shakes her head.

"Good morning, Savvy."

She scoffs, her hot breath fanning across my skin since I like to sleep without a shirt on.

"What's the matter? Don't like when I call you that?"

She shrugs. "Doesn't matter to me."

I take her arms to lift her off me and topple her over onto her back. She yelps at the fast movement.

"Quit," I begin, and place a kiss on her cheek. "Calling me..." A kiss on her jaw. "British Guy." Another kiss on her neck. I graze my teeth against the skin there and she arches off the bed.

"Or what?" she challenges, like the first time we woke up together with her cuddling me.

I laugh and crawl out of bed. Her eyes drop to my cock growing hard in my boxer briefs.

"I got something for you," I say and walk to my dresser.

"You got me a gift?"

"It's more so a gift for you *and* me."

Taking the box from the top drawer, I hand it to Savannah, who's now sitting up in bed. Her cleavage pours out of the tank top she wore to sleep in. I want to push the fabric aside and take her breast in my mouth. I want to suck that hard nipple and bite it and lap it with my tongue.

"Butt plugs?" she asks with confusion.

I sit on the bed and take the box back to open it. I hand her the three sizes of plugs and a bottle of lube.

"It's to stretch you out."

"Stretch... me out?"

She's inspecting the sex toys as if she's never seen one before. Wait... maybe she hasn't.

I lift her chin with my finger and thumb. Her large green eyes—full of excitement and hesitation—find my heated stare.

"You were so eager to take my finger up your arse. Did you enjoy it?"

"Yes," she breathes out.

"What about my cock? Do you want my cock up your arse too?"

She nods and licks her lips, and I almost follow the movement and lick them too.

"Then we need to prepare that tight little hole." I hold up the smallest. "We start with this one, then size up as your body adjusts."

She clenches her sheet-covered thighs together.

"You like the sound of that, don't you, Savannah?"

She nods again, nibbling on her lip. How I love when she nibbles on her plump bottom lip.

"Don't think I've forgotten about all those kinks you listed from your romance books. I plan to take advantage of every single one."

She groans and I can't hold back anymore. I lean over to kiss her. She almost falls into the kiss before pulling back.

"Put one in me now."

I raise a brow. "Yeah?"

"I've never had one... there. I'm intrigued."

I give her one more kiss. "Lie down."

I stand, checking the doors to make sure they're locked. I peek at Addy's nanny cam and she's in her room watching cartoons.

Back in bed, I settle between Savannah's legs.

"Take these off," I say and tug at her sleep shorts.

She's quick to remove them, leaving me faced with a half-naked, gloriously beautiful woman before me.

I could dive in right now and feast on her.

I tease the opening to her pussy with my fingertip, and she tries to clamp her legs on my arm. I push them back apart, then dip a finger inside her. She moans and slaps her palms over her mouth to muffle her pleasurable sounds. I pump into her a few more times before moving a finger to the puckered ring of muscles.

I let her own pleasure coat the entrance before I push the tip inside, just an inch.

She fists the sheets at her side.

"Oh yes, you like that. Savannah, you're doing such a good job."

She whines at the praise, and I move my finger in and out of a hole that's been neglected her entire life. I add a second finger and repeat, relishing her soft whimpers.

"Are you ready?" I ask after I'm sure she's stretched out enough for the plug.

She nods fast, matching her labored breathing.

I remove my fingers, grab the smallest plug, and drench it in lube. I nudge it in, slowly.

"Relax. It won't hurt."

"Are you sure?"

"I am. It might feel slightly uncomfortable at first, but that will pass quickly."

My words ease her worries and I slide the plug in completely. She gasps and arches her back before slowly lowering to the bed.

"That's it. It's in."

She lets out a quick breath. "It's in?"

"Yep."

I don't give her time to think about the fact that her arse is filled with a sex toy, because I want her to *feel* it.

My mouth covers her clit, and I suck hard. Her reflexes are fast enough that she grabs a pillow to cover her mouth just in time to muffle her loud scream.

"Oh my God, yes, yes, Reynold. That feels good," she mumbles against the pillow.

While working her clit with my mouth, I fuck her with two fingers. Her pussy clenches hard around the digits as I thrust them in and out, unrelenting.

"Fuck," she says and shudders with an orgasm.

She removes the pillow from her face after coming down from that high.

"I've never come so fast in my life." She smiles down at me with bliss. "The plug, your fingers... it was overwhelming, but in a good way."

My fingers are still inside her, and I start pumping. She sucks in a breath and fists the sheets beside her once again.

"Just wait until my cock is inside you while you wear that plug," I say and take her clit into my mouth, drawing it in to lap the tip of my tongue over the sensitive nerves. "Then... when you're all stretched out... you'll take my cock like a good girl, won't you Savannah?"

She groans and nods, unable to speak because I'm thrusting my fingers viciously into her. One of her hands moves to her breast, and she plays with her nipple. Her cunt tightens as she rolls it between her fingers.

She digs her heels into my back and grabs my hair to pull my face closer to her pussy while I eat her out for a second time.

It doesn't take her long to reach another orgasm, and she erupts underneath me.

Once she's done shaking, I remove my fingers and lick them clean.

The move prompts her to sit up suddenly and kiss me, deep and rough. I moan into her mouth as her hand slips into my boxer briefs and she grabs my dick. I jolt at her warm hands wrapping around my length. She uses my pre-cum as lubricant and slides her fist up and down. She squeezes, not too hard but applying just enough pressure that I can already feel my release building. She doesn't hold back.

Her talented tongue massages my own. Her lips are soft yet demanding as they dance over my mouth. Pressure builds in my lower spine, and I freeze.

Savannah pulls back but still doesn't stop fisting me. "Tell me where you want it."

"In your mouth."

She leans down, opening those swollen, red lips just in time for me to explode ropes of cum onto her tongue. Some gets on her lips, her chin, her cheek and she uses her finger to lap it all up back into her mouth where it belongs.

"Fuck, Savannah. That was beautiful." I kiss her and groan as I taste myself.

When we finally part, I rest my forehead on hers.

"We should get up and make breakfast for Adeline."

"Is she awake?" Savannah asks, some concern in her voice.

"Yes. She's watching cartoons in her room."

"What's the plan for today? You're off right? Today and tomorrow?"

"Today and tomorrow."

We get out of bed and stand before each other. I relish the way Savannah's lips still look swollen and red, her blonde hair ratted and sticking up around her head, and her sleep clothes wrinkled.

"How's the butt plug?" I ask and smile when her eyes widen.

"I forgot it was in there," she says and covers her mouth with her palms.

"Good. Let's leave it in for an hour. Then tonight..."

She swallows hard. "Tonight?"

"Tonight, when Adeline is out at a Broadway show with Mylan, Lana, Eloise, and Kelly, I'll put it back in and fuck you with it inside you. Once you're well adjusted, we'll go up a size."

She frowns. "I want to go to a Broadway show."

I tilt my head back with a laugh.

"Yeah? You want to skip tonight?"

She blushes and bites her bottom lip like she loves to do.

"Hell no."

I grab her and tug her against my body, giving her a sweet and drawn-out kiss. "Good," I whisper against her lips. "Because we have the place to ourselves all night long. Addy isn't returning until tomorrow afternoon. Do you know how much we can do between now and then?"

Chapter 14 - Savannah

Mylan, Lana, Eloise, and Kelly show up around four to pick up Adeline. They're going to dinner at Junior's Restaurant & Cheesecake before seeing *The Lion King*. I'm super jealous and almost change my mind about tonight, but I'm too worked up. I wore the butt plug for an hour and squirmed every time I moved or sat down because it shifted and hit the right nerves. I need Reynold inside me to relieve this built-up pressure as soon as possible. Not to mention how he's been whispering his praises in my ear all day. My pussy has been clenching around nothing all day long and I'm so wet I've ruined my underwear.

I'm about to burst.

"You okay, Savvy?" Eloise asks, a knowing smile growing across her face.

We're all standing in the kitchen chatting. Adeline is in the living room, watching cartoons while waiting to leave.

"I'm great."

"Your cheeks are flushed. Are you still sick?" Lana adds.

Mylan, who is talking with Reynold about a scene they're excited to film, turns to look at me and tilts his head. "Huh... your face is the color of a tomato. Are you hot?"

"Probably hot and bothered," Kelly mumbles under their breath, which garners a united snort from Eloise and Lana.

"Bothered? About what?" Mylan asks, pinging his attention from his wife to Eloise and Kelly.

Of course, them pointing out that I'm flustered has me getting even *more* flustered. And paranoid. Certainly, they can't know I have a sex toy in my ass. Yeah, Reynold put it back in before they arrived. He's trying to get me used to it. It's been in there three times now. I'd forgotten about it earlier when I helped Addy pack. It took us about an hour because she wanted me to help with a puzzle, then she had me listen to her play her violin. It sounded like a wailing cat, but I smiled and clapped when she finished. After the violin, she showed me a game on her iPad. There were other things that kept her distracted from actually packing. It wasn't until we'd sat down for lunch, and I let out a sexual 'oh,' that I remembered the butt plug in my ass.

Addy giggled, and Reynold's eyes widened.

He'd been thinking about that 'oh' all throughout lunch. Once we finished eating, he snuck us away while Addy watched a movie, then ate me out in my bedroom... with the butt plug still inside me.

"You're right," I begin, ready to put an end to their teasing. "I am bothered because you're all still here. I know you know that Reynold and I are about to..." I pause and glance into the living room. Addy is on the couch, engrossed in the show she's watching. I'm not entirely sure she's not listening to every word we're saying in here.

"Shag?" Kelly says in a poorly done British accent.

"Have a bonk," Eloise chimes in with an equally bad British accent.

Lana doesn't even attempt an accent. "Bang it out."

"Get your oats," Mylan adds in a near flawless accent.

"I hate you all," I say, not able to hold back a smile.

"Every one of your accents was rubbish," Reynold says.

"Hey! I didn't even do one," Lana grumbles at the same time Mylan says, "Mine was perfect."

"You lot." Rey points to the hallway leading out of the apartment. "Out. Now."

Everyone acts offended and horrified at Reynold's insistence despite the humor on his face. I can't help giggling at this entire situation.

Addy turns off the television and runs into the kitchen. "Is it time to go see the lions now?"

Lana brushes an orange red curl out of her face. "It sure is, honey. Are you excited?"

Adeline jumps up and down. "Yes! I wish Dad and Savvy were coming, though."

"Oh, you'll be coming," Mylan whispers to Reynold, who is standing next to him.

"Inappropriate," Lana says and punches him in the shoulder.

"Ow, Donut. She doesn't even know what that means."

I smile at Mylan's nickname for Lana. They've talked about it in interviews before saying Lana loves donuts, and he loves her, therefore she's his donut. I know it's because Lana told Mylan that donuts are better than sex and Mylan said 'wanna bet?'

The five of them finally leave the apartment and I turn to Reynold. "You sure you're okay with them taking Addy again for the night? This is different from them taking her when we were sick."

When Lana watched over Addy, they went to the chocolate stores in Times Square as promised. They explored Central Park with Banana and other public places. The paparazzi found them and snapped photos, but no one seemed to recognize her as Rey Michaelson's daughter. Probably because Lana put a blonde wig on her, which Adeline kept and now wears around the penthouse all the time.

Still, tonight's different. They won't be in disguise. People will ask about the little girl spotted with Mylan and Lana. They've talked about adopting in interviews before. Will the public assume she's theirs? Or will they recognize her as Rey's and wonder why he's not with them?

While Reynold has been protective of Adeline and wants to keep her out of the spotlight, he said he trusts Lana and Mylan. He's also talked to Addy about the paparazzi, and she said she's not scared of them. She didn't care if they took her picture.

The older she gets, the harder it will be to shield her from the public. He knows he can't keep her hidden forever. He can't stop her from enjoying life. The paparazzi will take pictures and articles will be written.

Like when the media got shots of me out with Lana at the Statue of Liberty. Then shots of me and Lana with Adeline at the Brooklyn Bridge. I was the mystery woman who Rey's team later confirmed was his daughter's new nanny.

"Five years, Savannah."

"Five.... years?" He's said this before. I know it's been five years since he's been with anyone, but I'm playing dumb to get a reaction out of him.

He grabs me by the waist and tugs our bodies flush. His hard dick grinds into my stomach. "That's how long it's been since I've fucked anyone. That's how long it's been since I've *wanted* to fuck anyone. And believe me, plenty of my past hookups have called or texted me, offering to 'console' me over the past five years."

"Well, that's definitely not something I want to hear right now."

He tilts his head down to nuzzle my neck, blowing his hot breath on my skin and nibbling my jaw. "But they weren't you. No one has ever made me feel this way."

"And... and how do I make you feel?"

"Like I belong." He moves his mouth to place a kiss on my lips. "I belong with you." More kisses along my jaw. "I belong to you."

A trail of kisses down my neck.

"And tonight," he adds, "I belong between your legs."

"Tonight? Not right now?"

He steps back and wags his finger at me. "Dinner first. I need you fueled. It's going to be a long night."

I groan when he pulls away and takes my hand to lead me to a stool, whimpering when I sit down because the plug adjusts in my ass.

Reynold's only response to the sexual sound is kissing me, then he spins around to find two wine glasses. He opens the bottle of red he'd set out for tonight.

He's planned everything, including torturing me by slowly drawing out and building up my pleasure.

He fills both glasses with wine, then clinks his with mine. It's bitter but not too bad with hints of cherries. I'm not really a wine drinker, but Reynold is, and sharing this with him makes me eager to try all of them.

"Now," he says, setting his glass on the marble countertop, "I'm going to cook dinner for us, and you're going to sit there and watch."

He holds up that stupid, yet talented, finger when I open my mouth to protest.

"You'll do nothing but watch because tonight is about you. I want to take care of you. I want you to know how worthy you are because I bet that wanker Brett—"

"Brad."

"—didn't do shit for you."

He's right. Brad did the bare minimum in our relationship.

I cross my arms and raise my brow. "Okay, fine. I'll watch. But only if you take your shirt off."

He stares at me, deadpan, no emotion across his face as he slides his shirt off in one slick move using just one hand. His pants and boxer briefs follow.

Reynold stands in the middle of the kitchen naked.

"That's what I'm talking about," I say, my cheeks aching with how much this man makes me smile.

He walks to the pantry, takes out an apron, and puts it on.

"To protect the goods from splattering oil and what not," he says and winks.

"Of course."

Reynold gets to work, slicing veggies, searing steaks, and mashing potatoes. I can't help staring at his tight, muscular ass while he's turned away from me at the stove. He caught me a few times too.

While everything simmers and cooks, he commands his smart device to put on a music station that plays old school ballads. *(I Just) Died In Your Arms Tonight* by Cutting Crew plays and Reynold offers his hand.

We slow dance in the middle of the kitchen—something I've never done before. Life is crazy like that. I'm thirty-five years old and yet I'm still experiencing firsts.

With one hand on Reynold's bare waist, the other folded into his, I rest my head on his shoulder. We sway to the smooth notes and powerhouse voice of the song. He buries his nose into my hair and rubs his palm along my back, from the middle, then up and back down again.

He really likes touching me. I've never been a fan of touching, but I think it's because I wasn't used to it. Brad didn't do it, especially in public. He hated holding hands. He'd never steal a kiss from me in passing. Reynold is the opposite. He can barely go five minutes without touching me in some way. Even if it's a graze of his finger along my jaw or pushing a piece of hair off my face.

Once the food is done, Reynold puts his clothes back on (I insisted, so he wasn't sitting bare ass on the stool). Then he plates our meals with such precision, flaring the sauce he made for the steak, as if he's the chef of a Michelin star restaurant. I've never felt so fancy eating steak and potatoes.

Sitting next to each other so Reynold can run his palm up and down my thigh, we did little talking as we savored our food. Once our stomachs are full and the bottle of wine is empty (and I'm flush and somewhat tipsy from the alcohol), Reynold stands.

"Will you shower with me?"

"Hell yes."

We leave the mess in the kitchen and Reynold leads me down the hallway to his bathroom. Despite no one else being in the penthouse, he locks all the doors and turns to face me.

"Strip for me, Savannah," he says, his voice soft and full of demand and passion.

I'm wearing a simple sundress, no bra or panties because I knew I wouldn't be wearing the outfit for long. The fabric falls to the floor in a puddle, and I stand there, naked in front of a fully clothed Reynold.

"Fuck. You're beautiful."

His blue eyes light with desire and his dick rises as he takes in my body, making my stomach clench with anticipation. He steps close and I inhale his musk; hints of sweat infused with a wooden, spicy scent. Warm. Welcoming. I lick my lips and realize I'm gawking at the man. Does he see how much I need him right now? He must because he strips faster than I can blink.

I lift my hand to his chest. "May I?"

"Please," he breathes.

He closes his eyes as my hand spreads over every inch. I leave no patch untouched, appreciating his sculpted body over his broad shoulders and brawny chest.

"Are you okay?"

He nods. "I haven't been touched like this in a long time. It's intoxicating. Keep going."

He tightens his abs the moment my fingertips graze over them. I trace down to that V-shape and flatten my palms to slice them back up his stomach and over the muscles rippling across his shoulders. He flexes his meaty pecks with a wicked smile.

"Are you taunting me, British Guy?"

He ignores the nickname and leaves me to turn on the shower. He tests the water to make sure it's warm enough. When satisfied, he holds out his hand to me.

I eagerly take it and he twists me around to stand me underneath the stream.

Not warm... *cold*.

"Fucking bastard," I growl and slap at him, jolting away from the freezing water.

"That's for calling me British Guy again." He chuckles and adjusts the knob until warmer water spews out. Reynold pulls me flush to his body. My soft chest and stomach smash against all his hard lines and defined muscles.

"My turn to touch," Reynold says next to my ear, walking me backwards until we're both getting soaked. "Tell me where you want my hands, Savannah."

My head tilts back, and he brushes a kiss against my lips. "Everywhere. Touch me everywhere."

I've never said those words to a man. It's something no man has ever offered me. Dating has been exhausting for this reason. Men want to sleep with me, but they don't want to be seen with me. They don't want to touch me, but they want to fuck me and get their pleasure, then leave me unsatisfied.

I've always been the guilty pleasure.

Not anymore.

Reynold's hand finds my breast, and he squeezes appreciatively before his fingertips tease the nipple. I arch into the touch, and he leans down, covering his mouth over the peak.

His tongue laps over the sensitive tip, and I dig my nails into his back.

He hisses at the pain, but his mouth continues to work my breast.

"Sorry," I breathe out.

"Never be sorry," he says and moves a hand down to cup my pussy.

He slides a finger inside me, groaning at how wet I am. His thrusts are slow at first, allowing him to put pressure on my clit. Then he speeds up.

"Yes, Rey, please."

My breathing becomes fast, my walls closing in around him. I feel so full with his fingers and the butt plug inside me. But seconds before I orgasm, he stops.

"No," I whine.

"What's my name, Savannah?"

He leaves his finger deep inside me and my walls throb around him. Is he punishing me for calling him Rey just now?

"Fuck!"

He chuckles against my cheek. "No, my love," he says with his velvet accent that makes me melt.

My love? My heart beats faster because he's never said that to me. I know he doesn't mean *love* love but to hear the word come out of his mouth...

"Reynold, please," I groan and squirm, hoping to satisfy the ache he's causing.

He rubs his thumb in circles over my clit, and my knees almost give out. I grip his shoulders for leverage as he pumps his fingers again. His mouth covers mine and that talented tongue takes over.

The water skirts the line of too hot, or maybe it's because heat rushes through my body as my orgasm builds once again from Reynold putting the right amount of pressure against my clit.

"I'm close," I cry out. "Don't stop."

But he does stop. The fucker. Like last time, he thrusts his finger deep inside me and just stays there. He curls the tip and grazes that evasive spot he always seems to know how to find. He teases it, putting me on edge.

I gasp. "You're edging me!"

He kisses me, long and languid, and hums against my mouth. "It's one of your kinks, is it not?"

He removes his finger and shoves it in his mouth, relishing the taste of me as if I was the dessert after our meal tonight.

"I told you; I didn't forget about your books. How many of those kinks can we get through tonight?" He moves me back underneath the stream of water. "I'm going to take this plug out now, then wash your hair and your body. Then I'm going to take you into my room, and I'll put the next size in you before fucking you. You'll be so wound up from edging, you'll see stars when you eventually come. Do you want that, Savannah?"

I nod and whimper.

"Good girl."

Chapter 15 - Reynold

I can't remember the last time I showered with a woman. I forgot how wonderful and euphoric the experience is. How my hands slick down her body through the lathering soap. How she moans when I wash her hair and scratch her scalp. The kisses I steal when it's her turn to wash me.

Our hands explore every inch of each other's bodies. Her palms indulging the creases of my abs, her tiny hands wrapping around my biceps and squeezing, her fingertips digging into my rock-hard ass.

My palms cupping her breasts, fitting perfectly because they're not too big. My fingertips grazing over the stretch marks along her stomach and hips and thighs. My hands squeezing the plumpness of her ass and kneading it, never wanting to stop because it's my favorite part of her body.

After we shower, I dry her off, then she dries me off, and it's such an intimate thing to do with someone. With Savannah, it feels natural, comforting.

I lead her out of the bathroom and into my room, placing her at the foot of the bed. I tug on her towel, and it falls to the ground. She does the same to me and my dick pops up, hard and leaking pre-cum.

It's been hard ever since she stripped for our shower.

I step to her and palm her cheek. She leans into my touch, and I inhale deeply, stifling a groan because she smells like me after I used my shampoo and body wash on her.

"Crawl into bed and get on your hands and knees," I say and kiss her gently.

She smiles against my mouth then follows my order.

I take out the middle size butt plug from the box and soak the teardrop shape with lubricant before stepping up behind her.

I rub my palm over her ass cheek, and she pushes back against it, as if telling me she's ready. "I need a word, Savannah. Something you can say if you've reached your limit. Can you do that for me?"

She looks at me over her shoulder and bites her lip while thinking. "Boundaries."

"Of course you'd choose that." I slap her ass, not too hard, but she wasn't expecting it and gasps. "You will say that word anytime you feel overwhelmed or when anything I'm doing becomes too much. Do you understand?"

She nods.

"I'm going to need you to say it, Savannah."

"I understand, sir."

She's mocking me. I squeeze her ass hard, and she lets out a soft moan.

"I'm putting this inside you now. Relax for me."

She relaxes, but barely. I spread her cheeks apart, and she sucks in a breath. I nudge the soft, pointed tip to the puckered hole and slowly inch it in. She tenses.

"This one is bigger, but you can take it. You're doing such a great job."

Her body melts at my praise, and I push the plug in until it's fully inside.

"Beautiful, Savannah." I spank her harder this time and she bucks away from the pleasurable pain. "I'm going to do some more of those things from your books. Maybe not all tonight, but we have so much time to play. So, tell me, what would you like? Want me to spank you? Harder than I just did? Tie you up and blindfold you, then bring you to the edge until you're panting and begging? Choke you while fucking you until you struggle to breathe? Do you want me to do all these things to you?"

"Yes, sir, please."

"So obedient." I kiss her lower back. "Roll over."

"I'm not a dog," she says, amused, still on her hands and knees.

My hand crashes down on her ass, and she falls to the bed. "Fuck, Reynold."

"You liked that, didn't you?"

"Yes. Please."

I take a condom out of the box in my top dresser drawer (recently purchased for this moment) and roll it on. Then I crawl on top of her and spread her legs. I run my finger along the slit of her pussy.

She's fucking soaked.

"I love that I do this to you."

I sink my finger in, and she arches off the bed. I pump in and out, fast and unrelenting. I add another and her walls are quick to latch on with how much I've already built her up. My thumb pushes down on her clit, and I massage it while I fuck her with my fingers. She's panting and moaning—such wonderful sounds.

But I can't let her come yet.

I pull out of her, and she whines.

"Boundaries?"

She shakes her head fast as I get on my knees. I pull her body down to the edge of the bed so I can bury my face in her cunt. I flatten my tongue over her opening and lick, drawing out a moan from her. My mouth covers her clit and I suck as hard as I can, then flick my tongue over it while thrusting my fingers inside her once more.

"Reynold, please," she pants.

I reach my free hand up to pinch a nipple, and that almost causes her to come. I remove my fingers and stand. Taking hold of my cock, I slide the tip through her pleasure, up and down.

"Now, Reynold, I'm begging."

I grin at her, enjoying the sight before me: flushed cheeks and red spreading across her neck and chest.

"I do love it when you beg," I say and plunge inside her in one slick move.

She screams out and fists the sheets. I stay seated, waiting for her to adjust.

When her back falls to the bed, I pull out, then slam back inside her. "You feel so fucking good, Savannah."

I pick up my speed, pounding into her at a damning pace. "You're taking me so well."

Her pussy clamps down at my praise and I can tell she's about to break. I expected her to come quickly after not letting her for the past thirty minutes. When I reach down between our bodies to massage her clit, she stiffens, preparing to orgasm.

Not yet.

I pull out of her and flip her over. Before she can complain, I'm fucking her from behind. I crash my hand down as I ream into her, and she jerks at the sudden pain. I do it again on the other side and she moans my name. Then I repeat the spanks, five more times on each cheek.

"Boundaries?" I ask. She shakes her head, which she has buried into the mattress. "Give me your arms."

She reaches them back at my command and I take hold of her wrists with one hand, binding them behind her. I pull on them enough that it lifts her body off the bed as I pound into her.

"Please, Reynold," Savannah begs, barely able to get the words out through her pleasure.

I unleash more spanks in rhythm with my thrusts, relishing the bright red her cheeks turn.

Fuck, I'm getting close too.

Savannah's pussy constricts around my cock. She's ready to burst. "Okay, Savannah. I want you to come for me."

I pound into her harder and harder until she's screaming out her orgasm. Her body shakes and I pause to let the pleasure consume her. When she relaxes, I let go of her arms and she falls to the bed. She rolls over and gives me an intoxicating grin.

"Good job, my love." I crawl up her body and kiss her deeply. She weaves her fingers into my hair and tugs on the strands hard enough it's painful. Payback perhaps?

I return between her legs where I belong and line up my hard dick to her opening. "Now give me another one. I know you can."

I don't let her respond and thrust into her. She whimpers, still sensitive from her first orgasm, but those whimpers quickly turn to moans.

"I'm going to choke you now. I want you to tap on my arm twice when you need air, okay?" I bring my hands to her neck. She nods, her eyes filling with excitement.

I wrap my fingers around her throat and squeeze, not too hard at first, just enough so she can get used to the pressure. As my thrusts pick up speed, my hold around her neck tightens. Her eyes roll into the back of her head, and she digs her nails into my wrists.

Her face turns bright red the longer she goes without air, but at the same time, her pussy clamps down on my cock, building up to another orgasm.

That was fast.

My thrusts are brutal at this point. Her entire body bounces and I stare down at her tits as they move with every pump into her.

Then she taps. Twice.

I let go, and she comes as air fills her lungs. I join her seconds later, burying my head into the crook of her neck.

"Fuck," I groan, out of breath.

I fall onto my back beside her.

"That was the best sex I've ever had," Savannah says, cuddling up to my side. "The butt plug amplifies everything."

I kiss the top of her head, which lies on my chest, and I run my hand up and down her bare arm. She hums, content, and I move my palm to her arse, squeezing generously. She whimpers, her skin likely still stinging from my spankings.

I can't get enough of her. I never want to stop touching her. But she needs aftercare and from what she's told me about that loser ex of hers, he never provided it.

"I'm going to take the plug out of you then clean you up, okay?"

She hums again, sounding sleepy. Her eyes are closed, and I'm certain she's about to fall asleep.

I toss the condom into the rubbish and return with a cloth. Her legs are wide open for me, tempting me to take her again. She smirks, knowing it's crossed my mind.

My lips trace along her inner calf, up past her knee, then along her thick thighs that have adorable dimples. She holds her breath when I run my finger up and down her slit. I'm distracting her so I can remove the toy. She gasps when I pull it out.

She watches me with awe as I take care of her, wiping away her pleasure. When I finish and throw the cloth in the laundry, I return to her side and pull her against me.

"This is nice," she whispers, sounding surprised.

"Are you tired?"

"No, just... satisfied." She lifts her head and smiles. "I want ice cream."

"It's not breakfast, though. I thought ice cream was only for breakfast."

She rolls her eyes. "Fine, let's make waffles for dessert."

"With peanut butter, bananas, and maple syrup?"

"And lots of whipped cream."

Chapter 16 - Savannah

Waffles got messy. Reynold intentionally splattered the batter all over my face and hair. Then he added a whipped cream crown. He covered my mouth with the sweet topping and kissed it clean.

Our first batch burned because he laid me on top of the counter to eat me out. The second batch also burned because I demanded to blow him as a reward for giving me multiple orgasms tonight.

Finally, after nearly an hour, we have the perfect set of waffles topped with peanut butter, bananas, and drowned in maple syrup. Our favorite combination.

We eat in silence, savoring the breakfast-inspired dessert. Once our plates are clean, he leans back and rubs his flat tummy. I rest my chin on my palm and watch him. He blows out a breath of satisfaction.

He's so dang adorable.

He's got a bit of whipped cream on the corner of his mouth. I reach out my thumb and wipe it away. As I pull my hand back, Reynold takes my wrist and licks the cream off the tip before I can.

"Tell me about your parents," I say, trying to ignore my stomach cartwheeling at the sexual move. He flinches at my question and releases my wrist. "Sorry, that came out of nowhere. You don't have to..."

He sighs and that stiffness in his posture loosens, almost as if he's relieved. "It's not that I don't want to. It's just... I haven't talked to anyone about them in a very long time. Not since Annalee was alive."

I take his hand and thread my fingers with his.

"They were wonderful parents."

His voice is quiet and full of anguish as he pauses to gather his thoughts. Or maybe to rein in his emotions.

"I always knew I wanted to be an actor. I grew up memorizing lines from my favorite TV shows or movies, then I'd act them out for my parents and Annalee in the living room after dinner. All of them were so supportive. Mum took me to my first audition when I was twelve. I got the job. It was for a commercial, and I was only in it for maybe ten seconds, but we celebrated as if it was a lead role. We celebrated anytime I landed a role, big or small, either by going out to dinner or cooking a meal together as a family. One time, when I was thirteen and cast a major film, my biggest role to date, I came home to my dad and sister wearing party hats and blowing noisemakers. They decorated the living room with streamers and even had a cake for me."

He smiles fondly at the memory.

"I was making decent money when they died. Mum got the flu, and that turned into pneumonia, which she didn't survive. They did an autopsy and said her heart failed. Maybe heart problems run in our family. I get mine checked routinely. Adeline's too, just to be sure.

He stops talking, and I squeeze his hand to remind him I'm here, listening.

"After mum passed, my father sank into a deep depression. My sister had to take care of me. She'd make sure I ate breakfast every morning, then drive me to school or to auditions. He got better after a couple of months. He'd at least join Annalee and me for dinner and wasn't holing himself up in his room as much. But he must not have been sleeping well because one night—he worked late nights—he was driving home and dozed off. His car veered off the road and he hit a tree. His head hit hard enough to kill him instantly."

"Oh Reynold, I'm so sorry." He doesn't respond to that and keeps talking.

"I poured my grief into my acting because it's what mum told me to do. I think she knew she was going to die. The day before she passed, she told me to grieve her but not let her death hold me back from living my life. So I didn't.

"We lived off their life insurance and my income from modeling and acting. Annalee saved what we didn't use for bills. She wanted to move us here to the states where I'd have more opportunities for my career. She handled everything as far as visas. She's the one who submitted our applications for citizenship. Now I have dual citizenship."

"When's the last time you went back to England?"

He sighs. "I haven't been back. Not for a proper visit. I've had a few movie premieres in London, but my busy schedule only allowed for me to stay a night or two." He circles his thumb on the inside of my palm. "I want to take Adeline; she should know where her mother grew up. I started showing her pictures a couple of years ago, and I talk about Annalee all the time. She understands I'm not her biological father.

"Annalee and I... we grieved our parents by being there for each other. They gave us a wonderful, loving life, and they'd want us to keep living as if they were still with us. Then when she passed, I grieved for her by taking care of Addy and loving her as my own.

"I cry when I think of my family, but then I smile at happy memories and feel proud of my accomplishments. I wouldn't be where I am today without them. Grief is strange and different for everyone. For me, it's not about the past, it's about the future."

"That's beautiful, Reynold."

He brings our clasped hands to his mouth and kisses my knuckles.

"What about your parents? You don't talk about them much. You mentioned they live in Georgia. Let me guess, in Savannah?"

"Yeah. They love it there, hence my name. Original right?" I laugh. "My parents are the best. They raised me to love myself no matter what and were supportive in every decision I made. They didn't care that I never wanted to go to college or have some fancy, high-paying job. I always found it more exciting to take life day by day and live in the moment.

"I feel bad that I don't visit enough. I told you I was ashamed to see them after not breaking up with Brad, but I also couldn't afford to take off work. They offered to pay for my flight, but I didn't get vacation pay so I would have lost money by visiting. I also think I was scared I wouldn't want to return to Arkansas and, until now, I wasn't ready to deal with starting a new life.

"Brad was also the reason I didn't visit as much. He always guilted me into going to his family's place for the holidays. I'm a jerk. I should have put my foot down and made him go or went without him."

"Why did you tolerate him for so long?"

"He wasn't always bad. He was sweet in the beginning and said all the right things. Sometimes he'd bring home flowers or make dinner. Bare minimum, I know. Like I told you, after our fight over Ginger's wedding, he changed. He was hiding something, but I just didn't care. A part of me always knew he was cheating. We weren't having sex as much and it wasn't even good to begin with, so I didn't fight for him."

Fuck him. He doesn't deserve any more space in my head.

"Him cheating was the best thing to happen to me. It made me realize I was wasting my life in Arkansas, and it was time to make a big change."

"What *do* you want to do with your life?"

"You know... I'm not sure. But New York seems like the best place to figure it out."

"What's something you love?"

I tap my finger on my chin. I always thought I'd be working at Lilies Bar & Grill for the rest of my life. Or be a stay-at-home mom to some husband I pretended to love. Not that there is anything wrong with those roles (aside from the not loving my husband part) but I'm at a point in my life where I can be anything. I can *do* anything.

"I love fashion. I love pushing trends and making them my own."

Reynold's eyes fall to my skintight tank and my pushed-up cleavage.

"Oh yes, my love." He tugs the straps, tracing his finger up and down. "Your outfits are always flawless and sexy as fuck. You could be a stylist."

"You think? That'd be a dream."

"I could recommend you to some agencies. Or if you want to be your own boss, I have former colleagues who would love to be styled by you."

My eyes water, which catches me off guard. I don't cry often. I try to stay away from things that make me sad. My tears are typically happy, like when I watch videos of kittens being rescued or the game show contestant wins the big prize.

Now I cry because this man is too good to be true. He's already helped me beyond what I deserve. He's given me a home and a job and a new life. Now he wants to pave a path for my future? One that I never gave enough thought to because I never believed I'd be following any of my dreams.

"You don't have to..."

He leans in and takes my head in his hands. "I want to."

He kisses me before I can argue. Not that I would have. The kiss is soft and slow, as if he's savoring this moment and turning it into a memory.

We pull apart and he boops my nose, which makes me giggle like a girl with a crush.

I am a girl with a crush.

"So... this new nickname..."

He stands to clear our dishes from the island.

"Whatever do you mean, my love?"

I point at him. "That. That nickname!"

He laughs, setting the dishes in the dishwasher. "Would you like me to stop?"

"I mean... no... but you saying it doesn't mean... um... it's just we haven't known each other that long, so to say... *that* word."

It took me almost a year to say it to Brad, but to be fair, Brad never made me feel the way Reynold does.

He shuts the dishwasher and leans against the counter, arms folded over his broad chest.

"I don't say that word easily, Savannah. In fact, it's a word I haven't said to anyone who wasn't my family or my friends. For you, love seems possible for the first time in my life. And you are correct, we barely know each other. So, for now, I use the word as a term of endearment for the woman who is currently making me happy."

T wo full days with this man. It didn't seem real. We spent every moment together: eating, sleeping, fucking, showering together. It was like when we were sick, but no gross coughing and feeling like shit.

The amount of sex we had... my poor vagina rarely got a break. Not that I'm complaining; it's the type of ache I crave.

Reynold returns to work and I'm back on nanny duty. Lana came over for breakfast, then walked with me to take Addy to preschool. After dropping her off, we headed to the Metropolitan Museum of Art a couple of blocks away. I'm not too worried about being spotted with Lana since she's wearing one of her famous wigs. This one is a black bob with bangs. We sit on the stone steps, enjoying the warm day while looking at photos from Addy's sleepover with Mylan, Lana, and Banana.

"She's been begging Rey for a dog ever since," I say.

"He should get her one. Every child needs a pet." She swipes to a picture of them standing outside the Minskoff Theatre before seeing *The Lion King*. People crowd around them, ecstatic to be near celebrities.

Except one person.

I point at her phone. "That man..."

She brings the phone close to her face and zooms in on the picture. He's staring at Lana, Mylan, and Addy with a look of disgust.

"Is that...?" I ask, scared to hear her answer.

"The man from Adeline's preschool and the Brooklyn Bridge? Yeah, that's him."

My heart flutters in my chest.

"Lana. I think you have a stalker."

She frowns. Two of her bodyguards standing next to us give each other a look.

"We saw him a lot when we had Adeline while you and Rey were sick, and again when we were out these past couple of days. He stays back and watches. It's super creepy, but technically, he's done nothing wrong."

She blows out a long breath.

"My security team keeps an eye on him."

"Does Rey know about this?"

Lana nods. "It's why you have extra protection too."

I open my mouth, confused.

"Oh," Lana adds. "You haven't spotted them yet."

I scan the area, only seeing my two bodyguards.

Lana points at a man in athletic gear, stretching near a tree. "That's one." She points to a woman dressed in a simple t-shirt and jeans, standing near a bus stop on her phone. "Her too."

"Unbelievable. I told him not to hire extra bodyguards."

"He was just worried. You can't be mad at him for caring."

I snap my mouth shut because how can I argue with that? He *does* care. So goddamn much. I told him not to hire extra protection, but what do I know? This is his world. He knows the dangers better than I ever could.

I still wish we had talked about this, though.

As if his ears were burning from us talking about him, my phone lights up with a text.

Hot British Guy

I miss you

I'm going to leave him on read. Let him sweat a little for not communicating with me over the extra bodyguard situation.

"What are you up to?" Lana asks as I smile deviously at my phone.

"Just pushing his buttons," I say, standing. Lana follows suit and we ascend the stairs into the Met. It's on my list of tourist adventures in New York City.

Once we're inside and we've been slowly making our way through the first area of exhibits, my phone vibrates in my jeans pocket.

Hot British Guy

You must be having fun out with Lana. Text me when you can

I heart the first text and thumbs up the second. I giggle and tuck my phone back in my pocket.

I've never been to a museum so massive. In high school, my science teacher took us on a field trip to Little Rock to the Museum of Discovery. We learned about the science behind things like electricity, cars, and tornadoes. But I'm pretty sure there aren't any art museums in Arkansas, at least none like this one.

We slowly make our way through the exhibits, stopping when something piques our interest. Lana's favorite were the sculptures—how all body types were considered beautiful back then. My favorite exhibits were the European paintings. Artists painted people of all sizes, just like the sculptures. Women with curves laying half naked across a chaise or being fawned over by men.

If only it were still like that, and the world didn't hate fat bodies.

After about three hours, Lana and I tire of walking around. We could spend all day inside the Met and still not see everything. I definitely plan to return. We stop at one of the museum's cafés and snack on pastries and iced coffee. I check my phone and see Reynold has been filling it with text messages.

Hot British Guy

> I'm bored. These resets are taking forever

He sends a selfie of him and Mylan.

Hot British Guy

> What are you ladies up to today?

> Seeing the sights?

> I can't stop thinking about you

> I can't stop thinking about fucking you

> You're okay, right? You haven't been kidnapped?

> Fine. I know you haven't been kidnapped because I've been checking in with Sarah and Henry. You're at the Met

> They sent me pictures

> You and Lana laughing. You and Lana admiring a beautiful piece of art. You smiling at your phone. I know you're getting my texts!

I react with double exclamation points. He sends an eye roll emoji.

Hot British Guy

What's with the reactions but no responses?

Oh, I see what you're doing

You having a laugh?

I giggle.

Hot British Guy

Just you wait until I get home tonight

I respond with an angel emoji, and he sends back a devil.

"You two are so smitten with each other," Lana says and pops a bite of donut in her mouth.

"It doesn't seem real."

Lana's smile softens. "I still pinch myself, thinking I'm dreaming. A celebrity was the last person I imagined myself falling in love with."

"I haven't really experienced the fame part of his life yet. Not going to lie, I'm terrified."

Lana swallows her last bite of donut and washes it down with her iced coffee. She stands and I follow her to toss our trash before we make our way back to the front of the museum to exit.

"It's annoying as hell, but I've been dealing with it ever since Rebecca wrote *Tyler's Team* and it was picked up by a celebrity book club."

I didn't know Lana when that happened, but I remember the chaos that followed. Strangers would come into the coffee shop I worked at and ask where to find Lana Young, the woman from the book. The fans weren't far behind. The world became obsessed with Lana and Tyler's love story. It got so bad; she had to sell her house and shut down her social media presence. As far as I know, she still doesn't have online accounts.

Mylan does, though, and he chronicles their life together frequently. I giggle every time he posts a picture of Lana flipping off the camera.

Reynold has social media accounts, but he hasn't posted on them in years. My stomach flutters with the thought of a picture of me and him being the first he posts upon his return. That would make 'us' official. People would find my pages. I only have a couple dozen followers—all family and friends. I've been quiet online the past few months, making my big move to escape small town life.

I'm sure by now everyone in Silo Springs knows I live in New York City. They're probably taking bets on how long I'll last because everyone who moves away always finds their way back.

Not me. There's no way. If I leave New York, it'd be to move to Georgia with my parents.

Besides, I don't plan to leave NYC now that Reynold and I are... together? Fucking? Whatever we're doing, I want to see it through.

Chapter 17 - Reynold

Giggles pour into the apartment as the elevator down the hall opens. Adeline's tiny feet pitter patter as she runs down the hallway.

"Dad! You're home," she says, spotting me stretched out on the couch in the living area, reading a script.

"I sure am Poppy." I sit up, set the script on the coffee table, and stand. "Did you have fun at school today?"

"Of course, I had fun, Dad. I love school."

Oh, well, excuse me, Miss Sassy Pants.

Savannah walks into the kitchen and freezes. Her mouth hangs open, surprised to see me home early. I was supposed to be on set until midnight, but it's about to storm, and the rain is lasting all night, so they rescheduled our outdoor scenes for tomorrow.

Addy runs back to Savannah and takes her hand. She guides her to the living room where I stand.

Savannah's face turns a dark shade of red, and I know she's thinking about my threat after being a brat today. She looks anywhere but at me, scanning the room as if she's never been in here before. Her eyes linger on the white curtains along the wall of windows that face Central Park. I keep them open, letting the sun pour through to brighten the space, but now, with the storm moving in, the cloudy sky gives the room a somewhat ominous feel.

Addy places Savannah on the white couch. The living room is set up in a square formation. The couch, a matching love seat and chair, and a flat screen television and entertainment center complete the square. Floor to ceiling bookcases fill the far corner of the room. The shelves are packed with odd memorabilia from movie sets, photographs of my family and friends, and other random items the decorator thought fit the design aesthetic.

Addy takes my hand and sits me next to Savannah.

"What are you doing, Poppy?"

"I want to play Mario Car."

"It's Mario Kart," I muse.

"Dad set up his old Ninteeno in here," Adeline tells Savannah, ignoring me.

"Nintendo 64," I mumble under my breath.

"I'm not very good at the game, but it's still fun." She distributes all the controllers, one for me, Savvy, and her.

"Adeline," I sigh. "Can we play after dinner? I really need to talk to Savannah."

Savannah's green eyes fall on mine, and I raise a brow.

"Don't you want to *talk*, Savannah?"

My daughter's shoulders drop and a twinge of guilt rips through my stomach. She didn't have many friends growing up. Just the kids at the park when the nanny brought her there. She's never had a sleepover or friends over to play. I'm still hesitant about that. I suppose Savannah is the closest to a friend she has. It's all my fault as I tried to keep her hidden and protected from the media.

The best decision I made was enrolling her into preschool, where she can be around other kids her age. I need to reach out to the other parents to arrange play dates. Most of the kids that go there are the products of the rich and famous. They all want privacy as much as me.

"Dad, please. Savvy promised we could play when we got home."

"Oh, did she?"

"Yeah, Daddy, please let us play. We have plenty of time to *talk* later," Savannah says. She bites her lip when I narrow my eyes at her. She knows exactly what she's doing calling me that. Glad to see she's no longer acting nervous. It's more fun when she pushes my buttons and fights with me.

Addy bounces on the couch. "Yay!"

"I'm going to kick your ass," Savannah says out of the corner of her mouth, quiet enough so Addy doesn't hear.

"I've been playing this game all my life, my love. You're toast."

An hour.

That's how long we played Mario Kart. My face hurts from smiling. Savannah and Adeline giggled nonstop and every time their cart took a curve, they'd lean their bodies left or right as if that would help maneuver it. Savannah and I both let Adeline win. Then we'd battle it out for second place.

She plays dirty, tossing banana peels and shells at me nonstop.

I won *one* game out of ten. One!

We battled for fifteen minutes before realizing Addy vanished to the loo and never returned. I have a feeling my daughter did that on purpose. She's being a little matchmaker.

"You're so fucking proud of yourself, aren't you?" I say, plating the dinner Shirley prepared for us. I'd just checked

Addy's nanny cam, and she's in her bedroom, dressed in her knight's costume and wearing the blonde wig Lana gave her.

"You don't understand," she begins, her eyes bright with victory. She grabs a cherry tomato from the salad bowl and pops it in her mouth. "Growing up, my parents didn't make a lot of money, but on my tenth birthday, they splurged and bought me a Nintendo 64. It was the biggest and bestest gift I ever got—"

"Is bestest a word?"

She ignores me.

"My friends would come over all the time and we played that thing until it crapped out ten years later. Mario Kart was my all-time favorite."

"Mine too. I have an Atari and a Sega Genesis in my room."

Savannah gasps. "When we talked about our love of old gaming systems, you didn't tell me you own a Sega. This guy I dated in high school had one and it's so fun to play."

I swallow that damn jealous feeling at her mentioning another man. I'm not one to be jealous. So why with this woman?

"Tell me we can play Sonic the Hedgehog."

I laugh. "The consoles are in a glass bookcase in my room. I rarely bring them out. I'm too scared they'll get broken."

"Please, Daddy? For me?"

I freeze, holding two plates in each hand, about to walk past her to take them to the table.

"Savannah," I growl. Her cheeks redden and she bites her lip.

Placing the plates on the island, I walk over to where she leans against the cabinets. I take her by the throat, and she sucks in a breath. Her pupils expand, letting me know just how much she likes this.

"That's the second time tonight you've called me that."

She grimaces. "Sorry. Is it weird? I'll stop. Plus, I'm older than you. Maybe you should call me mommy."

"Let me make a couple of things clear." I squeeze enough to make her whimper. "You calling me daddy is not weird. I only told you to stop because it's time to eat dinner. The sooner we eat, the sooner we can get Adeline to bed, and I can punish you for being a fucking brat earlier today."

She parts her plump lips and runs her tongue across them.

"And *never* be embarrassed about the things that bring you pleasure. Do you understand?"

She nods, and I crush my mouth against hers. Her hands latch onto the fabric of my shirt, and she fists it as I stroke my tongue, massaging her own. She tastes like the sweet wine I bought her because she's not a fan of the bitter stuff.

Addy's laughter pours out of her room from down the hall. I end the kiss but keep my hold on her neck.

"Your mouth was made for me. I can't wait until after dinner when you have it around my cock."

She whimpers.

"Do you want that? Do you want me to fuck your mouth?"

"And punish me," she adds. "I've been wanting you to punish me since we met on the plane."

I tsk. "Such a dirty girl."

"Your dirty girl," she purrs.

I almost lose it right then. Savannah is a firecracker. She's vibrant and strong and beautiful, but she's also submissive. She knows what she wants in the bedroom, and I've been quite eager to reward her for giving me all the control. I've always been dominant, but it's been well over five years now since I've allowed this side of me to come out to play.

Savannah also knows what *I* need. She feeds into it to a point that I forget about responsibilities. I was ready to devour her right here in the kitchen, even though Adeline could have walked in on us at any moment.

I come to my senses and release her. She rubs her neck and smiles, clearly loving how my fingers bit into her skin. It's now bright red, and I wouldn't be surprised if it bruises too.

"Now, if you want to call me daddy, do it. But I'd much rather you call me sir."

"Yes, Sir," she whispers before I walk out of the room to get Adeline for dinner.

Chapter 18 - Savannah

Dinner was agonizing. Addy took forever to eat because she talked nonstop about any and everything. She wanted something sweet for dessert, so we made chocolate chip cookies. Reynold kept giving me heated looks, and I'd clench my thighs together to contain the ache he's causing. Not to mention that I can still feel his fingers gripping my neck.

Who knew I was into choking? The minor breath play from the first time we fucked was euphoric, and I'd never come so hard in my life.

This is what I love about Reynold. He helps me explore my sexual curiosity, and with his experience, I'm reaping the benefits.

My heart has been thundering in my chest all night, thinking about what his punishment could be for not responding to his text messages earlier today.

Wait... love?

Did I seriously just think that?

I didn't mean love, love. I meant—

"What are you thinking about over there, Savannah?"

I snap my head up at the sound of Reynold's deep voice.

"Nothing. No one."

"No one? The only person you should think about is me," he warns.

"And me," Adeline sings, oblivious to this very adult conversation we're having.

"Adeline, it's almost bedtime. Finish that cookie and drink the rest of your milk so you can take a bath and go to bed."

She's playing with her two last bites like they're dolls, parading them around on the plate and giving them conversations. She frowns at her dad and the look he sends back means no nonsense. It has me squirming in my seat. Thankfully, he doesn't notice because he's too busy disciplining his daughter.

I need to be patient. My discipline will come.

With what has to be the biggest sigh on record, Addy eats the rest of her cookie and downs the milk before hopping off the chair. She gives me a hug.

"Goodnight, Savvy."

"Goodnight."

Reynold follows her, but before passing me, he leans down to whisper next to my ear.

"In my bedroom. On the bed. Naked. Now."

My heart kicks into full speed, my face heating and my entire body sizzling with desire. I force myself to walk—even though I want to run—to his bedroom and strip out of the sundress I wore today. I need a shower. Can I shower first? He didn't say I could shower.

Maybe we'll shower together.

My bra and panties hit the floor next, and I lay down in the middle of his bed.

I wait.

And wait and wait and wait.

The jerk left me in here, turned on as fuck, for nearly an hour before he walks in. I lean up on my elbows and frown at him.

"Whatever is wrong, my love?"

"I'm no longer in the mood," I lie. He knows I'm lying because my chest and cheeks are still bright red with lust and my nipples are hard as fuck.

He silently walks to his closet and disappears for a few seconds, returning with two ties.

"What are you doing with those?"

He says nothing as he joins me on the bed. The silence is so goddamn frustrating, but that doesn't stop my excitement from pooling between my legs.

He takes my right arm.

"Are you going to tie me up?" I whisper.

Gripping my chin in his hand, he leans in so his mouth hovers mine. "I am, and I need you to tell me right now if that's not okay."

"It's okay. It's more than okay. Please."

"Please, what, Savannah?"

"Please tie me up, Sir."

"Good girl."

God. Why do I love it when he says that?

He slowly, torturously, secures my right arm to the headboard, then does the same with my left arm.

"Your punishment for being a brat is to let me fuck your mouth. I'm going to come down your throat and you're going to take every last drop. Then I'm going to eat you out, tied up just like this so you're not able to touch me or yourself. I'm going to bring you to the cusp of orgasm, but you won't come until I say so. Do you understand?"

I nod and whimper and my pussy clenches around nothing.

"You're doing such a good job, Savannah. What's your word?"

"Boundaries."

He tests my binds, then brushes a piece of hair out of my eyes. I pull on the ties and they tighten around my wrist.

"Ah, ah. The more you struggle, the tighter they'll get."

Noted.

When he's satisfied with how I'm placed before him, he strips naked and gets on the bed to stand over me.

He fists his rock-hard cock up and down until pre-cum leaks from the tip, which he wipes over my lips. I open my mouth for him.

"So eager for me," he growls and slides the head in. He pulls it out and I attempt to grab him, but forget I'm tied up.

Reynold takes hold of my ponytail to stop me from moving.

"Ready, my love?"

I nod.

He thrusts his cock in my mouth, clutching my hair so hard, my scalp burns. I wrap my lips around his length as he brutally pumps into me.

"Yes, that's good. Just like that," he says.

My eyes water and I gag as he goes too deep, but I'm loving every second. Reynold's grunts and moans encourage me. I hum and clamp my lips harder, putting slightly more pressure on his cock.

"Ahh! Fuck, Savannah, that almost made me come."

I chuckle and he grips my hair harder. The need to touch him grows and I pull on the binds once again, wincing as the fabric tightens around my wrists.

Reynold doesn't let up and pistons into my mouth while I keep humming and suctioning my lips around him.

It doesn't take long before he gives one last thrust to let his warm cum pour down my throat. I swallow as fast as I can.

Every. Last. Drop.

He removes himself and swipes his thumb over my lips. "So thirsty, swallowing all my cum."

I smile up at him and he kisses me, sweeping his tongue over mine in the most delectable way.

Can he taste himself?

He kneels between my legs and slides a finger inside me. I buck off the bed and moan and try to slap my hand over my mouth. Instead, I feel the tie bite into my skin.

"I'm being too loud," I gasp when he pumps two fingers in and out of my pussy.

"She can't hear us. I plugged in her headphones and put music on. She passed out listening to it."

He leans down and covers my clit with his mouth, grazing his teeth over it while he continues to fuck me with his fingers.

My release builds, my walls clamping down.

He slows his thrusts, and I whine.

"Remember what I said. No coming, Savannah."

The tear of plastic foil pierces the air—I didn't even see him grab a condom—and he rolls it on his cock, which is already getting hard despite me draining it minutes ago.

For the next thirty minutes, he edges me until I'm sweating and panting and begging him to let me orgasm.

"Please, Reynold. Let me come."

He smirks, like he's about to ignore my pleas, then he takes me by the hips and lifts my ass off the bed. He slides into me in one brutal thrust.

"Yes," I gasp.

Then he doesn't move while inside me. He's to the hilt, letting my aching pussy spasm around him.

He smooths his palm up my stomach, to one of my nipples, and pinches it before slapping it. I arch my back.

"Fuck you," I growl.

"Well, if you insist."

He starts moving, slowly. I pull at the binds and the pain feels amazing as it mixes with the pleasure of his cock driving in and out.

"You want to come?" he asks. I nod, my voice claimed by ecstasy.

"Okay. I'll allow it. Come for me, Savannah."

He picks up his speed, fucking me in such a feral way that it only takes me less than a minute before I'm shaking underneath him and he's chasing his orgasm seconds later.

"That's my girl," he says and pulls out of me. "You took your punishment so well. I had to reward you for being obedient."

I close my eyes at his praises and lean my head on the pillow.

I'm going to ignore his texts more often if this is what happens.

Chapter 19 - Reynold

It's been a month of bliss with Savannah. I'd go to set and film for an ungodly number of hours, then return home late at night and crawl into bed with her. No Addy in sight since she stopped waking up wanting to sleep in my bed.

Some days I'd finish filming early enough to eat dinner with them. Afterward, we'd all pile onto the couch to watch a movie Addy picked out.

While I see Savannah every day, it's been a struggle getting time alone with her to worship her body. We only fucked a handful of times over the past month, and they were all quick and dirty. My call times have been all over the place. I'd return home too exhausted to give her what she deserves.

Having her near and not being able to *have* her was a special kind of torture. I'd steal kisses any chance I could, mostly in the mornings when Adeline was watching cartoons in her room.

"What are you thinking about?"

I glance up at Savannah's question and a knowing smile spreads across her beautiful face.

We're sitting at the island, a script I'm paying no attention to is in my hand. Savannah is reading one of her romance books. It must be getting to a good part because she's been fidgeting in her seat for the past five minutes. If I didn't have to leave soon for set, I'd help relieve her of that built-up tension.

"I'm thinking about how it's been too long since I've properly been inside you and how I want to lock us in my bedroom and fuck you until we're both dead to the world."

"That sounds intense. A bit dramatic."

"Am I not an actor? I live for dramatics."

She shakes her head and closes her book, setting it on the countertop. Addy is in her room, picking out her outfit to wear today. It's the end of June. This is her last week in preschool before the break for summer.

Then she'll be in kindergarten.

She's growing up too fast. I should be home spending more time with her instead of being on set for twelve to sixteen hours a day.

"Whoa, what happened there? Your face went from turned on to sad pretty fast," Savannah says, crossing her arms and furrowing her brows.

I sigh because nothing gets past this woman. We've been around each other enough to learn facial expressions. Like how she chews on her bottom lip when she's nervous, or thinking about something sexual, or thinking in general. How she blushes so easily when embarrassed or turned on. How her eyes open wide, like a doe, and she blinks rapidly when she's lying. She's a horrible liar.

I wonder what my tells are.

"This is Adeline's last week in preschool. She'll be in kindergarten next year. Before I know it, she'll be graduating from high school." I stand to pack up the script in my bag.

Savannah walks to me. I wrap my arms around her and rest my cheek on her head.

"You've done such a great job raising her. She's going to need you for the rest of her life. There will be times she hates you, but I guarantee she'll never forget the love you gave her."

I inhale her sweet scent and squeeze her hard. I am never letting this woman go.

I lean back and meet her gaze. "Will you go on a date with me?"

"Really?" she asks, her face lighting up at the idea.

"I have a short filming day on Friday. I want to spend that night eating junk food and watching movies with Addy to celebrate her last day of school. Then Saturday, I'm off, and you're all mine. I'll have to find someone to watch Adeline, though. Lana goes back to L.A. tomorrow, but I'm hoping Eloise and Kelly will be around."

They just bought a loft in Brooklyn.

Savannah peels herself out of my arms and returns to sit on the stool. "But what about the paparazzi?"

"What about them?"

"They'll... take our pictures and write stuff. They'll assume stuff."

"Then let's not let them assume. I'll have my team release a statement to confirm we're in a relationship. They'll 'leak' a sighting, sending the paparazzi to where we'll be on our date. We'll hold hands, flirt, and kiss in public. And I'll handle all the questions."

"That seems... terrifying."

"It will be at first, but you'll get used to it. I just... really want to experience the city with you. And Adeline. She had such a fun time out with Mylan and Lana. I want to take you both to Broadway shows or maybe to a baseball game at Yankee Stadium."

"Ooo! Yes, please! I've never been to a professional baseball game."

"I want to take you out to dinner at a rooftop restaurant overlooking the city. We could go see an outdoor movie at Bryant Park and cuddle up on a blanket. Or what about a picnic in Central Park?"

"Yes. I want it all."

"Or maybe we can go sing karaoke. I know a great place in Midtown East."

"I knew it. You're a good singer, aren't you?"

Savannah sits with her back leaned up against the island. I step between her legs, and she grabs my sides.

"I'm an okay singer."

"Only good singers say that!" she huffs. "I'm horrible so I will *not* be singing karaoke. But I'd love to hear you."

I smooth a piece of hair out of her eyes. "So, is that a yes? You'll go on a date with me?"

"It's a yes... but do we have to alert the paparazzi? Can't we just go out and see what happens?"

"We can, but they might go feral over an unannounced public appearance, especially since it will be my first outing with a woman in five years. If I have my PR team leak our location, we can set boundaries."

"I do like boundaries," she says, and sighs. I wrap my arms around her when she rests her head on my shoulder. I've never been more certain that she belongs there. When she looks back up at me, her brows furrow in thought as she runs her bottom lip between her teeth. I want to kiss her to stop the bad habit.

As if reading my thoughts, she grabs my nape and kisses me. A quick kiss that has me yearning for more.

The week dragged on. I spent a lot of downtime on set in my trailer, practicing songs on my guitar. I saw the way Savannah's eyes lit up that first day when she walked into my office and saw my guitar. Then she mentioned how she wants to hear me sing at karaoke. Better yet... I'll *play* and sing to her.

We also texted a lot. She'd share her day with Adeline after picking her up from preschool, but it was the texts when she was alone in the penthouse that made work sufferable.

We exchanged dirty texts until I couldn't take it anymore and I called her to *hear* her words. We Face Timed so I could *see* her fall apart while demanding she touch herself for me.

Now it's Saturday. Date night. Addy is staying at Eloise and Kelly's new place. My friends have been saviors. They're all too eager to watch Adeline. Something I never thought I'd be okay with. Five years raising her, and now I'm sending her off without a second thought. A part of me wants to feel guilty, but as Mylan reassured me, I need to look after myself. Adeline doesn't need me like she used to. Now I can focus on other parts of my life. And right now, that's dating Savannah.

I have her all to myself tonight.

I've never been more nervous. All the red carpets and awards shows I've been to, and the famous names I've worked alongside, have never conjured such wavering confidence.

What if she hates the date? The places we go, the food we eat at the restaurant I choose. What if the paparazzi terrify her and she packs up her belongings and leaves me?

Leaves us.

The door to Savannah's room creaks open. My heart beats faster with every soft step down the hallway. She rounds the corner to the kitchen, and I suck in a breath.

She's styled her blonde hair up in a tight bun. Her makeup is light and natural. She's wearing silver flats since she's not a fan of heels. The outfit she chose is a classic little black dress that clings to her body like static electricity that pushes her breasts into round globes and puts every single curve on display.

How lucky am I that this woman allows me to touch her, kiss her, worship her?

"If you keep looking at me like that, we'll never make it out of the penthouse."

She stops in front of me, and I inhale her cherry and crème scent. I scoop her into my arms, planting the hungriest of kisses upon her lips. I force her mouth open so I can taste her. She moans as I stroke and suck and caress.

My hands roam across her backside, squeezing with fervor as they find her plump ass. She slides her palms up my chest and around to grip my nape. Her fingers latch on to my hair and she tugs me towards her as if we could get any closer.

I want to make out with her all night, but her kisses slow down, and she gently pushes me away.

"Save some for later, BG!"

I slap her ass, and she yelps before falling into a fit of giggles.

The buzz of my phone on the counter lets me know Xavier has arrived with the car.

"Time to go." I offer her my arm. "M'lady."

She rolls her eyes with the biggest grin I've ever seen, and she wraps her fingers around my bicep.

"Are you nervous?" I ask once we're inside the car.

"Not as nervous as you," she laughs.

"I don't know what you mean."

"You sweat when you're nervous. And you pick at your hangnails."

I tuck my hands under my legs to stop exactly what she caught me doing.

"So... where are we going tonight?"

"You'll see."

Traffic isn't too bad. We pull up to a line of red and white brick buildings in the East Village and exit the car.

"Italian?" Savannah asks.

"Your favorite." I tug her hand to lead us into the building.

I give the hostess my name. Reservations for this place book months in advance, but I name dropped—not even ashamed of that—and got us a spot for tonight. The woman takes us to a semi-private booth in back.

Once settled, Savannah lets out a tiny giggle.

"What?"

"That woman was trying so hard to get your attention. Swaying her hips, licking her lips, and pushing out her tits."

"I couldn't even tell you the color of her hair or outfit." I lean in for a kiss, hoping that woman sees, but Savannah pulls away and her eyes dart around the restaurant.

"Are they here?"

"The paparazzi will be outside waiting for us when we leave. Though it wouldn't surprise me if someone in here takes a few photos of us."

She winces. "I don't want to be caught stuffing tortellini in my face."

I bark out a laugh. "You should see some shots they've taken of me. Their goal sometimes is to get the worst facial expressions or poses. One time I was out on... um..."

I hesitate to continue because we've yet to share our body counts with each other.

"On a date?"

"Yes... And they got me picking lettuce out of my teeth."

"How many women have you been with?"

My back straightens. Okay. Guess we're finally discussing past relationships.

"I've been in one serious relationship that lasted a year. After that, I only dated casually."

"You mean slept around?"

"Yes."

"How many?"

"Do you really want to know?"

"Why not? I'm not ashamed. Sex is natural. If I hadn't been in a relationship with Brad for as long as I was, my number would be higher."

"Would it now?"

"Yes. Though, the ten men I've slept with were shit in bed compared to you, so I might have given up on seeking good sex."

My dick jumps at her words, very much wanting to prove to her I am the best and all she'll ever need.

"Fifty. My body count is fifty. At least... it was when I stopped counting."

I blow out a long breath, waiting for her reaction.

"See? That explains why you're so good. You're far more experienced than I am."

I clutch her chin and bring her lips to mine. "You're my favorite, by far."

"I better be," she says and nips at my lips.

We kiss far too inappropriately for public. I try to slip my hand between her legs and underneath her tight dress, wondering if she's wearing panties, but she slaps my hand away.

When we pull apart, our server arrives to take our drink order. I select a bottle of Bartolo Mascarello from 1971.

"That costs $3,600!" Savannah gasps.

"It's well worth it. Trust me."

She favors sweet wine, and the one I chose has notes of black and red cherries. I assumed it'd be sweet enough for Savannah. Nope. She hated it. Not that she told me. Her face gave her away. Her nostrils flared and the corners of her mouth turned down almost comically.

She gives me a thumbs up.

God, she's adorable.

Dinner went smoothly. They didn't have tortellini, so she ordered Bolognese parmigiana she said was "to die for."

I had a pancetta and chilies dish. Both of us staying away from anything with a lot of garlic and onions.

We shared a bourbon gelato and after nearly two hours, we're ready to leave for the next part of the date.

"This is it," I say, leading her to the front of the restaurant. The paparazzi gather like a horde of zombies, peering in at their meal. "Are you ready?"

"I'm ready. Let's do this."

Chapter 20 - Savannah

T he door opens to blinding flashes and frantic voices
yelling over each other.

"Rey, who are you with?"

"Rey, tell us about fatherhood."

"Rey, how's filming?"

"Rey, has Mylan fallen off the wagon yet?"

What the actual fuck with that last one?

Cameras and microphones are shoved in my face.

"Who are you? What's your name?"

"Aren't you the lady on the plane?"

Wait, what? How did they know? Were there pictures? I
never looked and Reynold didn't tell me. I only know about
the pictures of me out with Lana. I didn't even read the
article that reported those photos.

We stop before getting into the car and turn to face the
mob. Reynold prepared me for some questions they might

ask. He even told me how he'd answer them because 'who' I am to Rey Michaelson, famous actor, is the most important one.

"This is my girlfriend, Savannah. Fatherhood is the best thing that's ever happened to me. Filming is going well. And fuck you to whoever asked that question about Mylan."

The vultures aren't even phased.

"Is it true you two met on a plane?" a woman asks, her eyes on me.

"Yes," I answer before Reynold can. "He asked me to be his nanny for Adeline."

A few eyes widen, some photographers chuckle.

"Lowering your standards, aren't ya, Rey?" some asshole in the back quips.

My face heats, and my heart roars inside my chest. Reynold starts for the man, but I hold him back by the elbow with shaky hands.

"Who said that?" I ask and the men in front of me shrink back slightly. I lock eyes with the only guy smirking. "Was it you?"

He shrugs.

"Explain to me what you mean by that."

His smile falters, but he holds his chin up high. "I mean he's an A-list celebrity and you're just some fa—"

"I'm going to stop you before you say a word that will piss me off. Because I punched the last guy who pissed me off."

A chorus of "ooo's" spread through the photographers.

"You seem unhappy. A sad, sad man. An adult bully and that's embarrassing. I'm embarrassed for you."

The man's face darkens red.

"If you think your words can bring me down, just remember that I'm the one dating a movie star. I'm the one who's living my best life while you're just some troll hiding behind a camera, putting others down to make yourself feel better. Do you?"

He gulps. "Do I... what?"

"Feel better about yourself? Knowing that the world will look at you and see a coward full of hate?"

I don't even let him answer. I turn away from the gaggle and the door to the car is already open for me. Someone shuts it behind me. One of Reynold's bodyguards, maybe. I hadn't even noticed them there.

My ears ring and I'm feeling lightheaded. I can't believe that just happened. What did I say? Did it even make sense? Was my comeback good enough?

Before I can ask myself any more questions, a hand grabs my arm and I'm tugged across the leather seat.

Reynold kisses my temple and wraps his arm around my shoulders.

"That was fucking beautiful, my love."

He rubs his palm up and down my arm and buries his nose in my hair.

Tears pool in my eyes as my adrenaline fades, but Reynold's words quickly ignite my body with lust.

I leap out of my seat and settle in his lap. My dress rides up in a puddle at my waist. What follows is a mess of kisses and his hands everywhere. I grind on his dick, which gets harder with each frenzied move I make.

"Fuck me, Reynold. Right here in the back of your car."

"Say less," he groans between kisses.

A window rolls up and I'm guessing it's a privacy screen shutting out the driver. Reynold smashes a button somewhere because loud rock music plays. My hands fumble with his buckle and the zipper of his dress pants. He's not wearing underwear, so I grab his cock and fist it up and down.

His head falls back and hits the headrest.

I push aside the thin strip of my thong and adjust myself to line up the head of his dick with my pussy. I'm already soaked.

"Condom?"

"Not unless you want to. I'm disease free and I have an IUD."

He answers by thrusting up into me. I cry out from the pleasure packed pain because he's bigger than I'm used to, and I have to adjust to his size. His hands squeeze my ass, encouraging me to move.

I use his shoulders as leverage and lift my body before slamming back down. He moans and fists my hair to hold my head in place. He kisses me like a starving man who didn't just eat a full course meal.

I move up and down, going as fast as my body will allow, but it must not be enough. Reynold holds me so he can thrust up into me at a damning pace.

"Fuck, yes, Reynold."

My head falls to the crook of his neck where my lips work his skin. I suck and bite and he groans next to my ear.

"You feel so good," he gasps and reams into me faster. "Are you going to come for me like a good girl?"

"Yes," I whimper.

I'm close. My pussy constricts around his cock, and he moans, digging his fingers into my ass cheeks.

He pauses, fully seated in me, and sticks a finger in my mouth.

"Suck."

I do. Down to his knuckle.

He removes his finger and slides it into my asshole. I arch my back at the sensation that I swear I'll never get used to.

"Let me hear how good I fuck you, Savannah."

He resumes thrusting. Once he's got a good rhythm going, he pumps his finger in and out of my ass. The combination breaks me. I come undone. Stars burst across my vision and Reynold grunts as he pistons through my orgasm until he's filling me up with his cum.

He removes his finger from my ass, and we sit there panting for at least a minute.

"We're almost at our next destination," Reynold says, rubbing my back.

"Mhm." It's all I can say. I'm too satisfied. I could nap right here in his lap, his dick inside me where it belongs, and my head resting on his shoulder.

His hands move up and down my spine before he slides them down to my ass. He squeezes generously then slaps once: my cue to get off him. He's ready with a napkin to clean up his cum as it leaks out of me.

I rarely experienced aftercare in my past relationships. I can never go back. Reynold has spoiled sex for everyone else.

You don't want anyone else.

The thought has lingered in my head for weeks now. I try to convince myself that it'd never work with Reynold. Our lives are too different. And that paparazzo's comment outside the restaurant is just the tip of the iceberg.

Lana offered to be there for me to talk about this part of dating a celebrity, but she has her own life. She and Mylan are considering adoption to begin a family. Ginger is about to give birth and I haven't met Jensen yet. Anyone who could be there for me would be too busy.

"Are you okay?" Reynold asks, either seeing or sensing my sudden mood change.

"I'm fantastic." It's true enough. "Just trying not to fall into an orgasm coma."

He chuckles and takes my hand, kissing the knuckles.

"We're here."

The car pulls up to a tall building with red awnings and banners hung all over.

"The Strand? Oh my God. I've been wanting to go to this place!"

He took me to a bookstore. A four-story one. I could literally spend all day here picking out books to add to my ever growing 'to be read' pile. I still haven't read all the books he bought and stocked in his library.

"Wait... those books you bought me. How did you know which ones to get?"

"I found your wishlist on your social media pages. You keep it up to date despite not posting content. So, I went through your list and bought some of the books on it."

"What about my perfume? You bought Amber Romance. How'd you know that's one of my favs?"

He shrugs. "Lana. When I called her for a reference, I explained how you moved here with next to nothing. I told her I was going to buy you everything you needed, and she remembered how much you loved that perfume."

"The towels? Did she tell you to buy the bigger ones?"

"She did."

"You're too good to me."

"Oh, my love, I'm only getting started. I plan to spoil you and worship you and give you any and everything you could ever ask for."

"That's a bit dramatic, don't you think?" I tease. "Kinda obsessive. Do I need to file a restraining order?"

He growls in the most delicious way and grabs me by the throat to attack me with rough kisses. My panties melt and I'm suddenly ready for round two of car sex (that was my first time fucking someone in a car and I will definitely do it again with this man.)

He releases me, and I'm not even going to think about my swollen and red lips as we exit the SUV.

"Let's go get you some spicy romance books," Reynold says, walking behind me.

I glance around, but the paparazzi are nowhere to be found. This stop must not have been on the approved sighting list. We enter the double doors to a massive space lit up bright and packed with tall bookcases and tables filled with books.

"Where's everyone at?" I scan the store but find no customers. I only spot a couple of employees standing at checkout.

"They closed an hour ago. The owner was happy to keep the store open for us after my sizable donation. I also made a matching donation to some local reading programs. I promised a nice write up about it in Entertainment Now next week too."

"You're so disgustingly rich," I snort.

"Disgusting, huh?" He grabs me by the waist and tugs my body against his.

"Yeah. So gross. Too rich for my blood."

He rubs his palms up and down my back and grinds his cock into my stomach, already getting hard despite fucking in the car just minutes ago.

"But," I add, "you're also not selfish with your wealth. You pay your staff exorbitantly and donate to a lot of charities. So, I'll forgive you."

"And how do you know all this? I thought you didn't Google me."

I shrug. "I might have caved. And I had a nice conversation with your house manager, Brenda. The amount you're paying me was... a lot. Too much, honestly. I wanted to know if that's just what you do. And... it is."

He leans in and kisses me deeply.

Men I've dated were never into PDA. I always thought it was because they were ashamed to be with me. But Reynold? He's almost too eager to show me off. When we part, I peer over at the employees.

"Let them watch. Let them take photos and share them with the world. Let them see how absolutely obsessed I am with you."

"I knew it. I'm getting that restraining order tomorrow."

He smiles wide, his blue eyes lighting up and crinkles form around the edges. That half-moon dimple on one side makes an appearance. He's too adorable. How did I get so lucky?

Reynold takes my hand. I lead him through the store, wandering aisle to aisle, scanning every display, and reading the backs of dozens of books. He holds a basket for all the ones I want to buy. I tell him I'm paying, and we argue over it for at least ten minutes. I know he won't let me pay, but I'm having fun messing with him.

We take the elevator up to the top floor and enter the rare books room. The space is big. Shelves full of classics worth hundreds to thousands of dollars line the walls. I didn't find anything I absolutely needed, but Reynold grabbed an Andy

Warhol book to add to his impressive rare books collection
in his library.

Downstairs in the basement, we find tables full of records
for sale. Reynold flips through them—since he has a record
player in his office—while I peruse some more shelves of
books.

I might need another basket. And where am I putting
these? Do I add them to ones Reynold bought and shelved
in his library? Are we sharing space like that now? It almost
seems... intimate. Like I've moved in with him even though
I technically already live with him.

It's nearing ten when we finish shopping. I'm surprised it
only took an hour to walk through the place. I suppose it
helped that no one else was here getting in the way.

We check out. I don't look at the total, but I know it's got
to be four digits. The employees ask for photos with Rey, and
he happily agrees. He introduces me as his girlfriend and my
stomach flutters at the word coming out of his mouth for
the second time tonight.

We already agreed to label this relationship as such, but
hearing it said is exhilarating.

"Now what?" I ask once we're back inside his car.

"One last stop before I take you home and finish what we
started in this backseat."

My face heats at the promise and I reach for his pants, intending to go for round two and give him a blow job, but he stops me.

"The things I plan to do to you tonight deserve more than the backseat of a car."

"And what exactly do you have planned?"

He pulls me into the middle seat next to him, buckling me up and tucking me to his side.

"Those spicy romance books you love so much? Think of one you've read with a scene that turned you on. That made you touch yourself. I want to reenact that scene with you, Savannah."

My heart explodes with anticipation at his words. Fuck. There are too many spicy books I've read one handed. I'm too turned on now. I need to calm down before we step back out in public. I rest my head on his shoulder as classical music plays over the speakers. Reynold traces his fingertips over my bare arms, and I close my eyes.

I love that he always needs to be touching me.

It takes about twenty minutes to get to Midtown from the East Village. We're let out at Rockefeller Center. Reynold pulls me against his body, protecting me as we weave through the crowd. We enter the towering building and take stairs down to an underground concourse. We're walking fast and I'm thankful my legs are long enough to keep up. I understand why we're moving so quickly when curious heads turn our way.

We stop at the entrance to Top of the Rock.

"Hi. Rey Michaelson. I spoke to someone named Jules about an escort."

The woman with a tablet looks up, and her eyes grow wide with awe.

"Yes. Of course. Right this way Mister Michaelson."

The star struck woman, who can't be older than twenty, takes us to an elevator. We ascend one floor and exit. After bypassing security, we end up at another elevator. We're the only ones who get on.

I didn't miss all the phones pointed at us, taking photos or videos as we made our way past the people waiting in line.

We reach the seventieth floor and an employee meets us to escort us through the crowd. Reynold has two bodyguards, one on either side of us, and another bringing up the rear. I don't recognize them, so they must be part-time security because Sarah and Henry deserve time off too.

Most people ignore us, but the massive presence of the protection and employee escort has some curious folks following. I tighten my hold on Reynold, and he responds with a kiss to my temple.

"This is intense," I whisper.

We take an escalator up to another level and exit to an outside space. And the most breathtaking view of the New York City skyline.

"Most tourists go to the Empire State Building because it's iconic," Reynold begins, leading me to the plexiglass barrier. "I've always loved Top of the Rock because you actually get to *see* the famous landmark."

The clear night sky allows for the perfect view of The Empire State Building. It's lit up in beautiful shades of light pink and deep blue. It twinkles and transforms between the colors.

Reynold's hand rests on my back as he inches us toward the glass barrier, where we wait to take pictures. I sigh, content as fuck, and lean my head on his shoulder. Our security detail keeps us barricaded from people who recognize him and gather near us.

After a couple of minutes, we find an open spot for our turn with the magnificent view. Reynold takes some photos of me with the skyline in the background. Then we snap some selfies. Next, he hands his phone to a woman who I met once. Rey must have told his assistant to meet us here to help with the chaos. She certainly hadn't been with us the entire night.

Her name is Hailey, and she's an adorable short woman who's in her early twenties. She's tiny but fierce because she's scowling at anyone who gets too close. She even yelled at a couple of people who tried to push past her.

It feels like we've been taking pictures for ages. Reynold poses us in every way imaginable, including plenty of shots of him kissing me or snuggling into my neck. He even did one of those prom pictures where he's behind me, his arms around my waist.

"These are going all over my social media pages."

I roll my eyes playfully because he showed me the ones he took of us earlier. He posted two of them. One photo was of us in front of a mirror back at the penthouse. He's behind me in his blue suit, opened to reveal his black V-neck shirt. His hand is snaked around my stomach in a possessive way. In the other photo, he's leaning down and kissing my neck.

He captioned the post "mine" with a ton of hashtags including girlfriend and my love and it already has a million likes and tens of thousands of comments. I will never read those comments. Reynold said he has people going through them now, searching for death threats or bullying that his team will report and remove.

Lana told me she went through the same thing with Mylan.

Once we're done taking photos, Reynold places a sweet and short kiss on my lips.

"I have to say hi to my fans."

I nod and he leaves me with one of his bodyguards so the other two can protect him amongst the horde. Hailey stays by his side, managing the demand. He takes selfies and signs autographs and answers a million questions, including some about me. I get a few dirty looks from people, but I also have several women and young girls who look like me and have my body type come up and say hi.

I expect them to ask how I did it. How the sexy movie star fell for the fat girl. It's a silent question that will eventually be voiced. The only way I can answer is that not everyone in this hateful world believes the horrible things said about us. Some people are decent and have their own opinions and interests.

I just happened to find a man who sees me through his eyes and not the world's.

ENTERTAINMENT NOW

REY MICHAELSON'S NIGHT OUT
By Angela Borrows

Action star Rey Michaelson was spotted out in New York City Saturday night with a gorgeous plus-size woman on his arm. Michaelson posted pictures of the two on his social media pages with the caption: mine. Entertainment Now has confirmed the mystery woman's name is Savannah Monroe. She's not only his new girlfriend, but he hired her to be the nanny for his daughter, Adeline.

Monroe is the same woman spotted on the plane, sitting in the same row as Michaelson and his daughter. She hails from Silo Springs, Arkansas and is friends with Lana Young-Andrews and Ginger Stein.

This is the first time in five years Michaelson has been seen in public with a woman. The new romance comes as the 30-year-old returns to acting and the spotlight.

Chapter 21 – Reynold

The date was perfect. Savannah was perfect. I feared she'd hate the spotlight and decide she wanted to end things with me. I know better. That's not who Savannah is. She's strong and fierce. She punches men who try to kiss her without her permission and beats up gropers at bars and gets arrested for fighting for her rights.

She threatens cowardly paparazzi.

Savannah hesitated to put herself out there for the world's unfair judgement, but she lifted her head high and didn't let any fear show. She welcomed my fans with open arms, even the ones who tried giving her the cold shoulder. She smiled at them and made sure they knew that I'm *hers*.

"Why are you looking at me like you're about to devour me?"

We're back at the penthouse, just inside the door where she's slipping off her flats at the shoe stand built into the wall. She rubs the back of her neck, then stretches it side to side.

"Because I am." I shoo her hands away so I can massage her sore muscles.

She moans the moment my fingers bite into the muscles and my cock jumps at the sound.

"Have you thought about that book, Savannah?"

"Mhm."

"Do you own it?"

"It's one that you bought me. I've read it before."

I lean in, my breath fanning her neck. "Go get it and meet me in our bedroom."

"Our bedroom?"

"I said what I said."

Her cheeks blush with anticipation before she turns and leaves.

I prepare everything I hope to use on her tonight, lining up the toys on top of my dresser. Lube and nipple clamps (something Savannah told me she'd be interested in trying. I didn't have any, so I had to order them). Two of my ties and a butt plug (though I'd rather have my cock up her ass tonight). And finally, a dildo and vibrator (which I also had to order).

She returns within a couple of minutes, her face glowing with eagerness. She shyly holds up a paperback of a woman with pink hair wearing a white sports bra on the cover.

"It's a Why Choose. Enemies to lovers. The FMC's father sold her to a gang leader to pay off his debts."

I smirk. Of course, she'd choose enemies to lovers. Because she loves pushing my buttons.

"Tell me what 'why choose' means." I have an idea, but I want to hear her explain it.

"The main character has multiple lovers and doesn't choose."

I stalk toward her. "Is there a group scene?"

"Yes."

I grab her waist when I reach her, tugging her flush against my body. My hands squeeze her ass, still in the tight wrap dress that I desperately need gone so I can feel her silky skin underneath my touch.

"I'm only one man, Savannah," I say and place a soft kiss on her plump lips.

"You're all I need," she whispers against my mouth.

I smile, knowing that all the toys I plan to use on her tonight will make her feel as if she's in a group sex scene from one of her books. All her beautiful holes will be filled.

"Let's shower."

I tug her into the bathroom and strip her out of her dress. She's wearing the sexiest red lacy bra and matching thong. She preens at my response from seeing her like this. Slowly, I unclasp the bra and let it fall down her arms. Her thong goes next and when I kneel to help her step out of the fabric, I decide I can't wait.

I push her up against the sink, throw one of her legs over my shoulder, and cover her clit with my mouth. Her hands bury into my hair, tugging and pulling as I work my tongue over the sensitive nerves.

"Fuck, Reynold," she moans as I slide my finger inside her.

She grinds her pussy into my face, trying to reach her release faster. I pick up the pace, adding another finger. I take my time going through a combination of grazing my teeth over her clit, sucking and licking it viciously.

She tugs painfully on my hair, and that's when I know she's about to come. She screams and stills, letting the orgasm wash over her.

After I remove my fingers and lick her pleasure off them, she drags me up her body and covers my mouth with hers. She whimpers, tasting herself on my lips and tongue and doesn't stop kissing me until she's sure it's all gone.

"Come on," I say. "We're just getting started."

I let her undress me and we step into the warm water. We take turns washing each other. She tries to kneel to suck me off, but the next time I come; I want it to be inside her.

The shower is fast, both of us eager to lose ourselves to one another, and we quickly dry each other off. I can get used to this equality of taking care of each other. It's something I didn't know I needed.

"Have you been a good girl wearing the butt plug like I asked?" I bring her to the bed, both of us naked. Her eyes fall to my rock-hard dick and her pupils dilate, leaving a thin ring of green.

"Yes," she rasps, her lust almost too much for her to speak. "I'm at the biggest size now."

Those long days on set have made for some exciting sext conversations between the two of us. Including me, demanding she wear a plug while home alone. To touch herself and tell me how it felt to come with her arse full.

"I'm so proud of you, Savannah."

She blushes, the pink spreading over her cheeks, neck, and down her chest.

"Get in the middle of the bed. Grab your book and find a sex scene."

She doesn't hesitate to follow my command. Precum leaks out of my dick at her obedience. She flips through the pages until stopping halfway through.

"Now what?"

"Now... read it. Out loud."

I grab the vibrator as she talks about one of the love interests going down on the female main character. I crawl between her legs, spreading them wide, and push a button to turn the toy on.

She stops reading, her eyes widening at the sound.

"I didn't say stop."

I lower the round head to her clit and press it down hard enough to garner a whimper from her as the vibrations massage and coax her pleasure to the surface. Her words are strained as she continues reading, her breathing becoming labored.

"You like that, don't you?"

"Mhm," she hums and bites her lip.

"Keep reading."

She goes on and gets to a part mentioning nipple play.

Perfect.

She whines when I suddenly pull the vibrator away so I can grab the clamps from the dresser.

"You said you've never used these before?"

She nods.

"It might be too much. If that's the case, I'll need you to say your safe word, okay? Tell me what it is again."

"Boundaries."

"Good girl. Now... keep reading."

She lifts the book so I can have access to her breasts. I carefully put the first clamp on as she reads words about sucking, flicking, and biting down on the hardened tips. She inhales sharply when the clamp closes but the blush across her cheeks deepens. Once I have the other one in place, I reward her with a small tug on the chain connecting the clamps.

"Fuck," she screams and tries to grab her breasts. I slap her hands away.

"Was that good or bad?"

"Good. Fuck, it was good."

"That's my girl."

I return to between her legs and turn the vibrator back on.

"Read."

Another man has joined the sex scene in the book and while one plays with the FMC's pussy, the other fucks her mouth. When the vibrator hits Savannah's clit this time, at full strength, she bucks off the bed. I splay my hand over her lower stomach, holding her down. She's still reading, obedient as ever, but her words jumble.

She's getting close.

"You're not allowed to come until I say so. Do you under-stand, Savannah?"

She whimpers—my favorite sound—but nods her head in agreement.

I massage the vibrator in circles over her clit and slide two fingers inside her at the same time the character in the book does. She arches off the bed again, but I'm out of hands to push her back down. My fingers fuck her slowly, certainly torturing her.

She stops reading. "Reynold, please."

"Please, what, Savannah? What do you need?"

"Please let me come."

Her walls tighten around my fingers, making it hard for me to continue pumping them. She's going to climax soon, but I can't let that happen.

I pull my fingers out and turn off the vibrator.

"No," she whines.

"I told you. You're not coming until I let you." I slap her sensitive pussy and she yelps. "Flip over. On your hands and knees. Take this."

I hand her the vibrator, and she eagerly grabs it and tosses the book off the bed in the process. Okay, guess we're done with that. Once she's in place, my hand crashes down on her arse. She groans and I relish the red outline it leaves.

Her pleasure leaks from her pussy and I take it to use as lubricant and push my finger into her arse. She tries to move away, but I grab her hip with my free hand to hold her in place. I pump into the tight opening, getting it ready for my cock. Then I remove my finger and replace it with my mouth.

"Oh," Savannah gasps.

I plunge my tongue in and out of her hole, keeping her cheeks spread apart to give me more depth.

"Reynold, fuck. That's... strange. But good. Oh, God."

She's never had this done to her before, so I fuck her puckered hole with my tongue viciously to show her what she's been missing.

"Turn the vibrator on and put it on your clit," I say, then get back to work.

She groans the moment she presses the vibrator to her clit while I eat out her arse. Her release is already building up to the breaking point.

"Please, Sir, can I come?"

I almost let her because I love the sound of 'sir' coming out of her mouth, but I stop and pull away.

"Goddamn it, Rey."

She gets another spanking for calling me Rey, which she enjoys too much.

"On your back again."

She huffs but rolls over. I tease her opening with my finger. She's soaked. The edging has made her more than ready for me.

I line up my cock to her heat. "Is this what you want?"

"Yes, please."

I slam into her, and she arches her back at the swift movement. I stay put until she adjusts to my size before pulling out and slamming into her again. My thrusts are slow, and I know it's frustrating her. She's chewing on her bottom lip, her cheeks bright pink as she holds back her curses.

I pick up the vibrator from where she set it down and turn it back on, then press it to her clit. Her pussy closes around my cock at the over stimulation. Savannah squirms beneath me, urging me to go faster. She fists the sheets in frustration.

I grab the silver chain connecting the nipple clamps and tug at it.

She gasps and reaches for her breasts as if forgetting they were on. Then that shot of pain transforms into pleasure and her hands return to the sheets.

I need to do something about those hands.

Leaving a panting Savannah in the middle of the bed, I grab the two ties from my dresser where I laid out all the toys and return to the bed. I secure one of her hands above her head to my headboard with one tie and put the other tie over her eyes.

Then I grab the bottle of lube and pour a line onto my dick.

"Are you ready, Savannah?" I ask, returning to between her legs. "I'm going to fuck your arse now."

"Yes, please. I need you."

The moment I press the tip against her puckered hole, she tenses.

"Relax. Breathe. This is going to feel so fucking good, Savannah."

She nods, letting out a long stream of breath, and I push in past the outer ring. Her back arches at the sudden intrusion.

"You're doing amazing, Savannah. Do you know that? So fucking beautiful."

I use the praise to distract her and push halfway in. She moans, showing no signs of discomfort, so I sink into her more, inch by inch, until I'm all the way seated inside her.

"You take me so well, Savannah."

I move my hips, slowly drawing out, then cautiously pushing back in. I want to go faster, but I know she's not ready for that. So, I take my time, letting her adjust to my size.

"You won't hurt me, Reynold. It feels incredible. Fuck me harder. Please."

I trust her to know her body and limits, and I do exactly what she begs of me. My thrusts pick up and I grab the vibrator and turn it on, then place it in her free hand.

"Put it on your clit," I demand, and she does. It takes her a couple seconds of adjustments to find the right spot.

I grab the dildo next, thankful she can't see what I'm doing beyond the blindfold.

"You want a group scene? You get me and all my toys."

I slow down my thrusts to slide the head of the dildo into her soaked pussy. She lets out a tiny 'oh' at the sensation and her legs spread wider, allowing better access. Once I let her adjust to having both holes filled, I start fucking her with the dildo, holding it with one hand just above my dick while I piston into her arse.

She won't last long with the overstimulation.

"Please, Reynold, I can't... I can't hold off much longer."

My palm smooths up her stomach and to the nipple clamp chain.

"I know, my love. You can come now."

I tug on the chain, and she explodes with an orgasm.

I grunt, fucking her through her release. Her arsehole sucks my cock so fiercely that I can no longer hold back and pour my cum inside her.

"You look so good coming underneath me."

When I've let every last drop out, I remove my cock and the dildo. She already dropped the vibrator. It's still on, jumping around the mattress.

I take off her blindfold and untie her binds, then fall onto my back beside her. I pull her on top of me, both of us drenched in sweat. Her head rests on my chest, and she runs her palms up and down my stomach. I kiss the top of her head.

"I think I blacked out for a second," she says. "I definitely saw God. Or some God. A sex God, maybe?"

"Are you tired?"

"Mmm. No. Just well fucked."

"Good. I have plans for you tonight."

"Is that a threat or a promise?"

"Both."

She giggles and I squeeze her closer to my body.

Fuck. I think I'm in love with this woman.

But as much as I want to tell her right now... I'm scared she'll think it's too soon.

BIRTH ANNOUNCEMENT

Bruno Stein and his wife, Ginger, welcomed a baby girl this weekend in Los Angeles. The couple met five years ago during the filming of Tyler's Team when Stein was Mylan Andrews's bodyguard. Ginger is best friends with Lana Young-Andrews, who returned to L.A. two weeks ago to be with Ginger for the birth.

Ginger and Bruno own a successful security firm that provides bodyguards to celebrities and high-profile individuals across the world. This is the first child for the two who got married in Hawaii last year. Ginger announced on social media that the little girl's name is Gracey, named after her mother, who passed away a few years ago. We're told mother and child are healthy and happy.

Chapter 22 - Savannah

It's been two months. Two wonderful months of being Reynold's girlfriend. The announcement of our relationship calmed down after a couple of weeks. Articles showcased all the pictures taken of us on our date and even some from fans who spotted us. I looked fantastic in most of those photos. And the way Reynold couldn't keep his eyes off me... it was as if I was the only one in the world, despite being surrounded by chaos.

He's accustomed to that chaos. Me, not so much. My sexy black dress and perfectly styled hair couldn't hide the concern, doubt, and fear on my face.

The video of my interaction with the fatphobic paparazzo went viral. I refused to watch it, experiencing it was enough. I also refused to read the comments. I knew a lot of them were bad. However, Reynold read me dozens of positive messages from people with bodies like mine. They thanked

SETTLE MYER

me for inspiring them to be confident and fight back against body shamers.

I also did an interview with Entertainment Now before reporters dug into my past and found my criminal history. I confessed every arrest and why I don't regret them. That article also went viral. People cheered my defiance and instead of becoming a villain, I'd become an unintentional role model.

Two months seem like a long time, but in Reynold's world, the days flew by. He was gone more than he was home. He'd film long hours and sometimes six days a week because they'd gotten behind schedule. We barely had time to see each other.

I'd fall asleep in his bed—our bed. Our room. It's been our room for two months. He made space in his closet for my clothes. I added pictures of my family and friends next to his.

Addy hasn't been waking up at night either. I have a feeling she only did that at the beginning to push me and Reynold together. As soon as we told her we're in a relationship (which she was super excited about), her late-night wakeups magically stopped.

Reynold would return home from set late and cuddle with me. We'd wake wrapped in each other's arms and make love before starting the day. I've never craved sex so much in my life. With this man, I never make an excuse not to have sex, and I definitely don't fake an orgasm.

Reynold hired a part-time nanny to watch Adeline so we could go on date nights. He began interviewing people the moment we made our relationship official. He even asked me and Addy to help. The woman we liked is older. Nadia's a grandmother whose grandchildren have all grown up. She nannied for rich and famous families before and loves spoiling young ones. One of Reynold's co-workers recommended her, only letting her go because their kids grew up.

Addy fell in love with her the minute she showed up with candy and a stuffed toy dog that looked like Banana.

Last week, Lana returned to New York City to visit for a few nights before heading back to L.A. for some events with the Tyler's Team Foundation. We met up with her and Mylan for karaoke at a bar in Midtown East called Cornerstone Tavern. They wore their silly disguises—telling us it's tradition. I sang *Wannabe,* by the Spice Girls, with Lana, who is a phenomenal singer, so I knew her voice would overpower mine.

No one paid us any attention until the boys decided to act up. Reynold requested the song *Mirrors* by Justin Timberlake. He placed a stool in the middle of the bar and brought me over to sit me on it. I was so confused at first but didn't question what he was doing. He had Mylan hold his phone up with the flashlight on to imitate a spotlight. Then he serenaded me with his velvety voice. It was sexy but also embarrassing because he rubbed up against me like he was the star of *Magic Mike* or something. The song wasn't even meant for lap dances, but Reynold didn't care.

Then it was Mylan's turn. He chose *Don't Stop Believin'* by Journey. He also tried to sit Lana on a stool in the middle of the bar, but she refused. He started off singing directly to her. Unlike Rey, Mylan's a horrible singer, but because he performs, the crowd ate it up. They sang along with him as Mylan walked up and down the bar—since there was no stage—and pointed the microphone in people's faces.

Mylan had brought on so much attention, people finally realized who we all were. They bombarded Lana, Mylan, and Reynold, asking for selfies. They even asked me to be in a few.

Lana and I stayed in touch over the past two months. We texted nonstop about the press and spotlight surrounding me becoming Reynold's girlfriend. I gave up all my social media pages. It was too overwhelming. I also had to change my number again because reporters somehow found it and called nonstop, asking for interviews. This time I only gave it to Reynold, his inner circle, and my parents. I told my best friend, Justine, if she needed to get a hold of me, she could email me. She understood.

The sudden fame wasn't the only reason I needed to change the number. Despite being blocked, my ex kept texting and calling me. Every week, he'd try using a different number. I thought eventually he'd run out of numbers, but nope. Now he can't call me at all.

His last text before I cut him off threatened to come to NYC and find me. I knew he was just blowing smoke out of his ass because Reynold has eyes on him in Silo Springs. He assured me that Brad was staying put in Arkansas. Probably because Justine told me that Cara Calloway is pregnant with his child now. Better her than me.

Reynold has six weeks of filming left. Today, Adeline and I are going to set to see him, which we've been doing all summer. We'd go at least once a week, sometimes twice, depending on how many days he was working. With Addy starting school again soon, Reynold wants to spend all the time he can with her.

He's missed out on a lot while filming this movie. The regret in his eyes when suggesting we carry on without him made my heart break. Like the day we took the train out to Coney Island. Addy and I hung out at the beach and in the water for hours and went on the rides at Luna Park. We played games and won stuffed animal prizes. Then we stopped at Nathan's and bought one of their famous hot dogs topped with chili and cheese.

That night when he came home, Reynold asked about our day, and we showed him pictures and videos. He'd swipe through, smiling and tearing up at the same time. Addy saw. She's such an observant little kid. She told him not to be sad. She told him she got to spend the first five years of her life with him and now it's my turn.

"Dad, I'm only five," she said. "We have plenty of time to hang out."

He wasn't so hard on himself after that day.

The paparazzi haven't been too horrible. They've yet to track down Reynold's home. Or maybe they have, but it's off limits. I really don't know how it works. I just know they never show up outside the apartment building. They only seem to find us when we're out in public. Coney Island was a mess because they hovered like seagulls waiting to steal our food. Sarah and Henry did a great job keeping them back.

One day, Addy and I tried to wear disguises like Lana and Mylan do, but that rarely works for them anymore and the rats found us pretty quickly.

Adeline had a blast trying to trick them, though, so we wore disguises a few more times just for fun. Thankfully, Reynold's overprotection kept us safe. He has four body-guards for us, but I only ever see Sarah and Henry.

"Savvy," a woman calls the moment we walk into the holding area. Victoria Bedford, the woman playing Rey's wife on the big screen, walks towards us.

I only met her once in the handful of times we've visited set because she isn't in a lot of scenes. Today they're filming on location at a pier near the Brooklyn Bridge. It's a flashback scene featuring Rey and Victoria's characters talking about her new job and how she has a bad feeling about her boss. Rey tells her it's probably 'new job' jitters. Then, this afternoon, Rey and Mylan will shoot flash forward scenes at the same spot. Mylan's character, the detective, will try to convince Rey's character not to do anything stupid like go after his wife's killers.

Victoria could be my sister. She has blonde hair and green eyes like me. Gorgeous. Flawless. I expected to feel threatened by her, to hate her, but she doesn't sneer at me or speak condescendingly like other women who find out I'm with Rey. She's not fake when we speak. She's a kind woman who welcomed me with open arms.

Reynold told me how flirty she was at the table read. The week before I met Victoria, tabloids published photos of her and Rey appearing intimate. He said it was for a scene they were shooting where they shared a kiss. Still, the media portrayed it as him "cheating" on me.

I knew it wasn't true, especially after he fucked me that night, leaving my legs weak and pussy aching.

"Rey and Mylan are going over some last-minute changes with the director, so I offered to keep you company."

She haunches down in front of Addy. "Hi Adeline. Do you remember me? I'm Victoria."

I expect Addy to hide behind my leg, but she doesn't. "You're my dad's fake wife."

Victoria laughs and stands. "That's right."

"My dad's going to marry Savvy."

I choke on my spit and start coughing. "Addy. You shouldn't be saying stuff that's not true."

She shrugs. "He loves you, though, right? And when you love someone, you get married."

"That's..." Oh my God. What am I supposed to say? Reynold hasn't said the 'L' word to me aside from 'my love' and he said it was just a term of endearment. I haven't told him I love him either. Do I think he cares for me? Absolutely. Do I care for him? More than anything in the world.

Do I love him?

Yes.

I'm too scared to say the word because the last person I thought I loved broke my heart.

But this is different. This love I have for Reynold is different. It's real. What I thought I felt for Brad could never amount to this feeling I have for Reynold. That overwhelming sense of need when he's not around. Security when in his arms. Fear that if I ever lost him, I wouldn't be able to function.

Victoria must sense my panic and waves her hands in front of my body. "You look wonderful. That outfit is to die for."

"Oh, thank you," I say, glancing down.

I'm wearing a simple black crop top, a short white flare skirt covered in black lace, fishnet leggings, and sketchers. My hair is up in a messy bun. It's an ode to my punk phase in my early twenties.

"Who is your stylist? I desperately need to update my wardrobe, and my current stylist is useless."

"I style myself," I say with a nervous laugh.

"Would you want to style me?" Her eyes light up with the idea.

"Sure. I mean, I'm not a professional, but I'd love to try."

She claps her hands together. "Wonderful."

She digs into her purse and extracts a card before handing it to me. "Call me. We'll set up a consultation. Email me your rates. If you're not sure what to charge, research the standard and charge me double."

I take the card, my eyes stinging with tears. This can't be real. Can it? "Did... Rey tell you to talk to me about styling?"

She tilts her head. "He didn't, but to be fair, we haven't filmed too many scenes together. Most of the flashbacks are scheduled for this month."

"Oh." So that means she saw me and liked my outfit?

"Is styling something you'd like to do?"

I shrug. "I didn't even think of it as an option. I just like wearing cute clothes and assembling outfits. Rey is the one who suggested it. He said he'd put me in touch with people."

She smiles softly at me.

"Of course he did. That man has it bad for you. I'm not going to lie; I had a crush on him. I mean, look at him. He's gorgeous, sweet, caring. What he did for Adeline..." She sighs as if he's Prince Charming riding in on a white horse. She's not telling me this to make me jealous. And I'm not jealous. If Reynold was interested in this woman, he wouldn't have fought so hard for me. "The first day we filmed together, he would not stop smiling at his phone. I've never seen a man blush and giggle at a phone like he did. It was adorable. I knew I'd never have a chance, and I'm not a conniving bitch who tries to take someone's man. As if I could have taken him from you."

Okay. I like this woman.

"She said a bad word," Addy whispers. Before I can respond and tell her that not everyone has to pay for saying bad words, Victoria keeps talking.

"Anyway, I need to head to wardrobe." She glances over her shoulder. Reynold is done with his meeting and walks toward us with a huge smile claiming his face. Victoria turns back to me. "Wow. I need someone who looks at me like that."

Addy runs to her father, and he lifts her up all the way over his head. He tickles her, and she erupts into a fit of giggles as he brings her back to the ground. When he reaches me, he grabs me by the nape and pulls me into a nearly inappropriate kiss. A clear sign of possessiveness in front of Victoria.

I am his, and he is mine.

"See you on set, Michaelson," Victoria says, shaking her head with a smile.

"Will you stay until lunch?" Reynold asks, taking Addy's hand while I take her other.

Crew members run around preparing the first scene of the day. Reynold weaves us through the chaos to the holding area where two chairs sit empty behind the cameras. He got us director's chairs with our names on it. He was so proud of himself when he showed us.

"Sure. We have no other plans today."

"Savvy, you said we could go watch a movie," Adeline whines.

"Shit. That's right."

"Bad word tax," Addy giggles, holding out her hand. "One dollar please."

"Add it to my tab." I finally explained what that meant to Adeline. We also came up with the official name: bad word tax. I think I owe her about twenty dollars by now, but Reynold is up to fifty.

"Fine," she sighs and rolls her eyes. She's entering a sassy phase and I'm here for it.

"We'll leave after lunch to catch an afternoon showing," I say to Reynold. "She wants to see some new animated movie."

He smiles, but it doesn't reach his eyes. I know he's thinking about how badly he wants to join us.

"We'll do a movie night on your next day off. Just the three of us."

That mournful smile brightens slightly, and he crushes me in an appreciative hug before a production assistant tears him away for his first film of the day.

Watching Reynold perform is an experience. He's captivating. Intense. He transforms into the character enough that I forget he's acting and believe he's a different person. While I could have stayed watching him all day, Addy got bored within the first hour.

We walk along the waterfront at Brooklyn Bridge Park. Sarah and Henry follow close behind, but it's not too busy and no one's paying attention to us. Most of the fans and paparazzi crowd around the set, hoping to catch glimpses of Rey or Mylan.

"Are we going on the carousel?" Addy asks, hopping next to me as we get closer to the iconic wooden attraction.

"We sure are."

We buy our tickets and find our horses, Sarah and Henry choosing ones behind us. The music starts up, and the ride goes round and round. Addy erupts in giggles, smiling bigger than her tiny face allows as the horse goes up and down. I snap a few pictures of her and take a video to send to Reynold later.

After the carousel, we casually head back to set, stopping at a roller rink inside the pier next to the one where Rey's filming today. I shoot him a quick text asking if it's okay to let Addy skate. He responds after a few minutes.

Hot British Guy

Of course. I trust you

My heart flutters at those three words. I trust you. I know he trusts me with his daughter, otherwise I wouldn't be his nanny, but to see those words is validating.

Addy has never skated before and the last time I did it was in high school. We may have fallen a time or two. Luckily, they had a helmet and crash pads for her to wear on her knees and elbows. They didn't have any for me, so I'll have to live with the scrapes and bruises.

Sarah drew the short stick and joined us in the rink, which means Henry was stuck with my phone, recording us from where he stood as a lookout.

After fifteen minutes of skating, and Addy's third fall, I decide we've skated enough.

When we get back to set, it's time for lunch. Reynold's assistant has our meals ready for us at a table. I chose a chicken Caesar wrap and chips. Addy got a hamburger and fries, just like her father, except the man has a bottomless stomach and he ate two burgers and fries, then stole some of Addy's fries too.

"Do you want to come over for dinner tonight?" Reynold asks Mylan, who joins us to eat. Mylan had been coming over on nights they'd get done filming early. Just so he didn't have to spend time by himself in the hotel room.

"Can't. Got an AA meeting." He holds up his hand the moment Reynold's mouth pops open. "I'm fine. I'm going to the meeting *because* I'm fine. This is just part of my recovery. I go to meetings back in L.A. too. Here I attend one once a week, sometimes twice. I don't have an urge to drink, and

I haven't in a very long time, but it's the first time Lana isn't here with me, by my side every day. So, I go to the meetings to talk about it with the group. I talk about *everything* I'm experiencing through my sobriety. Plus, you two inviting me over for dinner and keeping me company helps more than you know."

"That's good to hear, Mylan," Reynold says, slapping his hand on his friend's shoulder. "And you're welcome any-time."

The boys do their adorable handshake—the one Reynold told me they made up as teens—before Mylan stands.

"Time for hair and makeup."

We say goodbye and once Mylan's gone, Reynold sighs and pulls me in for a kiss on the cheek. "Did you two have fun exploring today?"

"Oh!" I grab my phone. "I forgot to send you the pictures and videos."

He scans through them the moment they come through to his phone. I watch over his shoulder, smiling at the video of us being silly on the carousel. People watch on from out-side of the glass that encases the ride, oblivious to who we are.

Except...

I swipe his phone out of his hand and replay the video, fast-forwarding to the part that caught my eye.

"What is it?"

In one shot, I spot a man wearing a hat and sunglasses staring directly at us. Every pass of the carousel, he's there, standing still except for his head, which moves as we pass by on the ride. I go through the other pictures and videos and he's in the background of a lot of them.

Watching.

He looks familiar, but I can't place him.

"You're scowling at the phone," Reynold says, concern in his voice.

I zoom in on the man and turn it around to show him. "Is this one of the extra bodyguards you hired that you hide from me and think I don't know about, but I know about?"

I've only seen them once when Lana pointed them out to me, but I can't remember what they look like.

Reynold's eyes widen slightly then he grins, not even feeling bad about having the overprotection. He takes the phone and squints at the image.

"No. That's not Larson or Melanie." He gives the phone back to me. "Why? What's wrong?"

Panic slips into his voice, but I don't want to worry him. At the same time...

"He's in a lot of these photos. I feel like I've seen him before."

He's not the man stalking Lana because, one, she's not with me and, two, it's a different guy. This man is sickly pale and has shoulder-length, dark red hair. He's also stick thin where Lana's stalker had shorter black hair and was built but not bulky.

Reynold selects all the videos and pictures from today and types out a message before sending them to my protection team.

He tells them to keep an eye out for the man.

"Don't worry," he says, pulling me close to kiss my temple. "This is why I hired more protection for you two. I expected some people would form a sick obsession once we went public. He must have just started following you around because the bodyguards would have spotted him by now."

I relax at his reassuring words, but my stomach stays sour. This is the part of Rey's life that I'm not a fan of. Will it get worse? Can I handle it if it does?

Chapter 23 - Savannah

T he next month and a half passes quickly. It's Friday and yesterday was Reynold's last day of filming. He has a meeting with his manager this afternoon, but he's free for the rest of the night. He wants to take me and Addy out to dinner and a Broadway show.

It's October, so that means Addy is back at school—a kindergartner now. She's done by three so at two forty-five, I leave to pick her up. Sarah and Henry follow close even though I haven't seen that creepy guy since the day we visited Reynold on set. While I wait inside the courtyard, Sarah and Henry stand just outside the fence, scoping out the area.

After about ten minutes, Addy runs out of the private school's entrance and slams into me with the biggest hug.

"I touched a snake today!"

I gasp. "A snake? Was it scary?"

"No! It was cool and weird and now I'm going to ask Dad if I can get a snake."

Dear Lord, I hope he says no. I've been terrified of snakes ever since I went camping with Justine in high school, and a copperhead tried to get into our tent. A group of guys camping nearby heard us screaming and saved us. They wrangled the venomous intruder and tossed it back into the woods, far, far away.

"I also pet a wolf."

Addy's class took a school trip to the Bronx Zoo today.

"That's pretty cool, Poppy."

Addy giggles at me using her father's nickname. The first time I said it, her eyes lit up, and she tackled me with a hug. She said only Reynold and I are allowed to call her Poppy.

"I can't wait to tell dad," Addy says as we walk out of the schoolyard and turn right to head back to the penthouse.

"He's not your real father, kiddo."

Instinctively, I grab Addy's arm and hide her behind me as I turn to face the asshole who dared to say that.

I expected it to be someone from the paparazzi who snuck by the bodyguards. Instead, it's the man from that day at the carousel. My stomach drops. I whip my head around, searching for Sarah and Henry. They're nowhere to be found.

Shit. Shit. Shit.

"They're incapacitated at the moment," the man says, answering my silent panic.

I scan the area, hoping to spot the backup bodyguards.

Where are they?

How the hell am I going to get away from this man? I'm freaking the fuck out and I can't focus.

"Who are you?"

"I'm Kyle. That little girl's real father."

My heart hurts at how fast it's beating.

Kyle. Addy's biological father. I'm not even going to call him her father. He's not. He's just a sperm donor. The asshole called her little girl, like he can't even say her name.

"Give me the kid and tell that rich boyfriend of yours he'll get her back when he pays me five million dollars."

I take a step back, trapping Addy between me and the fence surrounding the school. Parents walk past us, taking their kids home, oblivious to the danger we're in.

"I don't believe you. Kyle is supposed to be in prison."

"Savvy?" Adeline whispers behind me, her voice shaking.

Over the man's shoulder, I finally see the backup bodyguards. Larson and Melanie cautiously approach. Kyle took out Sarah and Henry, but he must not have known about my hidden protection.

"Yeah, well, I'm out and I'm here to collect what's mine. That bitch Annalee never told me about her rich brother. If he wants the kid back, he's going to have to pay me."

"You're insane. I'm not letting you take her."

I need to keep this creepo talking to buy time for Larson and Melanie to come up with a plan to save us. Should I yell? It's New York. People mind their business here. They'd probably keep walking with their head down or give us a wide berth to stay out of potential danger.

"You think Rey is just going to hand over money to you? The police will swarm you the moment it's in your hands. You're a fucking idiot."

He growls and pulls out a knife. My stomach sours and I cover my mouth to hold back bile. Okay, maybe I should have just kept my mouth shut. My eyes widen, darting frantically to Larson and Melanie, silently telling them to move in.

When Kyle lunges for me, I turn away, tucking Addy against my body to protect her. I vaguely register a burning pain across the back of my upper left arm.

Behind me, I hear grunts and scuffling as I assume the bodyguards are beating the asshole up. When he's cursing them out, demanding they let him go, I know it's over.

Sirens sound in the distance. Someone called the police. Damn, they responded fast. The adrenaline coursing through my body dissolves to relief. That's when the tears follow. I crumble to the ground, hugging Addy tight while I cry and rock her. She's shivering in my arms, sobbing right along with me.

"Savvy," a familiar voice echoes in my head. "You're bleeding."

I lift my head to see Sarah next to me. She's holding her side and has a cut over her right eye.

"What happened? Are you okay?" I ask.

She smiles and extends her hand to me. "Don't worry about me. Let's get you checked out."

I take her help and stand. Addy hugs my waist, her head buried into my side. I pet her hair, hoping to soothe her. I can't even imagine how scared and confused she must be right now. Sarah leads me to an ambulance that just pulled up. The burning sensation kicks back in. Blood trickles down the backside of my arm and onto my clothes on my left side.

That fucker slashed me.

The medic gestures for me to climb in so she can patch me up, but I shake my head.

"Help her first." I nod my chin to Sarah. She tries to argue but sways where she stands.

"Another ambulance is on the way," the medic says while keeping Sarah steady and helping her inside the rig.

I stand at the ambulance, watching Sarah get patched up as two uniformed officers lead Kyle to a cruiser in handcuffs. He spews hateful words and curses at anyone who will listen. I cover Adeline's ears and pay no attention to the wannabe kidnapper.

Henry—glad to see he's okay—and Larson stand off to the side with a detective in street clothes, perhaps giving him the rundown of what happened. I'm not even sure what happened.

Despite some minor cuts and bruises from the struggle with Kyle, Melanie resumes her bodyguard role and stands with me and Addy at the ambulance. After the scare at the carousel, I made Reynold introduce me to my hidden protectors. Melanie has a similar build to Sarah: tall with muscles and dark brown hair up in a ponytail.

I glance down at Addy, who sniffles against my hip. "You okay?" I ask softly.

She nods. "Yeah, but I was really scared."

"I know. Me too." Not so much scared for myself. I totally could have taken that guy. I broke up a lot of fights working at Lilies all those years. I was more worried about him trying to snatch Addy.

Larson and Henry finish talking to the cops and walk over to where we stand. Larson's face is full of anger. I don't blame him. He's got a couple cuts on his beefy arms where

Kyle slashed him too. A feat for such a thin and frail man like Kyle when Larson is probably twice his size.

Just before Henry opens his mouth to give me an update, I hear Reynold. He's shouting our names and running up the sidewalk, his face tight with fury. An officer tries to stop him from crossing the yellow police tape that was erected around the crime scene. A crowd has formed, curious onlookers wondering what happened. News crews are pulling up now too.

"That's my daughter and fiancée."

Fiancée?

The officer lets him through. He scoops both me and Addy in his arms and squeezes us tight, then kisses our heads. When Reynold releases us, he spots blood on his hand. He panics, searching Addy's body, then starts for me when he finds her injury free.

I hold up my arm to show him. "I'm fine. Don't worry."

"Savannah, you've bled all down your left side. It's too much blood. You've lost too much and you're slightly pale. You are *not* fine."

A second ambulance pulls up at that moment and Reynold takes Addy's hand, then presses his other to my lower back and leads us to the rig. The medic checks out the cut and tells me I'll need stitches. He covers the wound with a bandage and asks if I want a ride to the hospital.

"I'll take her," Reynold answers for me.

The drive to the hospital is silent. The adrenaline from the attack has left me exhausted. I rest my head on Reynold's shoulder. Adeline is asleep in his lap. The hospital isn't too far, so we're there in less than ten minutes, only held up by rush hour traffic.

Word spread fast about the attack. Paparazzi swarm the entrance to the emergency room. They barely leave a big enough path for us. Uniformed police officers struggle to push everyone back. Reynold's bodyguards help—Henry, Larson, Melanie, and three more that I see in rotation protecting him.

He called all hands on deck.

The emergency department isn't too crowded, and we're immediately taken to a room. I try to argue. My injury isn't serious, and I worry that I'm taking a spot from someone who needs help more than me. Reynold assures me we're in a special section of the hospital for VIP patients, where emergency room staff won't be needed.

I suppose that makes sense. High-profile people sitting in a waiting room would surely create a distraction. This must be a PR nightmare for the hospital. I hope the crowds aren't causing issues for people who actually need help.

329

We wait five minutes at most before a woman comes in to inspect my wound. She cleans it again and gives me a shot of lidocaine to numb the area.

"Can you find out if Sarah is okay?" I ask Reynold as the woman stitches me up. Fuck, it hurts, but I put on a brave face. If I don't, I might just crumble.

He sits in a chair next to where I'm perched on the bed. Addy is in his lap with her head on his chest. She's sucking her thumb. I've never seen her suck her thumb. Perhaps it's something she does when she's scared. Or when experiencing trauma.

Reynold types out a message on his phone. After about five minutes, it vibrates with a response.

"The knife missed vital organs. She's getting stitched up now."

The nurse or doctor, I'm not sure, finishes my stitches and gives me a tetanus shot as a precaution. Then she says she'll return with a prescription for pain.

Silence falls in the room. My thoughts are running on overdrive until I can no longer hold them in.

"You called me your fiancée," I say quietly.

He sucks in a sharp breath, then leans in to whisper something in Addy's ear. She nods and climbs off his lap, sitting in the chair after he stands.

He settles on the edge of the bed next to me and takes my hand.

"I did. I... don't know why." He pauses for the longest time and shakes his head. "Actually, I do know. Because I love you, Savannah. I have for a while, but I didn't want to say it too soon and scare you away. But after what happened..."

His voice cracks.

"I was terrified. It could have been a lot worse and the thought of losing you..." He takes in a deep breath. "Your instinct was to protect Adeline before yourself. I can never thank you enough for doing that. But if you let me, I will spend the rest of my life trying."

He lifts our embraced hands and kisses my knuckles. When he sees me crying, he moves closer so he can kiss the tears while cupping my face in his large hands.

"I love you too, Reynold."

His lips claim mine with a kiss packed full of hunger, relief, love, and *possession*.

We only part because Addy is in the room, not that she's paying attention to us. She found the remote and turned on the TV to watch cartoons.

"Yes," I whisper, palming his cheek.

It takes him a moment to understand what I mean, then he's kissing me all over again.

Chapter 24 – Reynold

I'm going to marry this woman. She said yes to the question I never officially asked her. She said yes to my slip up, calling her my fiancée because the moment I got the call from Larson saying to get to Addy's school immediately, my heart raced with fear. I knew right then I wanted Savannah to be more. Hell, I knew just weeks after meeting her, but hearing that she was possibly in danger validated everything I'd been feeling for her.

I never believed in soulmates but with Savannah...

It's almost as if she was put on that plane, in our row, in my path, because we were meant to meet and be together for the rest of our lives.

I want to kiss this woman forever, but we're interrupted by a knock on the private room's door. Henry, Larson, and Melanie walk in, followed by a detective who introduces himself as Bob. Bob is a burly man with light brown hair and a mustache. He's not too tall and has a permanent scowl on his face.

"Tell me everything," I demand.

Bob glances at Larson before answering.

"We've identified the man taken into custody as Kyle Scarsdale, Adeline's biological father."

Kyle? No fucking way. We'd never met, but Annalee showed me pictures of him. The Kyle I remember had short red hair and was bigger. The man I saw sitting in the back of the cop car was thin, sickly, almost. As if he's been wasting away in prison for the past five years.

My eyes dart to Addy, but all her attention is on cartoons dancing across the TV screen.

"He showed up and threatened to take your daughter. He implied he was going to hold her for ransom. He wasn't working alone. Another man, his younger brother Carl, lured Henry away by acting suspicious near the school's entrance. Henry chased after him and caught up to him. The two started fighting. Kyle disguised himself as a parent and approached Sarah while Henry was distracted. He stabbed her in the side and shoved her into some bushes near the gate, and she hit her head on the fence, leaving a cut just above her eyebrow. She was unconscious for a few minutes. That allowed him to get to Savvy and Adeline. Melanie was about to follow Henry to assist with the suspicious person, but that's when they noticed Kyle. They started moving in, but we're cautious. Didn't want to spook him in case he had a weapon."

"He was supposed to be serving a ten-year prison sentence," I growl. "Why the fuck wasn't I informed about his release?"

My lawyers were supposed to have been notified.

"He got out two months ago on good behavior and overcrowding. As for your lawyers not being notified," Bob shrugs. "His release may not have been entered into the system properly to prompt a notification. Or there's a backlog and notifications are going out late. Who knows? But the good news is he's confessing everything. Maybe he believes that'll get him points when he's on trial for aggravated assault, attempted kidnapping, and child endangerment charges. Anyway, he said earlier this year he read an article in an entertainment magazine—one from a stack the inmates get once a month. It was the article about your return to acting. It had a picture of your sister, Annalee, and then another picture of you and Adeline on the cover. He read about how you've been taking care of her since Annalee's death."

"I remember the article." Now I regret providing them with the damn pictures. "I assume he was pissed off about me calling him a lowlife twat?"

Bob nods with a smirk. "He had his younger brother track you down while he was in lockup."

"How?" I seethe. "The media couldn't even find where I lived or where Adeline went to school. How did that bastard manage to?"

"Pure luck. Carl was busted four years ago for running an underground gambling ring. He served a couple of years in jail and was released last year. Carl returned to his gambling ways and one of the men at the illegal casino he frequents, Sean, is a paparazzo. Carl started asking Sean questions, claiming he wanted to make money as a paparazzo. Sean sent him a list of celebrity hotspots and connected Carl with tipsters; people known to share celebrity sightings, planned or not. The day Lana Young-Andrews and Miss Monroe visited the Statue of Liberty, Carl was notified. He recognized the name. He knew Lana was connected to you, so he made his way to Battery Park, getting there just in time for Lana and Savannah to return and hop on the subway. He followed them to Adeline's preschool and then to the Brooklyn Bridge.

"Wait... Kyle's brother was the man we thought was stalking Lana?" Savannah asks.

The detective takes out his phone, taps a few times, then turns it around to show her. Savannah covers her mouth with her hand.

"That's him." She swallows hard. "But the man at the carousel was Kyle?"

Bob nods. "When Kyle got out, he already had his plan in place. He was going to kidnap Adeline because he didn't want to go through the trouble of finding a job and struggle to make money as a felon. He promised to share the ransom money with Carl if he helped. We believe they wanted to kidnap Adeline that day at the carousel."

"And we never saw him after either," Melanie says, pissed.

"He got spooked by Sarah and Henry and all the people in the park that day," Bob adds. "He realized he'd need to do it somewhere less public."

"And he's a dumbass too," I say. "All the times he watched us, watched Savannah and Adeline, he didn't notice the extra bodyguards I hired."

Bob shrugs.

"Did he really think he could pull this off?" Savannah asks.

"Desperation makes people do dumb things," Bob says and sighs.

Savannah sniffles and I take her hand. "I can't believe he did all this for money. He didn't even care about trying to be in Addy's life again?"

"Daddy?" Adeline says, her voice small and quiet.

"Oh, Poppy. Were you listening?"

She nods.

"You must be so confused right now."

"Why did that man want to hurt me and Savvy?"

I pause, thinking carefully before answering. "You see, sweetheart, that man is your biological father. I told you your mother was my sister, right? Well, she thought she loved that man and together they made you. But he left before you were born and when your mom died, he wasn't around to take custody of you, so I did."

She shakes her head. "That man is not my dad. *You* are."

I open my mouth to further explain, but Adeline grabs my face. Her tiny cold hands squeeze my cheeks enough to form a fish face.

"You're the only dad I've known. Not that scary man who tried to hurt me and Savvy."

I pull her into a hug. "I love you so much."

"I love you, too, Dad." She sighs, dramatically. "Can we go home now?"

Two weeks after the attack and the media attention has barely died down. The paparazzi finally found my penthouse. I'm surprised it took them this long. I put the lease under an LLC I created called Poppy's Trust. It's a common practice for celebrities when trying to keep their home purchases private.

We'd been careful about being followed home, but after the attack, it was impossible to ditch everyone. All it took was one time, and whichever media outlet tailed us shared their findings with the rest of the gaggle.

Because of the circus outside the building, Savannah, Addy, and I stayed inside the penthouse for the past two weeks. We had movie nights, all day read-a-thons, dress up parties, and Mario Kart competitions. We did a few living room karaoke performances. Savannah didn't lie about not being able to sing. She's not as bad as Mylan, but she sang with all his confidence—probably because we were in the living room and not in front of a crowd of strangers.

I also, finally, played my guitar for her. I swear I saw hearts in her eyes. She smiled and swooned and sighed, then pulled me to our room and showed me just how much she loved that solo performance.

Two weeks of wonderful memories, but we all have cabin fever.

Tonight was the premiere of Jensen's documentary of Rebecca's life. He took a step back from directing blockbuster movies to spend time with the woman he's been in love with for years. He documented her book tour for *Tyler's Team*, the book about her brother's battle with cancer and the good he did until his dying day. Jensen also made sure to tell Rebecca's story. One that was overlooked by her brother's diagnosis.

The red carpet was chaotic, as always. Paparazzi asked us questions about the attack, our engagement, and my next role. We kept our answers quick and simple.

"No comment."

"We are happy and excited to get married."

"I have my first romantic comedy role that starts filming in three months."

The documentary was ninety minutes long and fantastic. Savannah cried and laughed and grabbed my arm with joy when she spotted shots of Silo Springs, Arkansas—the town she grew up in.

Now we're back at the penthouse to change before heading to The Met Cloisters for the after party. It's a place I've been to many times. It's near where the Renaissance Faire is held every year.

Since the faire already took place a few weeks ago, Rebecca and Jensen created their own festival. I'm going as a knight, ditching the armor to don a black warrior tunic with black pants, black boots, and a belt for my sword.

Addy is also a knight, but her costume is made of soft fabrics sewn to appear as armor.

Then there's Savannah. The woman I love who takes my breath away... who makes my heart drum in my chest. She wears the sexiest green dress with a corset that pushes her breasts up generously. Her hair cascades over her shoulders in loose curls and a diamond crown sits atop her head.

A queen.

"If you keep staring at me like that, we'll never make it to the after party."

"I don't mind being late." I smirk and reach out to her. I run my hands up and down her arms, grazing my fingertips over the wound from the slashing. It's still raised and red. The stitches have since dissolved, leaving behind a scar.

I've been touching the wound a lot these past couple of days, as if reminding myself, or assuring myself, that she's alive.

My future wife.

Savannah steps into my arms like she's my missing piece, and I wrap them tightly around her. "I just need five minutes."

"Five?" She chews on her bottom lip, holding back a smile. Her eyes give it away, though. Bright with humor.

I lean in to press a kiss against her neck, just below her ear. "Trust me. I'll make you come twice in five minutes."

"Daaaad. Saaaavvy. Come on!" Adeline huffs at the end of the hallway, tapping her tiny foot.

"Okay little miss sassy pants," I muse.

"Ugh, Dad. Stop."

I press a kiss on Savannah's lips. "Is she supposed to be this sassy at five years old?"

"I'm five and a half!"

Shaking my head, I take Savannah's hand and lead my family out of the penthouse and down to the car.

My family.

It's been a long time since I could call more than one person my family. And I finally feel at home again.

Chapter 25 – Savannah

T he party is small, taking place in the museum's gardens. Fairy lights hang around the area with decorated tables spread throughout. We sit at a table with Eloise, Kelly, Lana, Mylan, Bruno, and Ginger (who left their new baby with Bruno's parents at the hotel.)

Lana told me Bruno moved his parents stateside from Germany after a loan shark kept trying to go after them for money, even though they already paid off their loan. Apparently, the asshole found out about Bruno's successful business and tried to scam more money out of them. They've been dealing with the man for nearly six years. Bruno had to bail them out a few times. He got tired of it and finally convinced his parents to move to L.A. It worked out perfectly since Karl and Sofia Stein wanted to be close to their grandbaby.

Eloise and Kelly whisper to each other, smiling and laughing and in love. They've been busy with their flourishing careers, booking jobs not only in L.A. and New York, but in Europe as well. They're flying out in a couple days to spend three weeks overseas working. Eloise is shooting a spread for Italian Vogue. She's also working Paris Fashion Week. Kelly will DJ at clubs in Paris and Milan or wherever else Eloise lands a gig.

Jensen and Rebecca sit at a separate table with both of their parents, who all flew in to attend the premiere. People I don't know sit at the four other tables. Reynold says they're people Jensen and Rebecca have worked with over the years.

Once everyone is settled, Jensen nods to the string quartet and they gradually stop playing.

"Thank you, everyone, for being here tonight," Jensen begins, standing next to Rebecca. She's gorgeous in her purple gown with a full, poofy skirt that has gold-laced trim, and a matching purple gemmed crown. Apart from the skirt, it's the same dress from the photoshoot with Jensen and Rey a year ago. Rey is also wearing the same outfit. I found the pictures online when I finally Googled him. He was a knight on a horse with a lance and shield. He looked sexy as fuck. When I told him just how sexy he was in that outfit, he wore it one night and we did a bit of role playing.

Jensen wears the same outfit from the shoot as well, a black tunic with purple trim, puffy sleeves, black pants.

"I am so honored that you all took time out of your lives to attend tonight's premiere. This documentary was personal. I got to follow the love of my life around the country, showcasing her passion. I got to tell her story through her eyes. I'm the luckiest man in the world."

The couple smile at each other lovingly and instead of the pang of jealousy I'd normally feel seeing a couple in love, my stomach flutters. Reynold takes my hand, weaving his fingers with mine.

"But we're not just celebrating the premiere tonight. We have some news to share," Rebecca adds, offering Jensen a mischievous smile. She flattens the massive skirt over her stomach, revealing a baby bump. "We're pregnant. Six months along. And we're also getting married. Tonight. Right now."

"Surprise!" they say together, arms spread open.

Gasps chorus through the small crowd. Lana covers her mouth, her eyes watering. Ginger's mouth hangs open. Mylan scowls at his best friend, Reynold shakes his head, and Bruno is chuckling with his meaty arms over his wide chest.

"Did you know?" I ask Reynold.

"I knew they were engaged. They never publicly announced it though. The pregnancy, however, I had no fucking idea," he says quietly next to my ear. Addy sits on my right and didn't hear him, otherwise she might have taxed him for cursing.

Now that I think about it, Rebecca's outfit for the premiere tonight also had a flowing skirt that hid her stomach.

Jensen keeps talking. "This ceremony will be quick and then we'll eat, drink—nonalcoholic drinks for Mylan and Rebecca—and party."

Mylan and Rebecca both flip the bird to Jensen before he takes his place at the front of next to his bride. Two ground lights turn on to illuminate the couple. An older man with stark white hair wearing a simple suit walks out to officiate the ceremony.

"They say that love at first sight exists," Rebecca begins. "However, this was not the case for us."

The crowd laughs.

"It might have been hate at first sight," she continues, "but damn you for finding a way into my heart like a parasite and never leaving."

"Your parasite," Jensen adds.

"I promise to always get on your nerves and fight whenever possible. Because it's how our relationship started out. It's what brought us together. And it's what will keep us strong from now until forever. I love you, Ani."

I giggle at her Star Wars themed nickname for Jensen. I love the movies and always enjoy meeting a fellow nerd.

"My Ami," Jensen says. "You're as beautiful as the first day I set eyes on you. But it's your soul that shines. You showed me you cared despite how cruel I was to you. You never let my darkness push you away, and I can never thank you enough for seeing the good within me. I can't wait for those annoying moments and the fights because it means the passion is still there. We fight for what we love, and I hope the day we lose that fight never comes. I love you."

The officiant asks if anyone objects. Thankfully, no one does. Then he pronounces them husband and wife. We cheer when Rebecca and Jensen kiss and kiss and kiss until Lana and Mylan stand to break them apart.

Dinner is served and halfway through when Mylan taps a spoon on his glass of non-alcoholic sparkling wine to get everyone's attention. "As Jensen's best friend, I have a few things I need to say. First of all, fuck you for not telling anyone about this."

Jensen flips him off again, sparking more laughter from the guests.

"Second, I am so proud of you, Jenny." Jensen's face drops at the nickname. He's not mad, but he looks like he's fighting back tears.

Mylan glances at Lana and she nods.

"Lana and I actually have a confession."

The crowd quiets. Only singing bugs in the gardens and trees on the property fill the air.

"We never told you this, but the hotel in Hawaii didn't mysteriously lose Rebecca's reservation. There was no glitch."

"What?" Rebecca says. "I don't understand."

"We canceled it," Lana finishes. "We knew you two were arriving around the same time, and Jensen had a spare room in his suite. We were tired of you two skating around your feelings for each other. We knew Jensen would offer to share his suite."

"And the sweet clerk, Vilonia, was more than happy to play along," Mylan says.

"It worked too." Lana smiles, too proud of herself.

Rebecca scoffs. "What if he didn't offer his suite? What if his flight got delayed and couldn't be there to offer me the room? I cannot believe you two did this. I'm going to kick your asses." Her words are laced with anger, but she beams with amusement.

"My biggest prank yet," Mylan adds, and Jensen shakes his head. Mylan lifts his glass. "To Jensen and Rebecca."

We all cheer and the newlyweds stand to give Lana and Mylan a hug.

Reynold stands too and holds out a hand to me. I don't question him and accept. He asks Eloise and Kelly to watch Addy. We walk over to where his friends and their partners gather. Lana gives me a hug and I wave at Rebecca since we only officially met at the premiere.

The three of us watch as Jensen, Rey, and Mylan partake in a three-way handshake of three palm slaps, two fist bumps, a fist to the chest over the heart.

"Mates," Rey says.

"Friends," Jensen counters.

"Brothers," Mylan concludes.

Epilogue – Reynold
One year, six months later

I've never been happier in my life. My career is thriving. I'm choosing more projects outside of my action-movie comfort zone. After finishing filming my first rom-com, I booked a minor role in Jensen's zombie flick. My character was the first to die, but I came back to life as the walking dead. I got to wear all the gory makeup and prosthetics. Then I chased Mylan around because he was the lead. I chose the minor role so I could spend more time with my family. It was nostalgic working with them again.

Savannah's career as a stylist is growing thanks to Victoria. After hiring her, Victoria found herself on every best dressed list. Word spread fast that Savannah was behind the trendy looks, and clients swarmed her with appointments, booking her out months in advance. She had to hire an employee to help her with the demand.

Kyle and Carl went to trial, and Savannah and I took the stand. The trial lasted for a few weeks, but the jury deliberations were quick. Both were sentenced to prison. Kyle will serve longer since he broke parole. He will serve the rest of his original sentence from the bank robbery. Then a twenty-five-year sentence for attempted kidnapping and two counts of assault for attacking Savannah and Sarah. No chance for early release. Carl will serve a ten-year sentence.

Adeline had nightmares after the attack, so Savannah and I sent her to a therapist who helped her work through the trauma. Addy also discussed other topics like growing up without her birth mum, me being famous, and her own fame because of me.

After each session, the therapist reports Adeline's progress. A year later, Addy is doing just fine. She skipped a grade in school because she's so goddamn smart. She's learned two languages already and knows how to play the piano and the violin.

She keeps begging me and Savannah for a brother or sister. We tell her to be patient because it's in the plan. Because before we have a child together, I need to marry the love of my life.

It's May. It's been exactly two years since I met Savannah. Two years since she boarded that plane and sat in our row, leaving behind a cheating ex and her life in Arkansas.

The wedding is being held in her namesake of Savannah, Georgia, at a beautiful outdoor gazebo near a pond in a park. Savannah always talked about not getting to see her parents often. Before I started filming my first romantic comedy, Savannah, Adeline, and I flew down to visit. After staying here for two weeks, I knew this was the right place for the ceremony. Also, because Savannah's dad is afraid of flying—which must be where she got her fear.

Her parents are tall like her, their Southern accents even thicker. They were nice and welcoming. More than I could ask for with in-laws. I almost forgot what it was like to be part of a family. The inside jokes and full belly laughter, the home-cooked meals and sharing life events. Her parents told stories about Savannah's childhood. How she was a 'Chatty Cathy' who liked to pick fights with schoolyard bullies.

Savannah learned more about my life through old family photos. I rarely take them out of storage, but that's because I've had no one to share them with. For our honeymoon, we're going to England and we're bringing Adeline with us. I can finally show them where I grew up and take them to all my favorite places. We'll spend two weeks there before sending Addy to stay with Savannah's parents while we go on a second honeymoon to Bali... just for us.

Our wedding is small, smaller than Jensen and Rebecca's.

Aside from Savannah's parents, and her best friend Justine—a short brunette plus-size woman who grilled me with a million questions and threatened to beat my arse if I hurt her best friend—our friend group are the only ones attending.

I make my way to the gazebo to stand with our officiant, Victoria, for the start of the ceremony. She and Savannah have become good friends. When we had her over for dinner one night, I mentioned we were searching for an officiant. We wanted a close friend or relative to do it since neither of us are religious. Victoria offered, saying she became ordained through one of those online churches so she could officiate her sister's wedding a few years ago.

Two columns of white chairs are placed on the green lawn before the gazebo—four chairs to each row, leaving an aisle for the bride to walk down. A string quartet plays a classical song as our guests find their seats.

Lana and Mylan take the first row on the groom's side. They have an adorable, raven-haired, blue-eyed boy named Zack in between them. They officially adopted the seven-year-old six months ago. Adeline is already in love with him and says they're going to get married someday.

Ginger and Bruno tote around their little girl Gracey, who is almost two years old now. They sit in the row behind Mylan and Lana, placing Gracey in Ginger's lap.

Rebecca and Jensen walk up the aisle next and sit on the bride's side with their son Luke, who is about fifteen months old now. He's feisty and energetic and squirming in Rebecca's arms, trying to escape so he can run all over the place.

Eloise and Kelly sit in two chairs behind Rebecca and Jensen. They eloped last month, not wanting the pomp and circumstance of a wedding. We were all pissed, but then they let us organize a reception at a rooftop bar overlooking the Empire State Building where we showered them with gifts and love.

The music changes over to an instrumental version of (*I Just) Died In Your Arms Tonight* by Cutting Crew. It was the song Savannah and I danced to in the kitchen the first night we made love. Savannah told me she never felt so cared for in that moment. That no one had ever slow danced with her in a kitchen. She knew that song would signify love and our relationship from that night on.

Adeline emerges from a building where the reception will be held. She's wearing a light orange dress, her curly red hair in pigtails. Carrying a white basket with flower petals inside, she walks down the aisle, picking one—only one—petal and tossing it to the ground. She repeats the action, pausing to concentrate on selecting the perfect petal.

"Come on, Poppy," I say, amused. "You're going to have to throw more than one at a time. Get a handful."

She rolls her eyes, but complies, and moves faster down the aisle. We hired a photographer recommended by Eloise and he snaps photos of Addy being an adorable flower girl. She runs out of flowers mid-way and turns back around to pick some up and puts them in her basket, causing a roar of laughter from our guests.

When she reaches the front, she sits next to Savannah's best friend, Justine, in the front row on the bride's side.

"Everyone please stand." Victoria announces.

Savannah appears in the doorway of the reception hall, her parents on each arm.

I suck in a sharp breath.

She's stunning.

She's wearing a ball gown wedding dress with a V-neck bodice and embroidered lace cascading down to a sparkling tulle skirt. It has short appliqué sleeves with floral designs. Her blonde hair falls in waves around her face.

She's absolutely magnificent.

Her parents walk her down the aisle, giving her kisses on the cheek before handing her off to me. I take her hand.

"My love," I say.

"My British Guy," she quips with a smile.

Victoria begins the ceremony, talking about love and soul-mates and other words that I pay no attention to because I'm distracted by the woman in front of me.

When it comes time for us to recite our vows, I'm sweating. I'm nervous because here I am about to bare my soul to the woman who brought me back to life.

"Savannah Beth Monroe, you're a thief in the night who walked into my life and stole my heart. From the moment we met, I knew you were special. I've never met another soul that spoke to my own. You challenge me and make me want to be a better man. You push my buttons and put me in line. You are my mirror because without you, there is no me to see. I can't wait to spend the rest of my life with you. I plan to spend every waking moment thanking you for seeing *me* and not the man made of fame. And thank you for opening your arms and accepting my daughter, Adeline, as your own. You are an excellent mother to her and you will be to all our future kids."

"All?" Savannah quips. "How many are we talking?"

Our guests laugh and I squeeze her hands. "As many as you'll give me."

Savannah's bottom lip shakes. She lets out a long breath, preparing herself for her vows.

"Reynold Michael Kane, you showed up in my life at an uncertain time when love had failed me. When I decided to leave my old life to start a new one, I considered other cities: New Orleans, Chicago, Miami... I kept coming back to New

York City. Something was calling to me and I think it was you."

She glances at Adeline.

"And Addy." Addy giggles and swings her legs in the white chair. "You offered me something I never dreamed I could have: true love. You took care of me, sometimes too much, and you protected me. You respected me and trusted me with the most important job in the world. I cannot wait to marry you, and I promise to always take care of you in return, to trust and respect you and protect you."

"You're going to protect me?" I muse.

She nods. "I'll protect you from being alone again. From never being without a family again. And I'll protect you from the fame because to the world you are Rey. To me? You're Reynold. The single dad on the plane who the media exploits because some bad things happened to him."

Still holding her hands, I tug and pull Savannah against my body so I can kiss her. She's crying and I'm crying, so I move my mouth to her cheeks to kiss the tears away.

Victoria clears her throat. "We're not at that part yet."

Laughter fills the air and I release my soon-to-be wife and step back.

"Sorry. Proceed."

Victoria rolls her eyes at me. "Can we please have the rings?"

Mylan stands and feels around his suit jacket. He puts on a show, pretending he doesn't have it. Savannah is giggling, but I'm glaring at him, letting my best friend know I will kick his ass. Mylan's face lights up and he extracts a box from his suit pocket. It'd been there the whole time, the wanker. He hands it to me.

Both of our rings are inside. Savannah takes the band meant for me and I take her gold band, then give the box to back to Mylan.

I put Savannah's ring on first.

"Reynold Michael Kane," Victoria begins. "Do you promise to love and cherish Savannah for the rest of your life until death do you part?"

"I do."

"Savannah Beth Monroe, do you promise to love and cherish Reynold for the rest of your life until death do you part?"

"I do."

"By the power vested in me and the state of Georgia, I now pronounce you husband and wife." Victoria announces. "*Now* you may kiss the bride."

She doesn't have to tell me twice. She didn't even have to tell me once. I scoop Savannah up in my arms and kiss her more deeply, more passionately than before. The crowd stands and cheers.

We part and I take Savannah's hand, weaving her fingers with mine. We walk down the aisle, heading to the reception hall where we'll celebrate.

Everyone in our friend group got their happily ever after in their own special way. Life is full of surprises. None of us thought we would be married with kids. We all grew up with hardships. We all faced loss. And we all found our own families to feel complete once again.

Then, there are my best friends. Mylan and Jensen. We are just three guys who fell in love with women who challenged us, who believed in us, and who gave us hope that there's more to life beyond the bright lights, the fame, and the spotlight.

The end

Thank You

Did you enjoy Savannah & Reynold's story? Please consider leaving a review for Beyond the Spotlight!
   Goodreads
   Amazon

Acknowledgments

Finishing this series has been an adventure. Three books featuring big bodies! I wrote these books to remind myself that as a fat woman, I matter. I belong and I deserve my own romance. Fat people should be main characters and while a few of us authors are trying to change the world's wicked view of us... we still have a long way to go. I have many more stories that will have plus-size main characters.

I'd like to thank my amazing alpha readers who offered their time amid their busy schedules to read this story in its roughest form. Xan Garcia, Stephanie Patton, and Maranda Perdue. Thank you for always being real with me and not holding back with your critiques.

To my beta readers—Kristyn Habick and Candice Hume—you were my final eyes before this story was sent to the editor. Thank you for pointing out any final inconsistencies.

To my editor Jenny at Owl Eyes Proofs & Edits—I'm so sorry about all the commas you had to add!

To Kate at Y'all That Graphic, thank you for making these amazing discreet covers. I'm obsessed!

And finally, to my readers and TikTok followers. You are the reason I keep writing. Thank you for all your support. To the ones who've been with me from the very beginning, I see you. I appreciate you.

F*ck the fatphobes. Flaunt your fatness.

Also by Settle Myer

The Off Script Series

Need to catch up? Beyond the Bright Lights is the first book in the Off Script series of standalone romances and features Lana & Mylan's story. Beyond the Fame is book two and features Rebecca & Jensen's story.

Find them on Amazon, KU, Audible & iTunes.

The Trinity Trilogy

If you love action & adventure, badass women with superpowers, diverse characters, found family, and fated mates—check out my sci-fi romance trilogy. Book 1 is a clean romance with some cursing and violence, but books 2 & 3 have a sprinkle of spice in them. Trinity Found, Trinity Returns, Trinity Rises. Find them on Amazon.

Social Media

Check out my website and sign up for my newsletter for updates on new books, discounts, and sneak peeks!

https://www.settlemyerauthor.com/

Join my readers group. Become a Settle Myer Star and be a part of the discussion with other fans. I also posts fun facts about my books, characters, and more!

Follow me on social media

tiktok.com/@settlemyerauthor

instagram.com/settlemyerauthor

facebook.com/settlemyerauthor

twitter.com/settle_myer

About the Author

Settle Myer lives in New York City with her cats, Zombie, Michonne, & Birdie. She's currently a TV News Producer who hopes to one day leave a world of death, disaster, and politics to write about worlds with plenty of forbidden romance, badass women with superpowers fighting violent villains. She loves all things zombies, cats, karaoke, and tattoos... but not necessarily in that order.